The Fighter

by

Lisa Fougère

For all the good humans in the world.

PROLOGUE

Victoria (me)

The lecture hall smelled of snow and sweat mixed with some student's overzealous application of cologne. I slunk in and took a seat at the very back, struggling to escape from my heavy winter coat. Something was off with the heating; it must have been eighty degrees in the room. People shed layers as they walked through the narrow aisles to take their seats. Once the din quieted, the professor, her suit jacket flung across the back of her chair and small sweat stains darkening the sleeves of her blouse, began her lecture. Today, we were discussing the literary theme of good vs. evil. I was excited. I was a big reader of fantasy fiction and loved a good hero.

"What makes a character great? Makes us want to invest in their story, share their emotions, believe their motives? Often it comes down to how relatable the character is to our own personal experience of life that captivates us. We readers want to see a bit of ourselves in the hero or villain on the pages. The theme of good vs. evil is one of the most common themes in literature, in part because it asks us to explore our own morality." The professor paused, looking around the room. "You've all seen some form of advertisement or cartoon presenting a person in the throes of making a difficult decision…and sitting on one shoulder, whispering in their ear, is an angel coaxing them to do the right thing, the moral thing – while a little horned devil sits at their other ear loudly trying to convince them to forgo morality for personal gain. To take the easy route, which is implied to be the 'bad' route. This theme resonates with all humans because we are perpetually facing decisions that include a trade-off of some kind. From something as insignificant as cutting in line at the grocery store, to lying on your resume or cheating on your spouse.

"Life is a series of choices along our subjective internal spectrums of good and evil. Most heroes and villains throughout history were not one hundred percent good or one hundred percent evil. There's a sliding scale if you will. But if we look at that old tale of Adam and Eve in the Garden of Eden, we're taught that humans have free will, a choice between being good and being evil. And that good things happen to us when we choose to do good, and bad things happen to us when we choose to do bad. A useful moral when you're a leader trying to maintain control over your subjects, don't you think?

"Let's pause now and think about our own personal definitions of what constitutes a 'good person'. Is it someone who always keeps their promises and never lies? Do they volunteer their time, help others, share wealth?" My professor gave us several moments to reflect before continuing. "Now what would you say makes someone a 'bad person'? Do they cheat, lie, steal? What if the reasons they choose to do something 'bad' are based on need or desperation? Before we move on, I'd like you to consider, just for a moment, where you would measure yourself on your own individual scale." She held her palms toward the ceiling and lifted them left then right to mimic a scale's weight shifting.

After a short pause, she proceeded with her lecture, but I was lost in my own personal turmoil. A pit in my stomach. My classification of a good person included someone who stood up for a cause, donated time to those in need, and helped the world in some appreciable way. This seemed perfectly acceptable and reasonable to me until I realized I was a person who did none of those things. I was someone who became terrified at the idea of standing out in any way or making any decision more difficult than my coffee order. I had always abstractly thought of myself as a 'good person', but can you still consider yourself good if you have done nothing, fought for nothing, sought nothing?

I left the lecture hall in a funk. Head down and crossing the snow-covered quad, I wished to believe there was potential for greatness somewhere inside me. Maybe all I needed was a test. Some trial to prove I wasn't just a lump of meat taking up space on the planet. Not destructive, but not contributing anything significant to the world. A waste of air. Almost the moment I finished my thought, a squeal erupted from up ahead. A woman walking about 30 feet in front of me was struggling with a man. In a quick move he grabbed her purse off her shoulder, shoved her to the ground and took off running. The woman had hit a patch of ice hard when she fell, and now held a hand to the back of her head as she slowly moved to sit up. Pink lines streaked the ice where her head had hit. I was frozen in place, staring at her hair now matted with dark red. She had been walking alone, and with horror I realized I must have been the closest person to her, yet I couldn't seem to move my feet. *Run to her, help her up!* My heart yelled. Then my mind yelled back, *You'll just screw something up if you go over there. Better for her if you stay out of it.* In the ten seconds of frozen debate, a guy from the other side of the quad had run over and was gingerly helping her stand. I hurried away, deeply ashamed. If a person never did anything at all, could they still be considered a good person? The pit in my stomach said no.

CENTURIES AGO

Chapter 1: Dike

A warm breeze lifted the leaves from their branches and dappled the sunlight shining down on Olympus. Lilacs in full bloom scented the air and a calming orchestra of birds and insects lent background music to Dike's thoughts. Her perch, a marble bench hidden within the branches of an ancient willow tree, caught the sunlight on its golden veins. Dike sighed in contentment and thought of everything she adored about Olympus, from the grand temples and gardens, to the vastness of the sky and Earth below. She even loved humankind. Yes, she was tasked with seeing the worst they could be. But you can't appreciate the brilliance of the light without understanding the depths of the dark.

The dark had seemed to be deeper than ever these last decades.

A thin white strip of cloth sat waiting in her lap. Once a source of familiar comfort, the threadbare linen now seemed foreboding. Reluctantly picking up the cloth, she placed it across her eyes and tied it behind her head. Abruptly, Dike's vision changed. Instead of seeing the lush garden and gently swaying willow branches, she was bombarded with horrific scene after scene. A battle raging and a greedy prince ordering his men into slaughter, a maid being violently raped in a tower staircase, a mother beating her child. The torrent of instances in which evil had overtaken the good in humans took Dike a long time to view and judge. Finally, she unwrapped her eyes and placed the cloth, now soiled with the evil of humankind, on the bench to her side. Once, the horrors men could inflict on one another would not remain swarming around her head after she'd removed the cloth. But feelings of sadness and frustration had been lingering throughout her days of late.

For centuries now, the human population had been growing exponentially, and Dike was finding her daily task of managing the balance of justice somewhat…unmanageable. Of course, never since the dawn of humankind was she intended to render justice on every single grave offense, on every human whose individual life shifted too far from good to bad. But, rather, her role was to maintain a balance so humankind as a whole didn't tilt too far toward evil. These days she was having to work harder and harder and was barely keeping up.

Dike breathed in the fragrant air and felt sorry for all those lost souls.

If only humans wouldn't forget their nature. They are born with the desire to be free and loved, happy and purposeful, yet they are raised by people who have become fearful, angry, and defeated. It was a terrible cycle she felt hopeless to break. She was the goddess of justice, not of love or health or wisdom. She had a role to play and was proud to help in her own way.

It wasn't just the humans' fault, of course. If only troublesome gods weren't constantly tempting them toward evil: like Eris, always sowing strife, and deceitful Apate spreading distrust. They never tired of their pursuits, toying with mortals as though their lives were meaningless simply because they were so short. An infinite supply of pawns to unwittingly play the games of the gods.

To add to her worries, the human world was now humming with anticipation for another man they labeled *prophet*. One who walked among them as a healer of the sick and champion of the poor. In truth, it was simply this man's ability to remember his inherent goodness that granted him the gift of healing. That filled him with light. It was their souls' recognition of the light that drew masses to him, this prophet who so many would follow and so many others would attempt to destroy. Dike knew his existence would inflame scores toward the emotions of evil – greed, envy, hubris. This peaceful leader would not only heal, but would ignite wars, and that would only lead to more work for her. Anytime a new belief system found its way into the minds of humans, battles would wage in its abolition or defense. It meant division and chaos for a few hundred, or even a few thousand, years.

Stretching her back and sliding on her sandals, she sighed again. The problem with humankind was that their weaknesses were preyed upon early in life, and those who had already succumbed to evil felt the need to share their misery with the next generation – a self-perpetuating cycle of hopelessness that fewer and fewer seemed able to escape. Dike knew her approach needed to change. And she had a plan. She picked up the cloth, left the sanctuary of the willow tree, and walked toward Zeus's temple.

Entering the great marbled hall, Dike made her way softly to her seat at the base of Zeus's throne, which was so large even he seemed dwarfed by its majesty. Gold carvings of all the gods and goddesses, each with a symbol of their power and sacred duty, adorned the base. Zeus was engrossed in conversation with a page, and Dike was content to sit and wait. Her seat was close enough to his throne to reach out and touch her own likeness, shrouded in the linen and holding the scales of justice. She secretly felt the artist was most skillful with her replica compared to those of the rest of her family. The fabric of her gown seemed alive with movement. The discussion wound down and Dike knew it would soon be her time to speak. She wasn't sure how Zeus would react to her proposal, and maintaining calm was the best way to keep the conversation rational.

"Dike, proceed," Zeus commanded.

She held the soiled linen up in her palms and methodically replayed her judgments before Zeus's eyes. Finally finished, he gave a curt nod and moved to focus on a papyrus to his side. Dike knew she must be swift in her speech.

"The humans are becoming too populous. I have watched, as have you, Zeus, as day after day, the number of judgments increases. I am troubled by this trend and find my duties to be overwhelming. The evil brought about by my fellow gods is too devious in its quest to overtake their hearts. It is my belief that justice will be better served with the aid of humans on the ground." Zeus shifted in his throne and gazed down at her with intensity. She knew he hated laziness in all forms, so she must make this about efficiency rather than overwork. "I want an army of fighters. Enhanced humans to become warriors or guides of justice on the earth. There is no reason for me to be the sole arbiter of good and evil. There are simple cases where a human could be swifter in execution."

"You wish to endow humans with the abilities of the gods?" his voice boomed.

"Not at all," she responded. "Their physical and mental capabilities would simply be enhanced. Those less suited for physical fighting could learn to influence through charisma." Dike maintained an even tone. "I would also bestow upon them the scales of justice, so that they would know immediately what the judgment should be. They will simply carry out the will of the scales, not decide each case for themselves. They would be guided and cared for. Imagine how much more efficient this could be for us both?" Dike returned Zeus's gaze as steadily as she could. She knew he had been tired of their meetings for at least a century.

"I admit I have grown weary of our consultations. But the humans are weak of heart. Their own emotions will get in the way of their duties. And they are so easily harmed or killed, you will constantly be losing them," Zeus replied.

Dike was nonplussed. "Yes, humans are fragile creatures, but there are many who possess a strong sense of justice. And I will choose among those whose lives have been stripped of loved ones and hope, so that their willingness to serve will be robust." Dike took a deep breath. "And I will give each an amulet. While wearing it, no physical harm will come to them."

"You are considering granting immortality to humans?" Zeus furrowed his brow. "The power will be too great—they will succumb to evil no matter how strong you believe their sense of justice to be."

"The scales will compel them," Dike argued.

"You have forgotten about free will. Humans must always have free will, which is why they are so easily tempted by the evil around them," he sighed.

"They may exercise their free will, of course. But the scales will be so compelling that as they carry out justice, there will be no doubt they are acting of their own choosing. They will feel as much desire as I do to bring judgment or to steer the course of history." Dike knew she was skirting the line of what Zeus felt appropriate when dealing with humans. "And I will be a little moth of encouragement flitting about their ears."

"And what about when one betrays you, as I suspect they will?" Zeus challenged.

"I am confident they will not, but if one does, I will strip them of their protection, and they will return to lead normal human lives. I will not offer any further interference." Dike would make it very difficult for her fighters to remember they had a choice at all. Anticipating his next question, she added, "They will still age as other humans. Still live governed by human laws, requiring food and sleep. Once I have chosen a fighter, they will train in combative and investigative arts and learn the powers of charisma and mental persuasion. No longer vulnerable and witless, I am certain they will become effective allies in my work. I simply need permission and power to put this plan into motion."

"And what of human guilt?" Zeus leaned further.

"I'm not sure I understand the question," Dike's mind raced. Where was he going with this?

"When your fighters betray you or grow older and can no longer serve, and you are ready to set them free, do you naively believe the actions they've done while ridding the world from evil won't impact them? That they won't feel too vulnerable without the amulets that have protected them? Humans are uniquely gifted among creatures to feel guilt over even the smallest perceived injuries. What do you imagine they'll experience after a lifetime of exacting mortal justice? Of being vulnerable to the world again? I do not believe you can simply take away their powers and protection and reinsert them into 'normal human life' as you call it. They will suffer tremendously." Zeus sat back in his throne and considered Dike. When she didn't immediately answer, he added, "It is as I assumed. You do not understand the humans as thoroughly as you might, Dike."

Dike would not be denied, and thought quickly. "You have brought up a valid argument, Zeus. But you are mistaken in your judgment of me. I would not want any humans, especially those assisting me in my sacred work, to suffer any affliction of the mind or heart. It is my intention to imbue them with an alternate history from which to source their memories. Nothing too grand or poor, a happy existence to recall and live the rest of their days within. They will ease out of service as they ease in. Their amulet will pass to another, and they will not remember its pull. This, of course, is only possible with the gift of power from you."

Zeus pulled at his long beard in thought and finally exhaled. "So be it. You have one hundred years to try this little experiment. If it fails, which I predict, you are to deal with the consequences." Zeus pulled a small shimmering length of gold, pulsing energy from his staff. "You may use a portion of my powers to endow your humans and create the amulets. But be warned, this will create an intimate link between you. You can affect them, and you are also open to being affected. Take care you do not forget what you are."

Dike fought to contain her excitement as she took the quivering energy. "I will not be swayed in my purpose. Thank you, Zeus." As she walked from the throne room, a slow smile formed on her face. Zeus had agreed. She was confident her plan would be successful. Why should she alone be required to oversee every case where a human tips the scales completely from good to evil? This would be much more impactful. She felt Zeus's power in her hand and laughed. As if a goddess could be affected by the weak spirits of humans.

2006:

A FIGHTER WAS CHOSEN

Chapter 2: Andrew

Andrew entered his family's restaurant to a familiar scene: His father, Zhang, behind the host stand, organizing the new menus. Andrew himself had illustrated the borders with lanterns and dragons and other stereotypical images found in Chinese restaurants. His mom had been the real artist in the family, but he must have inherited at least a bit of her abilities. The drawings weren't half bad. His father gushed with pride when Andrew showed him the finished sketches just the week before. Then he'd gotten quiet and traced his finger along the exaggerated tail of the dragon. "You have woven her name into the scales of the dragon's back, how very clever. Your mom would have been so proud."

Andrew's mom, Xiu Ying, had been gone two years, and it still felt strange not seeing her at the host stand or laughing with the regular customers. She was the heart and soul of the restaurant, while his dad was the substance and organization. It was a magical combination. When Xiu Ying found out she was pregnant, both she and Zhang were working high-level corporate jobs, he in finance and she in marketing, and regularly pulling sixty-hour work weeks. They decided to give that up and open the restaurant. If they were going to work that much, they figured they might as well be together as a family. It was a complicated birth, and, in the end, Andrew would be their only child. They were as close as a family could be, and Andrew grew up healthy and happy.

His mom's cancer diagnosis came when Andrew was just thirteen, and she died a hard year later. They closed the restaurant for a month to mourn her. Zhang had managed their money well, and the life insurance policy for Xiu Ying was enough to support them if they wanted to stay closed longer, but it turned out the restaurant was where her spirit lived on, and they felt better within its walls. As the customers made their way back in, with hugs and flowers and love, Zhang was comforted by the demands of the kitchen, while Andrew felt closer to his mom's memory spending time in the place she loved the most.

As he walked in now, sweaty from track practice, he smiled at his dad. It was still an hour before they'd open for dinner, and his only task was to get the floors cleaned up from lunch. Then he'd go home to shower, and return to help with the beginning of the dinner rush. He was used to spending evenings at the restaurant, but tonight he was leaving early. Tonight was his third date with Amber. The hours couldn't go by fast enough.

"Ah! Here he is, my famous artist son! Look at these menus…didn't they come out great?" Zhang held up a laminated, trifold menu covered in Andrew's illustrations.

Andrew took one and beamed. Though considerably shorter than Andrew's six feet, his father reached up and tousled his sweaty mop of hair. "People are going to absolutely love them. Oh, can you get the dishwasher loaded before you begin the floor?" Andrew nodded and pushed through the swaying door to the kitchen, greeted by the familiar scents of garlic, ginger and earthy peanut oil that seemed to live in the very air. Throwing his bag on a stack of extra chairs, he fished his earbuds out of his pockets, turned the music on high, and got to work. The sinks were full of dishes and loading the dishwasher took longer than expected. There were pots and pans coated in grease to scrub as well, and Andrew banged everything around in his haste to finish and get ready for his date.

About forty minutes later, finally finished with the chores, Andrew pushed through the swinging kitchen door to head home to shower. The door hit against something.

He peeked his head around to see what the obstacle was. His father lay on the floor in front of him, unmoving and bloody.

Andrew pulled the earbuds from his ears and dove to the floor. "Dad! Oh my God!" He couldn't understand what might have happened. His father's chest was covered with blood, and when Andrew grabbed his shoulders to lift his weight up from the floor, his arms and head pitched backwards. Stunned, Andrew abruptly let go, and his father's body slumped back with a sickening thud. Andrew recoiled, a sob rising in his throat. He could see now there was a dark circular wound in the middle of his dad's chest. Andrew's head swiveled around for some clue to what happened and locked eyes on a man, standing toward the entrance. He wore a black sweatshirt with the hood pulled down over his forehead, his mouth covered by a black bandana. His chest heaved up and down with effort and his eyes were wide as he stared back at Andrew. The man's arms were by his sides, and in his right hand, Andrew saw a gun pointed down at the ground.

"What?..." Andrew looked back and forth between his father and the man. "Why? Why?!" Andrew's shout broke the man from his stupor, and he turned to run out the door. Andrew shook his father once more but didn't get any response. He let out a horrible yell then leapt up and ran after the man.

The restaurant was in a strip mall, and as Andrew busted through the door, he screamed to the shoppers within earshot, "Someone call an ambulance! Help me! He shot my father!" The man was running at the end of the sidewalk far to his left, so Andrew took off after him.

The man had a head start, but Andrew had made it to state finals for track last year and immediately began closing the gap. He chased him through the end of the strip mall, nearly colliding with a car as he darted across the street. The man had turned into an alley behind the next strip of businesses, and Andrew followed. He finally caught up to him, throwing the full weight of his body at the man. They went rolling in the gravel, the gun falling aside. Andrew was high on adrenaline and grief and didn't feel the cuts and bruises. He immediately jumped up and straddled the man's chest.

"You shot him!" Andrew threw wild punches at the man as though possessed. "I'll kill you!"

The man raised his arms in front of his face and to defend himself from the blows. "I'm sorry! I'm so sorry! He tried to take the gun and it just went off!" the man blubbered. His voice broke a little while he yelled. He sounded young, and Andrew paused to rip the bandana off his face.

There was acne on his cheeks and chin, and the beginnings of facial hair above his lip. He was not a man, but just a teen, probably only Andrew's age. One of the punches had cut him above the eyebrow and a thin stream of blood snaked its way down his cheek, mixed with the saline of his tears.

"I'm sorry," the teen moaned. "I didn't mean for it to happen! He just grabbed the gun and it went off. I didn't want to hurt anyone." He shook his head back and forth. "They told me I had to get the money from the old man at the restaurant. If I got the money, they'd leave my sister alone. I'd be one of them and she'd be protected." He was sobbing now, and Andrew, confused by this response, sat heavy and still. "If I got the money, they wouldn't touch her," the teen whimpered. "I just wanted the money. I didn't want to hurt him. I didn't mean it."

Andrew felt the weight of what he'd just lost. His father, his lifeline, stolen from him. He wanted to kill this guy, to make him hurt like he did. The gun was lying just a few feet away. He could get it easily, and though he'd never fired one, Andrew was tempted to try. His body shook with fury.

The teen wept pitifully beneath him, no longer fighting, consumed with his own misery. If what he was saying was true, then he was too young to be given the choice he was given. Too young to have taken a life he never meant to take. Too young to spend the rest of his life in jail. Andrew unleashed a tortured scream to the sky, discharging all his adrenaline. Then, exhausted, rolled off the teen and stood up.

"Get out of here. Go," he said quietly.

The teen looked alarmed. "You're letting me go?" He cautiously got up and backed away from Andrew, unsure whether to trust him or not. Andrew took one long look at the person who ruined his life, then gestured with his arm for him to leave. Before turning and running, the teen said, "I really am sorry!" one last time.

Andrew watched until he was out of sight, then fell down on the hard ground to weep. What was he supposed to do now? An orphan at sixteen. The only person left in this world he loved was gone. He wished death would take him, too. Save him from this pain. He wanted to kill everyone, and he wanted to die, in equal measure. At that moment, he heard a low rumble, like thunder. A female voice broke through his consciousness.

You have been wronged, and you had the ability to avenge that wrong. Yet you chose to let him go because you knew he did what he did out of love for his sister. You have a strong sense of justice. You'll do very well.

Andrew bolted up from the ground, looking for the source of the voice, but there was no one. He assumed he'd gone delusional with grief. Then the voice continued speaking, and he closed his eyes and listened. When she was done, before even opening his eyes, Andrew answered, "Yes, I'll do it."

Suddenly there was a weight in his hand, and he opened his palm to look. As he unfurled his fingers, he saw a metal medallion on a chain. Then there was a dazzling flash of light.

CURRENT DAY: MONDAY

Chapter 3: Victoria (me)

The wind howled fiercely, and I turned to glance out the window. The sky had darkened, and the trees framing the manmade lake whipped left and right. It didn't seem possible they could bend as far as they did without snapping in two. The smaller branches that couldn't hold on were swept up with dead leaves and other debris into swirling eddies of air in the adjacent parking lot. I checked the time on my computer. Only 3:11 p.m. I sighed and hoped the storm wouldn't be upon me when 5:00 p.m. finally arrived.

Teniese poked her head over my cubicle wall, "I'm thinking about cutting out early," she started, her eyes darting toward our boss's office. "Do you think he'll care? It's the apocalypse out there!" she hissed.

Teniese and I were data entry specialists for a company that made steel fittings for food manufacturing equipment. I had been there over a year and a half and knew more about a specific set of widgets than anything I'd learned during my four previous years as an uninspired English major. Teniese started six months ago. Already she filled my ear with complaints about how *boring* the work was and wondering how I could have stayed there as long as I had. Her questions riled me because I knew I should have left by now. Though human resources had gone on and on about the "endless possibilities for advancement" throughout different departments in the company for those with "go-getter" attitudes, so far these opportunities hadn't presented themselves. And, frankly, being one rung up this particular ladder seemed just as mind-numbing a job as the one I'd already sacrificed more than a year of my life for.

I don't know why I've stayed, really. Or even took the job in the first place. Actually, that second statement is a lie. I took the job because it was offered to me, simple as that. There was no way I could go back to living at home after college. But as graduation approached, and I still had no plan, I was feeling desperate. A guy I dated that winter (it fizzled out amicably after a couple months, as these things tend to go with me) had been working in data entry here while attending classes at night. He offered to bring my resumé in one day in early March, saying it was a skilled paycheck for unskilled people and could earn me enough to stay in an apartment until I found a "real" job in my field. I chose it like I did most other things in my life: it was available and easy. He was already gone the week after I began.

If I'm being completely honest, I just might be a bit lazy and indecisive. Like my mom said to anyone who'd listen, "A well-fed sloth has ten times the ambition of my daughter." I often felt there must be something wrong deep in my DNA that made me this way. Made me stay home night after night because there was no one to call. Gave me heart palpitations at the thought of making a decision for myself. Of causing even the slightest ripple. What if it was the wrong one? If I didn't choose it, then it wasn't really my fault if I messed it up, right?

I looked at Teniese, who had returned her nervous gaze to the scene playing on the other side of the window. She anxiously twirled a finger through her curly dark hair. Just last week she confided in me that she'd made a second round of interviews for an entry-level position at an advertising agency in the city. Teniese had one foot out the door of this place already. Like other newbies I'd trained before, and toasted farewell to shortly thereafter, I knew she would be gone as soon as she was able.

"I think I'm just gonna leave and see if he even notices. 'Cause so what if he does, I'm done with this job anyway." She looked around the bland cubicle-land and grimaced. "You want to duck out with me?" she offered.

I did want to leave. This storm was going to get intense, judging by the weather alerts that kept beeping on my phone. I cut my eyes to the boss's office again before answering and heard Teniese sigh.

"Don't worry so much. What's the worst that can happen? We get fired?" she huffed. "This job is awful, and don't even argue. Maybe getting fired is exactly what you need to get you to move on with your life! I know you've got a brain in there." She tapped me on the head with her index finger. "Aren't you tired of not using it?"

I bristled. "I use my brain, Teniese. I just don't feel like losing my job," I retorted, offended. "You go ahead, there are less than two hours left in the day anyway. If he asks about you, I'll say you went to the bathroom." I wanted her to just leave, but she fixed her disapproving eyes on me and shook her head.

"Suit yourself," she added finally, before packing up her things and slinking away. I looked back out the window and shuddered as a plastic bag was lifted off the pavement of the parking lot and pulled twenty-five feet into the air.

Of course, I hated this job. Of course, I felt there was something more productive or enjoyable I could be doing with my time. I didn't need Teniese constantly pointing out what a dead end my life was. I slumped in my chair. Who was I kidding? I wouldn't go against authority, and I was too much of a loser to know how to start changing my life. I turned back to my data sheets and tried to ignore the self-loathing creeping in. Just around 4:30 p.m., I saw our boss, Franklin, don his coat and briefcase, take one sweeping look at the skeleton crew still at our desks, set his jaw and walk out. If he was a better man, he might have invited the rest of us to join him, but after a year and a half, I knew his character was not up to the task.

Once he was out of view, my remaining colleagues quickly assembled their belongings and ran out. During the last hour, the storm had really begun to settle in, and rain had joined the wind in wreaking havoc on the world outside. At 5:01 p.m. I shut down my computer and, as the last one standing, turned off the lights and headed for home. Though I could see it from the window, I wasn't prepared for the force of the wind as I stepped outside. It pushed me sideways, and the umbrella I wielded immediately turned inside out. I was completely soaked before I finished the ten-second trek from office building to car. Little puddles of rainwater squished under my toes as I fumbled my way into the driver's seat. *Damn, there go my new shoes.*

The storm swallowed the daylight, so that it might have been 8:00 p.m. instead of just past 5:00 p.m., and there was now an ominous green tinge to the sky. I shivered as the cold wetness soaked into my skin, and pulled slowly out of the office park. Very few other cars joined me on the street—people

23

obviously had more sense than I did and headed home earlier. I cursed as the car hit standing water and my tires locked up for a moment. The last two times I'd gotten my oil changed, the mechanic cautioned me about my balding tires. I guess I should have listened.

Lightning streaked across the sky to my right and a powerful boom followed almost immediately after. The storm had to be right overhead. I drove a little faster and gripped the wheel tightly. As I approached a yellow light and slowed to a stop, I saw a man hunched against the wind attempting to cross the street in front of me. What the hell was this idiot doing out in this storm? There was literally no one else around. I watched him struggle, so grateful it was him out there and not me. Just then, a massive gust of wind hit him, and he stumbled down.

"Shit!" I exclaimed, looking around to see if there might be anyone else, anyone other than me, who would come to his aid. Nope. It was just the two of us. "Shit!" I said again. "Get up, get up…" The man stayed down on the pavement. I counted to ten just to see if maybe some other car would arrive, then threw my car in park with my flashers on. Getting my door opened against the wind was more of a challenge than I expected, and it slammed hard the moment I was through it. Rivulets of water flowed down the street, and the rain battered my face, making it hard to see. I tripped on a pothole, falling hard onto one knee. Scrambling to get up, I tossed off my high heels – they weren't helping me anyway – and looked at the man, now just a handful of feet away. He was still on his side in the road, rocking back and forth.

"Sir!" I called out as I approached. "Sir, are you okay?" Another strip of lightning lit up the sky, and the roar of the thunder was so loud, the man on the street shot up to sitting. I leaned down to try to see his face without actually having to make physical contact. He looked up at me wild-eyed. I had expected an elderly man from the way he struggled across the street, but the man in front of me didn't look more than thirty. He was of Asian descent with a clean shaven face and full head of dark hair, and looked strong and young. He sat in a pothole not unlike the one I tripped on a moment ago. The water rushing down the street had increased, and it flowed over my feet and his legs. I moved in just a bit closer, "Are you hurt?" I shouted. "Can I help you up?" I gestured my arms forward to mime helping him, in case he couldn't hear me over the roar of the wind.

He thrust his arms out and grabbed each of mine in a vice grip, pulling me towards him. "You?" he bellowed, then turned his face upwards. "I am not ready, dammit!" He yelled to the sky. "I am not done here! I'm sorry, okay?" The sky replied with a powerful flash and boom, and he yanked me down to my knees until I was just inches away from his face. "Fine!" he screamed to the heavens, then moved his feverish gaze to me. "She wants you! You have to take it!" he screamed.

This guy was nuts! I tried to pull away but he tightened his grip and jerked me forward again. "Stop fighting!" He released one of my arms and began wrestling with the collar of his jacket, pulling loose a necklace of some kind. With my now free hand, I tried to wrench my other arm out, but his grip was way too strong. Having finally freed the necklace from his head, he yanked me forward again and tried looping it over mine.

I wriggled away from his outstretched hand. "What are you doing?" I yelled. "Let me go!" I batted futilely at the hand with the necklace.

"You don't have a choice!" he yelled in my face.

I was panicking now. "Stop!" I screamed. "Get away from me!"

"Just take it!" he screamed back.

At that moment, a flare flashed so bright, it blinded me.

MONDAY

Chapter 4: Victoria (me)

Two people hovered over me. I was still wet, but no rain was falling, and the wind appeared to have stopped. Red and yellow lights flashed all around.

"Her heartbeat is all over the place!" yelled the woman. "I'm charging the pads!"

"She's still too wet, give me a minute to dry her off!" answered the man next to her.

I was moving, being wheeled on some cart or something. Different people floated on either side of me and the flashing lights were gone. There were so many voices. A man to my left gazed down at my face with concern.

A steady beep and the sound of my mother's voice. "Honestly, Arthur. She's just doing this to annoy me. The doctor says she's absolutely fine! They have no clue why she isn't waking up! I am telling you, it's like it always is. This girl just loves attention."

I blinked my eyes open with some effort; my eyelids were heavy and seemed glued together. My mouth felt dry and thick, and I desperately wanted water. I took in my surroundings. The room was quiet and dark apart from a small yellow light off to my left. As my eyes adjusted, I recognized the sleeping form of my mother in a chair next to a large picture window. Her head lolled to the side, and a book with a booklight drooped down in her lap. She wore her hair in a short pixie cut, and I detected a red tint in the weak light. When had she done that? The last time I saw her it was shoulder length and gray. My eyes moved to the window. The blinds were up, revealing a dark sky with a bright crescent moon. *I guess the storm is over?* I thought. *What am I doing in a hospital?*

Shifting my weight to sit up, I assessed my body. Aside from extreme fatigue and thirst, I didn't notice anything wrong; certainly nothing that should warrant a visit to the hospital. I wiggled my toes and stretched my arms overhead. This upset a blood pressure cuff that was attached to my arm and rattled the side rail of the bed. My mother shifted awake and looked over at me.

"Oh! Victoria, you're awake at last!" she exclaimed. "I was starting to think we'd be here all night." Then as an aside, she added, "How are you feeling?"

"Mom? What happened? What are we doing in the hospital?" I asked.

"You don't remember anything? Well, I don't know what possessed you to be out and about in that storm, but the doctor says the ambulance drivers found you passed out in the middle of the street. They say you were struck by lightning, if you can believe that." She rolled her eyes. "Honestly, Victoria, of all the things." She tsk-ed at me. "It's 9:45 p.m. I've been here for nearly four hours waiting for you to rouse."

I remembered stopping to help the man. "A man had fallen in the middle of the street. I got out to help him," I answered, defensively.

"Nobody told me anything about a man, just that they found you there in the road, alone and barefoot. I had just started making dinner when they called. I had to *drive* in that storm, Victoria," she scolded. "The whole world knew to stay home except you."

"I was driving home from work, not out for a joy ride. Why didn't Dad come?" I asked, knowing my mom was a fearful driver even in a gentle sprinkle. There's no way she would have braved the storm unless there was no other option.

"Oh, his sciatica is bad again. That useless man hasn't gotten off the couch all day. Says it hurts too much to even stand up." She waved her hand dismissively. "Frankly, I think he just wants the excuse to watch tennis for hours on end. How he can spend all day watching a ball go back and forth is beyond me."

Fearing an unending tangent, I tried to shift the focus back. "So I was really hit by lightning? Shouldn't I be dead, or at least badly injured or something?" I wondered aloud. It seemed strange that I should feel no pain if that was true.

"That's what I said. But the doctor told me there's not a thing in the world wrong with you. That initially, your heartbeat was going berserk, but once it stabilized, it was as though it never even happened. The way they know it was lightning is because of some mark it left on your ankle…a 'Lichen mark' or something like that." She gestured toward my feet.

I pulled back the covers to look, but the room was too dark. "Could you turn on the light?" I flinched as the brightness hit my leaden eyes, reminding me of the huge blinding flash. I looked down. A red, feathered streak began on the top of my foot and wound its way to the outside of my ankle and up my calf, swirling this way and that, stopping just below the back of my knee. "What the hell?" I mused. It had tendrils that looked like a leafy vine snaking its way up my leg. I traced the scar with my finger, it was only slightly tender to the touch. "Wow. Mom, do you see this?" I asked her.

My mother moved in to inspect it closer. "Goodness, I didn't realize it was the whole lower leg! The doctor only showed me the ankle. It doesn't hurt you?"

"No, maybe it's a little itchy…" I replied.

"Well, I'm glad, but your beautiful legs! You'll never be able to wear shorts again." she moaned, shaking her head and settling next to me on the hospital bed.

"Actually, I think it's kind of cool," I returned, slightly ashamed how excited the idea that she thought I had perfect legs made me. Compliments from my mother were rare occurrences. "And this scar is what makes them know I was struck by lightning?"

"That's what the doctor said. Its shape supposedly mimics the bolt of lightning as it crosses the sky. It's a 'telltale mark.' " She made air quotes.

"It does look like a streak of lightning, doesn't it?" I marveled. "But how is the rest of me unharmed? And what about the man?"

"Victoria, who is this man you keep mentioning? Like I said, they told me they found you alone in the street. Your car was parked next to you with its flashers on, and you were just lying there." Her tone was growing impatient. "As to how you are otherwise unscathed, I don't have an answer. The doctor is quite mystified by it." She shifted her weight and I followed her gaze out the window. "Hard to believe the storm was only a few hours ago…it looks peaceful as a poem out there."

She made to move off the bed, and the book light caught on the side rail and dislodged from the book. It was a thick book, and I was drawn to the cover, a chaotic medieval war scene with men in robes and helmets, wielding swords and striking at one another. It did not look like the cozy mysteries my mom usually had in her grasp.

"What are you reading?"

"Oh!" she replied, straightening her spine. "Your brother's latest book, of course! It's an astonishing accomplishment. All about the Templar knights – did you know they basically invented banking?" she finished, triumphantly.

"Oh right! I hadn't seen the cover yet. It's very impressive."

My mother swelled. My older brother, the prodigal son, was a high school history teacher who lived a couple of hours away. He had decided to start writing historical fiction a few years back. Frankly, I found his characters boring and the storyline lacking in his first book, a product of spending your entire life in front of a computer in an office or classroom instead of out living life. But the rich history he infused throughout helped move the story along and at least make it readable. This current book looked nearly twice as thick as the first – it would probably take me a year to get through. But I would, of course.

"Thank you for coming to see if I was alright. I'm sorry you had to drive in the storm," I mumbled. "I like your hair by the way. It looks great."

My mother drew a self-conscious hand through her short, red hair. "Thanks, just trying something a little different." She turned her back to me and busied herself with her purse. "And, of course, I'm glad you're alright, even if it was foolish of you to be out."

I closed my eyes and breathed, letting that one go. "Now that I'm awake, do you think that means I can leave?"

"Well, I would imagine so. It wouldn't be worth the cost of an overnight stay if you can avoid it, the way insurance companies nickel and dime you," she replied. "I'll go see if the doctor is available."

I was able to be discharged when my mother promised to take me back to her house to keep an eye on me for the night. My car had been towed, anyway, so I was at her mercy for the short term. The car ride home was nearly silent except for some gasp or tsk about a downed tree in the road or a missing piece of a shop roof. Apparently, the storm had raged on while I slept it off at the hospital. The only physical sign I had marking that it had happened at all, aside from the tattoo nature decided to give me, was the extreme fatigue. It felt like I was moving through mud. My thoughts were all jumbled. And I couldn't get enough water in me; my cells were screaming for water.

Walking into my parents' house was not a nostalgic experience for me. Once my brother and I had (*finally*) both left for college, they quickly sold the home we'd grown up in and moved into a small ranch in my mother's hometown. She wanted to be closer to her sisters, and my father had just been let go from his IT job. This town was a lot more affordable, and my dad found work from home after not too long.

My brother's bedroom served as my dad's office, and my room became the sewing room when we were away. And, as these things go, when we were home, too. Philip stopped coming home for the summers as soon as the move was official, and then enrolled in graduate school the moment undergrad finished. I dutifully came home each summer and school break, and worked in my aunt's frozen yogurt shop. She needed cheap labor she could pay "off the books," and I needed something to get me out of the house and distract me from the fact that every friend I'd grown up with now lived four hours away. I couldn't wait to get back to college each break.

I had no real connection to this place, which made me pull even further away from my parents than I'd already begun to. But when you have no real ambition in life—as I had heard countless times— the problem is that you tend to just flow where the river chooses. Sometimes you get rapids that force you to fight or swim out…I was still waiting for mine. I lived and worked only twenty minutes from my parents, and every other member of my mom's side of the family: business owners, authors, nurses, and me…the data entry specialist with a BA in English lit.

We walked in the door to find my father still splayed out on the couch, the aforementioned tennis replaced with a book.

"Well, here we finally are!" announced my mother as she swept into the living room. "I convinced the doctor to release his prisoners as we were being held for no good reason! I am happy to say I won, and now we get to sleep in our own beds tonight. What a relief, right, Victoria?" She raised her eyebrows and looked at me triumphantly. I knew that was my cue to praise her on her genius and show gratitude for what was obviously her extreme cunning and careful saving. Unfortunately, she was the only one who would actually be in her own bed tonight: I had the lumpy, thin mattress in the sewing room to look forward to. This, I knew from experience, was not prudent to point out.

"Yes, thanks again, Mom. Hospitals are such dreary places," I conceded and walked over to plant a kiss on my father's forehead.

"Hey, Vickster," he said. "You gave us quite a scare. Are you sure you're alright?"

My mother answered for me, annoyed at the attention shift in my direction. "She's just fine, Arthur. I already told you when I called from the hospital, after talking to the doctors, remember. When *I* was *there*?" She couldn't resist a jab. "The doctors assured me Victoria is healthy as a porcupine."

"I'm sorry I couldn't go myself, Vic," my dad said. "This darned back has been so bad the last couple days…I've been worried sick since your mom left, about both of you." He cupped my face with one massive hand.

"For the last time, Arthur, Victoria is fine," my mother clucked. "And so am I, like I told you." Then to me she added, "I'll put a set of sheets on your bed, Victoria. Then I'm going to sleep, myself. I'm positively exhausted after that ordeal!" She left the room with her nose in the air. Somehow, I'd messed up again.

"Thank goodness she's gone," whispered my dad. "Let's make a run for the Toyota!" His eyes twinkled, replaying our old joke. Then he shifted up to his elbow, wincing slightly. "Hand me that pillow there, will you, Vic?" I grabbed it and propped it under his side so he had more support.

"Dad – this is pretty bad, huh? When's the last time you were this immobile?"

He waved a hand in dismissal, "I'll be fine in a day or two, don't you worry a smidge about me." Once he finished settling, he sighed, "There. Now, I want to hear from your own lips that you're fine. What the heck happened? Mom says the ambulance found you in the road unconscious – apparently struck by lightning? That sounds pretty extreme."

"I'm a little confused myself to be honest," I started. "I'm not a complete idiot, though. I didn't just leave my car in the middle of the road in a thunderstorm for no reason. I had stopped at a red light, and this guy was fighting his way across the road. Halfway there, he fell over – you wouldn't believe how crazy strong the wind was – so I got out to help him." I remembered his wild eyes as he grabbed at my arms, and I shuddered slightly.

"Was he okay?" my dad prompted.

"It was so weird," I began, "I think he must have been mentally ill, actually. He grabbed at my arms and shouted at me 'She has chosen you!' It was scary. But then the lightning struck, and I don't remember much between that moment and waking up in the hospital. I guess he must have taken off because I keep hearing how I was found lying alone."

"That bastard left you there? I'll kill him!" my father hissed, waving a menacing fist in the air.

I smiled at his protectiveness since he currently couldn't even stand up. "Thanks, Dad, but he was a complete loon. I'm thrilled he didn't stick around, or I might have been sacrificed to whomever it was who had 'chosen me.'" I chuckled, and shook off the mental images of all the potential ways it could have gone down differently. Thank goodness the ambulance found me.

"Well, as long as you're sure you're alright." He relaxed slightly. "Can I see the scar? Your mother lamented on the phone that your bare-legged days were toast," he winked.

I pulled up my pant leg, and my father let out a low whistle, "I've never seen anything like it. What's it called, again?"

"The doctor called it a Lichtenberg Figure. Apparently, it's a typical shape and it's how they knew it was a lightning strike that got me." I marveled again at the intricacy of the wound pattern—the winding vine with its fern—like tendrils extending from the top of my foot and around my ankle, finishing its dance at the back of my knee.

My father traced it gently, as well. "It's really quite beautiful, isn't it? Does it hurt?"

"Not any more than if I lightly scraped myself falling down or something," I replied. "That's the most surprising thing about it," I continued. "I would expect to be in a lot more pain. But, like Mom said, I'm fine. Just really tired."

"Well, I can't tell you how relieved I am to hear it, my darling girl. Get yourself to bed, and I'll see you in the morning." He pulled me in to kiss my forehead.

I headed to the bathroom and grabbed a spare toothbrush from the cabinet. When I finally got my leaden feet to my room, my exhaustion was so complete that the sweet relief of a bed, even an uncomfortable one, sounded like a miracle. Unfortunately for me, I found the mattress bare and a set of sheets and a comforter neatly folded on top. I struggled so much with the bottom sheet that I decided that was enough, pulled up the comforter, and immediately succumbed to deep sleep.

MONDAY

Chapter 5: Andrew

It seemed to Andrew that water was everywhere. He was lying in it, it flowed over his hands and feet, and it fell in buckets on his head. It wasn't an uncomfortable sensation, actually, almost soothing. But why was he sleeping in water? Andrew fought the sensation that he should be waking up now. Something important was happening, but the water was so comforting.

A memory from his childhood bobbed to the surface of his mind. Another day filled with water; his kindergarten graduation. His dad thought a graduation for kindergarten was ridiculous, but his mom couldn't stop taking his picture in his pint-sized cap and gown. Rain had threatened all that morning but so far held off as Andrew and his classmates made their way through the folding chairs set up for the parents on the school lawn. The first fat drops fell as the principal began calling kids by name to come up to the podium and accept their "diplomas." He tried to speed up the names, anticipating disaster as parents moved purses and programs over their heads as makeshift umbrellas. Right as Andrew stood poised, ready to walk up and have his turn, the sky opened up and unleashed a torrential downpour. Kids and parents went sprinting for the safety of the school, but Andrew had been frozen at the podium unsure what to do, confused because he hadn't gotten his piece of paper yet. His dad ran over and picked him up ready to run. But when they turned back around, there was Andrew's mom, laughing and dancing in a puddle, her clothes plastered to her body. She opened her arms and called to them. They stood and watched for just a moment before his dad turned to Andrew and shrugged. Then they both ran over and joined her, splattering the world with drops off their fingertips and covering themselves with mud.

A roll of thunder broke through his fog and awakened Andrew to the present. Shielding his eyes against the rain, he sat up and looked around, dazed. The dream of his mom and dad lingered like an emptiness in his chest. Andrew hadn't thought of that day in years, but it felt so real, so fresh. He looked down at his legs sitting in the flow of water in the potholed street until he could focus on the here and now. Something was wrong and he couldn't put his finger on it. Why was he in the middle of the street in the driving rain? He pressed his fists to his head to think. With a sinking dread, he remembered the attack, and the storm and…he looked to his right, and there in the street was the woman. His hands flew to his neck, and the absence of the amulet made him catch his breath. In nearly sixteen years, he hadn't taken it off. He was exposed without it. Untethered to his life and vulnerable. Andrew crawled over to the woman. She was slight, and her dark hair was stuck to her face with rainwater. Andrew felt for a pulse and looked to see if her chest was moving. She was alive at least, that much he could tell. More roughly than he should have, he pulled the collar of her shirt down, but there was no amulet. Her hands were empty as well. *Where the hell did it go?* Andrew moved his hands all around in the water at his feet to see if he could feel anything, but it was dark, and the streetlights weren't bright enough to illuminate the road. A sensation was taking over that Andrew hadn't experienced in a very long time – he was starting to panic.

Turning to the sky above, he yelled, "I want the amulet back! I still want to be a fighter!" But the wind and rain swallowed up his voice and she didn't respond. "Dike?" he shouted, but no sound entered his head. Since he had been a teenager, she was his frequent companion, and her sudden absence was disconcerting. Andrew could tell she was gone, not just ignoring him. As though their connection had been severed. And he felt more than alone – he felt empty. He turned his attention back to the woman lying in the road. What the hell was wrong with him that he couldn't think what to do next? He had always been clear about his actions. Andrew's gaze fell on her car sitting with its flashers on. *I can look for an ID*, he thought, swelling with the relief of something concrete to do. Before he could get there, however, he heard the sounds of sirens not far away and getting closer.

"Shit!" Andrew knew he couldn't be found there with this woman in the middle of the road. He took one more fruitless look in the water for the amulet, then ran off just as the lights from an ambulance came into view.

Andrew wove through and around buildings and streets to distance himself from the ambulance and give his mind time to work through what should happen next. He found his way back to the underground parking garage where he'd left his car in preparation for the attack. Once in his car, out of the rain but still dripping wet, Andrew let the full weight of what he'd done sink in. He had disobeyed her. Had chosen Ana over his duties. Chosen Ana over Dike. And what had it gotten him? He'd been abandoned. She took her presence, her guidance, and his purpose. *I'm such an idiot. What have I done*? Andrew sat in his car hyperventilating and terrified. If he could just focus on one action. Just one movement forward. One movement could lead to the next and then he'd have a direction. The simple idea that he should get dry clothes anchored him enough to calm down. Andrew turned the key in the ignition and pulled out of the garage to head home.

After taking a long, hot shower and dressing in dry clothes, Andrew sat down on the edge of his bed and opened the night table. The letter he'd written to Ana explaining his actions was still there. He hadn't known what would happen when he went against orders. The worst he could imagine was her killing him for his betrayal. The best was Dike would not punish him at all. After all, he knew from his studies that humans always had a choice. The gods could not force them to do something they wouldn't choose of their own free will. It seemed his punishment would be abandonment of everything he knows. Should he go to Ana and tell her what he'd done? Andrew was suddenly exhausted beyond words. He put the letter back in his night table drawer and lay down on the bed. Would she still even want him anymore? Just that morning, he'd opened up and revealed exactly who and what he was, and she'd lost her mind. Andrew squeezed his eyes tight, remembering the accusations she threw and the hurt in her face. These were the thoughts that accompanied him as he fell into a heavy, immediate sleep.

Nightmares. For the first time since Andrew was a child, he was having nightmares. But these were not like the ones of his youth. He wasn't being chased by a bear or falling from his bike. No, the images and experiences that plagued Andrew were the stuff of horror films: Anger and killing, blood and hurt. But worse than the images themselves was the knowledge that accompanied them. The knowledge that Andrew himself was the harbinger of all the destruction. It was by his hand that the people in his dreams died. By his will that they were struck down. Andrew threw off his covers and sat up heaving, trying to rub the images out of his eyes. He aggressively flipped on the light and paced the bedroom. Never once had he questioned his duty to Dike and the scales of justice. He knew he was helping rid the world of those who had been overcome by evil. Murderers, rapists, those who made hurting others their livelihood. But didn't that describe what he'd also been doing for the last sixteen years? Oh God…didn't that make him just as much a monster as them?

TUESDAY

Chapter 6: Victoria (me)

I woke up surrounded by clanging, and it took a minute to understand where I was. It sounded like a war was being waged on the other side of the door – but it was just my mother doing dishes because she'd decided we'd all slept long enough. Morning was seldom a quiet affair in my childhood.

I reached over and checked my phone. 7:40 a.m. Fabulous. She'd actually let me sleep in a little. I swung my legs around and sat up. My back and neck were stiff. Could that be from the lightning? More likely from the awful mattress and the fact that I didn't even have the energy to use pillows last night. I stretched my arms high overhead and breathed deeply. At least some of the heaviness from yesterday was gone. Accompanying my mother's pots and pans theatrics on the other side of the door was the low hum of the television. Yeah…my dad had no chance at sleeping late, either. I took in "my room." My mom had added a pegboard where all sorts of scissors and measuring tape hung cheerily as a backdrop to her sewing table. A pair of rattan baskets fit neatly beneath the table, filled with material scraps. Not one edge was out of place. My mom had taken up quilting when she and my dad moved back "home." Since the first blue ribbon she earned at the county fair a couple years back, her efforts had become like a full-time job.

The walls on either side of the pegboard held framed pictures of my mom smiling broadly and holding up a ribbon next to her winning creation. I had to admit, she did beautiful work. Beyond that was a bookshelf crammed with romance and mystery novels and peppered with occasional mementos of my youth. A clay pinch pot made when I was in the first grade, a framed picture of Philip and me one Halloween when we were six and four years old. I was a pumpkin and Philip a ghost (homemade costumes, of course). Then there was the photo I hated from the eighth grade. I went through horrible acne in my early teens. Coupled with my braces and the layer of baby fat I maintained well past when it was cute, it was not a flattering image. I had asked my mother to get rid of it the last time I was here. She just shooed me away and said I should not be so vain; it made her giggle. I grimaced and placed the frame face down.

That was the extent of my existence on display. A few more photos of Philip graced the shelves: Philip at graduation, Philip at another graduation, Philip and my mom in an embrace, laughing freely into the camera. I stuck my tongue out at their joyful figures and turned that frame face down, too. Then, thinking better of it, I put it back the way it was.

That last photo was taken at my own college graduation party. I hadn't wanted one at all, since I had no friends nearby, but my mother insisted on having the family over. I was hiding out in the basement for most of the party, my nose in a book as usual, when I heard my mom and my aunt Lucy talking at the landing at the top of the stairwell.

"Well, what do you think she'll do now that she's finished with school? Does she even have a job?" Lucy asked.

"She does, or so she says. Something to do with computers. She never tells me anything, you know. We'll see how it goes. Frankly, I'm not convinced she'll last more than a few months out in the real world," my mother replied. I closed my book and stayed motionless.

"Well, she's lucky you'll be here to pick up the pieces if she doesn't. How's the trucking business going? Is Arthur finally getting on his feet?"

My mother clicked her tongue. "Your guess is as good as mine. He and Victoria are like two peas in a pod. Neither of them can seem to get their acts together to save their lives." Just then, a third voice joined them and they all left the stairwell. I sat still as stone on that basement couch. Hadn't I just graduated from college? Wasn't this my party to celebrate that accomplishment? Didn't I have a job and an apartment lined up? Was none of it worth anything?

A few minutes later my dad came to the basement door and called down, "Vic? You down here?"

"Yup." I answered.

He quietly closed the door behind him and came down the stairs to join me. "Ah, hiding out, I see. What are you reading?" I showed him the cover – it was a fictional tale of an astronaut tasked with establishing and leading the first colony of humans on Mars. "That's my brilliant girl, always learning, always curious. Any good?" I nodded and curled up against his chest. "You know, your mother and I are so very proud of you, Vic."

"Thanks, Dad. I'm not so sure Mom is."

"Your mom has a difficult time showing emotions, but I know her heart. She is so very deeply proud of you." I didn't tell him what I'd heard her say to her sister just minutes before.

About me and him. No reason he should feel as rotten as I did. He really didn't know her at all.

I sighed, shaking the memory away, and put the photo frame back on the shelf. Then I caught a whiff of coffee and felt immense relief. One thing my mother and I had in common was our love of good coffee, and I could've wept at the prospect of it. Having slept in my clothes, I only needed to quickly make up the bed before heading out to the kitchen.

My mother had her back to me as she reached into the refrigerator. "Good morning!" I said brightly, hoping to catch her in a good mood. "The coffee smells wonderful!"

"Well!" She turned around and smiled broadly at me. "How nice of you to join us this morning, Victoria! I wasn't sure we'd see you before lunch!" she teased, sort of.

"Now, Marcia, she did get struck by lightning only last night," my dad countered, entering the room slowly. "I think it's remarkable she is awake before dinner!" He smiled at me.

"Dad! Does this mean your back is feeling better?" I walked over and gave him a giant hug.

"Not a hundred percent, no, but I can move around a bit again, and for that I'm grateful," he responded, going over to give my mother a kiss after my hug. "Thank you for taking such good care of things these last couple days, Marcia."

My mother's gaze softened and she waved him away gently after his kiss. "Go sit down, Arthur, the eggs are just about ready." Then after a moment she added, "And the doctor said Victoria is just fine."

I caught a sparkle at her ear. "Oh, I love your earrings, Mom. Are they new?" My mother has never been one to spend much on her appearance (too frivolous!), so the new hair and jewelry were interesting.

She quickly reached one hand up and covered the diamond hoop. "Somewhat." That was all she replied before disappearing back behind the door of the fridge.

I grabbed a mug from the cabinet, noticing it was one Philip had given my mother ages ago with his school picture emblazoned into the ceramic, and I put it back to choose a plain blue one. The coffee was beautifully hot, and I added just a dash of half and half before I sat down across from my dad at the worn kitchen table. Moments later, a large serving bowl of scrambled eggs was plopped in the middle of the table with a side stack of toast. Back when I was in kindergarten, my mother decided that a day begun with protein would jumpstart our brain activity, and she has served scrambled eggs almost every breakfast since. I loathed them. I grabbed a piece of toast and spread strawberry jam on it, hoping it would be enough. After all, I was twenty-four years old, surely I could choose my own breakfast by now.

"Victoria, don't forget your eggs," my mother warned. "You're looking unhealthy and underweight, frankly."

I sighed and dutifully spooned some eggs onto my plate. I mean, I *was* super hungry. Using my trick of not breathing through my nose while swallowing them down, I quickly got through it, to my mom's appraising gaze. It wasn't even the taste of the eggs…it was completely a texture thing. My mother either overcooked them to rubbery pellets or didn't cook them long enough and they were slick and slimy. You'd think after so many years she'd be an expert, but she didn't care enough to pay it any attention. Food for her was fuel. I didn't know why the coffee would be a different experience, but thank goodness, in that regard, flavor was paramount.

I didn't bother answering my mother's jab about my appearance. I *was* a little too thin right now. I just hadn't felt like eating much lately. In fact, nothing felt right recently. I had been restless these last several weeks. Teniese's words had gotten under my skin, and my usual numbing with wine in front of Netflix wasn't doing the trick anymore. My spirit was craving change…and it scared me.

Sitting at the kitchen table, I considered my parents. My looks favored my mother's Italian roots - olive skin and dark, straight hair. I stood a couple inches taller than her at 5'5", but otherwise we were pretty similar in body shape. Philip was the spitting image of my dad – fair hair and skin that seemed to maintain a constant ruddiness, bulbous nose, and a chest like a bear. Growing up, much to my delight, people had often commented aloud that we looked nothing alike. My big brother and I weren't the best of friends in our youth, and these days I hardly saw or spoke to him unless he was back in town visiting. I returned my attention to my parents, wondering if it was just habit that made a marriage last as long as theirs had. They certainly seemed polar opposites, and it appeared they squabbled more often than not, but I hadn't lived fully at home in years, so maybe I missed all the good parts.

I refilled my coffee and sat back down. An itch on my calf reminded me of the scar and I pulled up my pant leg to look again. My dad glanced over.

"Give us a look in the daylight, then." He leaned in as I moved my leg closer. My mother walked over to see as well. "Mother Nature sure wasn't messing around with you," remarked my dad. "It's a natural masterpiece…and you get to be its display case!" He beamed. Only my dad could find something in this situation to make him proud of me, even though all I did was pass out in a puddle. Thank God for my dad.

My mother rolled her eyes like she usually did when he found a reason to praise me. "Good grief, Arthur, always the dramatic one."

"I have the soul of a poet, Marcia," he teased, "and Vic here is my current muse."

"Anyway," my mother said as she turned to me, "once you're finished, we'll go get your car. I'm sure you're anxious about missing work."

"You're not staying the day?" my dad asked, hopefully.

My mother answered for me. "It's a Tuesday, Arthur. Why should she miss work when she's not ill?" she rebuked. "Goodness, Victoria! That's your fourth slice of toast!" I hadn't even realized I'd reached for another slice, but was already in the process of spreading it with jam.

"Marcia," my dad said, coming to my defense as always, "you just told the girl she looked too thin, now you're upset she's eating too much toast? Let her be." He finished gently, then turned to me. "Are you really feeling up to going to work today? No one would bat an eye if you took a day off after your ordeal, you know."

Work. Was the storm really only last night? It felt like a million years ago. I would love to play hooky today, but should I really waste a sick day when I am fine?

"Hardly an ordeal – she slept the whole time," my mother replied under her breath. I sighed.

If my choices were staying here with my mother or going to work, then data entry, here I come. "I'm fine, Dad. And, like Mom said, I shouldn't take a sick day if there's nothing wrong with me."

Thirty minutes later, we were in the car headed to the tow lot, and after another forty-five minutes of paperwork and payments, I was waving goodbye to my mother and driving away. Freedom.

After a rushed shower and change at home, I got into the office a little before 10:00 a.m. I had called ahead to say I'd be late, but I still got eyes from the receptionist when I walked through the door. Everyone expects drudgery to start on time. I didn't bother mentioning anything about the previous night's events; even to me it sounded like a fabrication. Teniese raised her eyebrows as I sat down.

"Look who decided to stroll in! I was about to send out a search party… I don't believe I have ever witnessed you being late for work." She gave me an expectant grin. Her teasing was the good-natured kind, unlike my mother's, which was one hundred percent the cutting kind that she tried to pass off as the good-natured kind. "Everything alright?"

I nodded. "Yeah, but I had a somewhat eventful night."

Her eyes twinkled. "Ooh…sounds juicy. Want to go to lunch today so you can tell me?"

"Definitely," I answered.

By noon, I was absolutely famished, and Teniese and I headed to the only lunch place within walking distance to the office park. They had decent sandwiches, and we ate there together at least once or twice each week. Actually, if I stopped to think about it, Teniese had become the person I spent the most time with in and out of work. *Was she my only friend?* I wondered as we found a seat near the front windows. Even though she was pushy with unsolicited opinions, I liked talking to Teniese. She actually listened. She was the daughter of immigrants; her dad from Jamaica and her mom from India, and she credited them for her positive 'take no bullshit' attitude in life, as well as her thick, curly black hair and long eyelashes.

The waitress came by, and I ordered the same tuna melt I've ordered every single time I'd eaten there. It was the first thing I tried when the shop opened, I liked it, so I just kept ordering it. I could rely on the tuna melt.

After we ordered, Teniese insisted I start talking. I told her what I remembered, and she sat listening, riveted.

"Can I see the scar?" she asked, and I pulled my pant leg up to show her. She was suitably impressed. "And they said you were laying in the road by yourself? What happened to the crazy man?"

"I guess he must have run off and left me there." The cowardice of that act seemed extreme since I had braved the storm to help him in the first place. "But I'm almost certain he was mentally ill or high on something."

I was so hungry I was considering eating my fork when the sandwiches were finally delivered to our table. But one look at the tuna melt and I was hit with a strong nausea. The smell was an assault on my senses. I pushed the plate away in despair. "I can't eat this!"

"Is something wrong with it?" Teniese leaned over the table to look closer. "Did you find a hair?" She curled her lip in disgust.

"No, the smell is just making me ill all of a sudden. Does it smell off to you?" I asked her.

Teniese leaned over and breathed in deeply over my sandwich. "No – totally normal, disgusting tuna smell. The same smell I endure every damn time we eat lunch here." She laughed and passed the plate back to me, but I recoiled.

"I have to get rid of this! What should I do?" I asked her.

"Just order something else." She waved our waitress over. "Hi, sorry, my friend here finally came to her senses and realized tuna fish is the devil's own spawn. She needs to order something else." She turned to me. "What do you want instead?"

"I'll have the Reuben on rye, please, lots of mustard. And I'll pay for the tuna as well…sorry about that." I quickly spat out. *Reuben? Have I ever had a Reuben in my life?*

Once the waitress left with the offending tuna melt, I turned to Teniese, "Okay, what's in a Reuben, again? I know I just ordered it, but I can't remember exactly what it is." *What the hell was wrong with me?*

Teniese squinted at me. "Seriously? It's a mound of corned beef with some kind of cheese and sauerkraut…I mean…some people might argue it smells as bad as a tuna fish sandwich when the person next to you is eating it." She rolled her eyes. "You're putting me through a Reuben and you don't even know if you like it? That electric shock you got last night has messed with your head…and your taste buds!" She shook her head and took a comically huge bite of her own turkey, cheddar, and avocado sandwich.

The Reuben arrived minutes later, and I widened my eyes at the mound of pink meat in the middle. I didn't know how I was going to eat it. But once the smell hit me, I swooned and snatched it up. When I looked up at Teniese again, one full half of the sandwich was gone. I had practically inhaled it.

"I guess you like Reubens, huh?" she asked.

"It may be the best thing I've ever eaten," I admitted, before picking up the other half. It was more food than I'd consumed in one sitting in a long time, and my stomach strained against my pants' waistband. Strange.

The rest of the day felt painfully slow, and when 5:00 p.m. came around, I was elated. A cold front had followed on the heels of last night's storm, and I threw on my coat to walk to my car. I hadn't worn it since the night before, and as I shoved my hands into the pockets and gathered it close against the chill, something hard grazed my fingers. I pulled out a chain with what looked like a thick coin attached to one end. The coin was a slightly misshapen circle about the size of a quarter, bronze-colored with faint green veins running through it. The face had a design of some kind and I drew it closer to see. It was somewhat degraded by age, or worn down as though someone had been rubbing at it. But I made out the image of a long sword between what looked like the plates of an old-fashioned scale. Two discs suspended by chains were joined at the top by a bar that slipped behind the sword. On the back was an erratic design shaped almost like a lightning bolt. It was heavier than it looked, and there was a small hole through the top where a chain was linked.

A loud car horn scared me half to death, and I jumped back. I hadn't realized I was still standing in the middle of the parking lot. I ran to my car and, once settled in the driver's seat, pulled forth the necklace again. *Where did it come from? The man in the street! This was the necklace he was trying to give me. But I didn't actually take it… did I? And if I did, wouldn't it have been in my hand when the ambulance found me? How the heck did it end up in my jacket pocket?* At least this meant I hadn't hallucinated him like my mother suggested. I turned the small metal ornament around in my palm. It looked valuable. That poor crazy man probably gave me a family heirloom or something. Then I groaned. I would have to try to find him and return it – it wouldn't be right to keep it. I reluctantly put it back in my coat pocket and drove out of the parking lot.

I stopped at the same streetlight as the evening before, and the contrast was startling. Yesterday, the sky was alive with electricity, and the light had been swallowed up by dark clouds and driving rain. Today, the sky above me was perfectly clear and only showed the beginnings of fading into twilight. Birds were singing, and the leaves on the trees that hadn't blown down sat perfectly still, not the slightest breeze to upset them. I scanned the surrounding area but didn't see anyone who could be the man. I drove for another twenty minutes looking for him, then gave up and headed home.

To be honest, I wasn't sure I could've picked him out of a lineup all that well. "Asian American, maybe thirty, penchant for dramatically yelling at the sky…" Not unless I was close enough to his face to see his wild eyes. It had happened too fast, and the wind and rain compounded things. As I pulled into my parking area, I was surprised to find the necklace in my hand. I hadn't remembered pulling it from my pocket again. I started to return it but experienced a slight nagging anxiety, so instead, I looped the chain around my head and let the medallion rest on my sternum. That felt better.

WEDNESDAY

Chapter 7: Victoria (me)

The next morning, I awoke with the sensation that I had blinked and the night was over. I had fallen hard into bed the night before and slept like the dead. That was two nights in a row now. Usually, I lie awake with my head spinning for a long while, then wake once or twice more in the night with the same issue. As I moved to sit up, I was surprised to find one hand clasping the medallion at my chest. Pulling it closer, I examined it in the morning light. The design of the sword and scale were even more intricate than they appeared yesterday, and the pattern on the back reminded me of my lightning scar. I twisted my body around to look at my calf, which I was surprised to find had completely healed overnight. Running my finger over the scar, I felt nothing. Not even the slight soreness that was there the day before. Surely a burn from a lightning strike couldn't be fully healed in just a couple days, could it? I held the medallion next to my scar for comparison. Though not the exact tendril patterns, they were very similar. How coincidental.

Bringing the medallion back into the morning light, I rubbed my fingers along the rounded outer edges. There were small flecks of darker copper red I hadn't noticed before, tucked into the creases of the raised image. A grumble in my stomach brought me to the present, and I begrudgingly got up to get ready for work. I left the necklace on, figuring it was safer around my neck than in my pocket, anyway. I would take another look around town today for the man.

My heart sank when I pulled into the parking lot at
work and saw a coworker sitting on the curb crying. This was
not a terribly unusual scene in the year and a half I'd been at the
company. Our boss had a cruel habit of letting people get
dressed and ready for a regular workday, then firing them first
thing, as all their coworkers were also arriving. He made it a
spectacle where he could observe the reactions of everyone else
in the room. This meant most people, myself included, ignored
whoever was being sacked and focused on looking as diligent as
possible at our own jobs, lest we be tagged as "less than loyal."
I, of course, felt badly for the person, but I was not about to risk
my team player status.

I recognized the victim this time; it was Jeannette from
the accounting office. Shoot. I really liked Jeannette. She had
been taking more time off than usual in the last few months
because she was in the middle of a terrible divorce. The story
going around the office was that her husband of ten years left
one day to move in with a woman he'd been seeing on the side.
Jeannette was completely blindsided and heartbroken. But the
worst part was that they had a five-year-old son with
developmental delays who was taking it devastatingly hard.
Jeannette had many sleepless nights these last weeks, and now
she would have unemployment to add to it.

I sighed and headed toward the office. I felt bad for
Jeannette, but, normally, I stayed out of the company's
business. I did not make waves, and Jeannette and I only knew
each other on the periphery. I wouldn't have called us friends.
These thoughts raced through my head as I started to walk past
her without even looking up. Then my legs stopped; I was
rooted in place. How could I just walk by when I know the pain
she's going through? What kind of person does that make me?

A person with a job, that's who. I answered myself the way I always had. But today, the words soured in my mouth. Is that really who I wanted to be? I had spent a lifetime feeling unimportant and wanting for someone to reach out and be a friend. Maybe Jeannette needed that, too. *Or maybe I should just stay out of it!*

Suddenly my body acted independently of my brain and I found myself walking toward her. Reaching her side I knelt down so we were level.

"Jeannette?" I started, "Hey, are you okay?"

Jeannette looked up at me surprised, then began frantically trying to wipe away tears and snot with her sleeves to compose herself now that she had an audience. "Vic? Oh, hey. Yeah. I just…I mean…I know I've been missing a lot of work lately. Anyway, I guess my work hasn't been up to par. I guess I knew I was slacking a little…" she trailed off. How could they do this to her? Surprisingly, my blood began to boil on her behalf. Yes, it was sad and would put Jeannette in an even worse place, but was that something I should really get so emotional about? I never would have before.

I was not a fighter. I had never been in a march or picket or protest line. Never complained when food arrived cold at a restaurant or if I got terrible service. Even though I might have believed something should change or was unfair, I felt there were others more suited to take up the cause. Who the hell was I anyway? No one who could make any real difference. I left the bravery to others. But, remarkably, here with Jeannette, feelings of sympathy, of overwhelming injustice, were bubbling up in a way I had never experienced before. I had to do something.

Really, Vic? What are you going to do about it? Don't be stupid. In defiance of my thoughts, my body moved to sit next to Jeannette on the curb, and I draped one arm around her. She flinched at the physical contact, then was overwhelmed with emotion and leaned into me to cry.

"What am I supposed to do now?" It came out as a squeak. "Adam dropped me from his insurance yesterday. I wasn't worried because I figured I could just enroll here. Now what? Do you know how expensive private insurance is? Henry is still under Adam's plan, but he's refusing to pay for counseling. Says our boy, who has started wetting the bed and yelling for his dad in the middle of the night, is just fine and doesn't need therapy. Henry is so confused by everything, he's been hitting himself. I found him this morning banging his head into the stair riser!" She cried with renewed vigor at the memory of her sweet boy's self-harm. "I had to leave him at daycare after that, knowing that I've already used all my sick days. And then to walk in only to be fired." She sobbed openly now. "He's suffered so much through this…thinks I'm the reason his daddy isn't at home anymore…what will I do without this job?"

My heart ached for Jeannette and I cried with her. I usually didn't show emotion in public, but the rage and helplessness I felt on her behalf was growing, and I held onto her until she was spent.

"Why did he say you were being fired?" I asked gently.

"I've made some mistakes lately. Nothing too bad, and they were caught before they were too serious. But that, coupled with the fact that I've been calling in so often…he said I wasn't being a 'team player.' That all of us have difficult situations we're dealing with in life, but we don't bring them into the office." She took a deep breath and tried to calm down. "I've been here five years and never received so much as one complaint about my work until now." She attempted a wry smile. "I guess seeing me cry at my desk was bad for company morale."

What do I say to that? I thought. I wasn't in the habit of comforting people, if only because I didn't have that many people in my life. "I'm so sorry, Jeannette. When did they give you the first warning?" I asked, remembering a previous colleague's experience with human resources. He was given a warning along with a list of 'issues' regarding his performance, then granted a month to meet certain criteria if he wanted to keep his position. He quit two weeks into his review month.

"What do you mean, warning?" she responded. "Franklin just called me into his office this morning and said I was fired. There was no warning."

"Wait, really? What did HR say when you met with them?" I asked.

"I was supposed to go to Cheryl's office directly from Franklin's, but I just couldn't. I was too upset," she lamented, propping her elbows on her knees and letting her head fall into her hands. "I think I'm just going to sit here for the rest of the day."

I stood up and faced her. "Come on, you need to see Cheryl. I don't think they are allowed to just fire you without giving you a warning period first."

"I can't go back in there. It's humiliating, and I'm not sure I'll be able to stop crying." She drew the already slimy shirt sleeve across her nose again.

Amazing myself, I replied, "I'm going with you to talk with Cheryl so you don't have to be there alone. What Franklin's done isn't fair."

Jeannette regarded me with a perplexed expression. We had never shared more than a few pleasantries in the entire time we worked together. She was right to be slightly confused by my sudden interest. I know I was.

Finally, she said, "That's very kind of you, Vic. I don't know if I can even think straight enough to have a coherent conversation. It will help having you there." As I pulled her up to her feet, she took a couple deep breaths and dried her face again, then we walked through the entry doors together.

Cheryl was the head of the three-person HR team, and we had to walk the entire length of cubicle-land to reach her office. I had my hand on Jeannette's arm for support and gave her a squeeze when I felt her wilt, trying to ignore all the eyes that tracked our progress. As we passed my desk, I threw a tiny glance toward Teniese, who mouthed, "What's happening?"

We finally arrived, and I knocked on the door.

"Come in!" I heard Cheryl yell from inside, and I opened the door, letting Jeannette walk in first. "Hi there!" Cheryl offered upon seeing us. "What can I help with?" She seemed awfully chipper in the face of poor Jeannette. Jeannette paused and looked at the ground a little too long. It was getting uncomfortable, so I stepped forward.

"Cheryl, Jeannette was fired this morning without being given any warning. I thought we had a policy that required a review period after someone was accused of underperforming. Why didn't she get that chance?" I was sweating and my voice faltered once. I couldn't believe I was initiating a confrontation. My stomach flipped, but I tried to look calm.

Cheryl furrowed her brow in confusion. "What do you mean, Jeannette was fired?"

He hadn't even consulted with HR before he fired her? This was not right. "This morning, Franklin fired her as soon as she arrived for work. Said she hadn't been a team player, and was bringing down company morale, right?" I turned to Jeannette who managed a nod in agreement.

At this Cheryl stood up, "Would you excuse me for a moment? Please take a seat, I'll be right back." She swept out of the office, and Jeannette raised her eyebrows at me. We sat and waited in patient silence, until Cheryl returned several minutes later. She was wringing her hands and didn't look at us until she was back in the safety behind her desk.

"It seems that there was some miscommunication this morning, and I'm sorry about it, Jeannette." Then she looked at me. "Thank you for your assistance, Vic, but I think you can probably head to your own desk now." She gave me a thin smile.

"Actually, I'd like her to stay with me, if that's okay. I will feel more comfortable having a witness to the remainder of this conversation." Jeannette had straightened her spine and lifted her head. Cheryl sighed and gave a slight nod.

"What Franklin *meant* to say is that you are being placed in a review period. I should have been present in the meeting, so I apologize for that as well." She looked weary. "Franklin will be sending me a list of his concerns by the end of day today, and then we'd like to have a meeting tomorrow morning to let you review them and talk about ways to address them."

"What happens at the end of the review period?" Jeannette asked.

"Then we'll have another meeting and assess how your performance has measured up to the expectations of the review period." She smiled. "I am sure you'll be able to rise to the challenge. Let's meet here tomorrow morning at 9:30 and we'll go from there, okay?"

Jeannette nodded and thanked Cheryl, and the moment we were out of the office, threw her arms around me in a big hug and whispered, "Thank you so much, Vic."

An unfamiliar emotion snaked out from my chest and wrapped me up: pride. She went over to her desk and focused on getting to work.

I arrived at my own desk and was just beginning to give Teniese the rundown, when Franklin emerged from his office. He locked dagger eyes with mine and summoned me gruffly. Instantly, the pride I'd felt from helping Jeannette was replaced with dread. I slowly got up and walked over. Sympathetic eyes followed my progression. Franklin hadn't waited for me at the door, he'd simply beckoned me over, then returned to his desk, leaving the door ajar. I reluctantly pushed it open to walk through. He was seated, shuffling a stack of papers to move to the side as I entered. I didn't sit, but stood waiting for him to speak.

Finally, he looked up and leaned back in his chair. He regarded me for a moment – he did not ask me to sit down. "Victoria, you have been here long enough to understand that I own this company, correct?" He paused. I guess he didn't mean to ask rhetorically.

"Yes, sir." I thought I might faint. I wondered if Franklin would even get up to check on me if I did.

"I understand you felt the need to intervene in a decision made for this company, by me, this morning that, really, didn't involve you at all, is that right?" He tented his fingertips together and touched them to his lips. It was clear he was expecting me to answer this condescending line of questioning, but I couldn't think of anything to say that wouldn't get me in trouble.

"I'm not sure 'intervening' is the right way to put it. I just helped Jeannette talk to Cheryl," I stammered.

"I value loyalty in my staff above all else, and you going behind my back makes me pause to question yours. I don't know what's changed, since you've always been a team player before, but..." He continued speaking, but I couldn't focus on his words. Another voice had taken root in my consciousness. A deep woman's voice drowned out the sound of Franklin. *He is wrong. He is not a good person. He does not deserve your respect.*

"Victoria, did you hear what I said?" Franklin's voice broke back through. "Are we clear?"

Christ, I hadn't heard him. I looked up and bowed my head slightly – it seemed the safest thing to do. He nodded once in return and swept his hand toward the door. I guess our little meeting was done.

I slunk back to my desk and caught Teniese's questioning glance. With a small shake of my head, I mouthed "lunch" to her. Franklin's door was still open, and I didn't need him catching me whispering with a coworker instead of doing my work. At lunch, Teniese and I had barely gotten through the restaurant door before she pounced on me.

"Okay, tell me everything, and start at the beginning!" I recapped the morning's events, and Teniese was my focused audience. "What a bastard. Did he threaten to fire you, too?"

"Possibly…to be honest, I didn't hear the end of his speech…my mind wandered," I said.

Teniese raised her eyebrows, "Are you serious? First, you stood up for Jeannette, and then our illustrious boss called you into his office to lecture you, and you let your mind wander? I'm not sure I know who you are anymore." Then she added, "So time to brush up your resumé, right? Because you know you have a big, red target on your back as far as Franklin is concerned."

I had seen it enough times to agree with her that once Franklin thinks he's been crossed, you are on your way out. I suddenly felt nauseous. I needed to make a decision, and that was not my strong suit. "I don't know what I'll do!" I moaned.

Teniese just looked at me like I was a complete idiot. "You don't know what you'll do? Vic, you are smart and loyal, and *this job* was never going to be your last job. It's time to get uncomfortable, accept that you have so much to offer, and bust your ass. Take some action!" She motioned for the waitress to bring our bill and gathered her things as I let her words find a small crack in my defenses.

That evening after leaving work, I spent half an hour driving around various streets looking for the man who gave me the necklace. My cell rang at one point, but seeing it was my mom, I let it go to voicemail. As I passed by a fast food restaurant, my stomach screamed with desire and my mouth watered. I pulled into a parking space and got out of the car. I was never one for fast food fare, and the voice of my mother lit up my brain: "When you give your body junk, your trunk is sunk." I had never been at this place, but my feet carried me forward without hesitation. I got in line, and my voice knew my order before I even looked up at the menu.

"Double cheeseburger with no pickles, large fries, Diet Coke," I heard myself rattle off to the girl behind the register. She was very familiar to me, and I looked at her name tag: Ana. Ana had bright eyes, and as she turned to get my soda cup, I had a flash of her sitting in an apartment with an older woman, the sound of people's voices, and traffic coming through the open window. I snapped back to the present as she handed me the cup and my receipt, and I moved over to the pickup line. I kept stealing glances at Ana, though, wondering what that vision was about and why she was so familiar.

Grabbing my tray, I filled my soda and sat down at a two-top near a window that I somehow knew gave the best view of the majority of the parking lot. Once seated, I unwrapped my burger and began shoveling it into my face. After three bites, however, I had to stop, feeling ill. Looking at my tray and my surroundings, I was completely baffled. What the hell was I doing here? I hate this kind of food…and my roiling stomach agreed. I looked over my shoulder at Ana, the cashier who took my order. Again, it felt like I knew her – like being here in this place, with these people, was familiar. The movement of my hand on the Diet Coke lever had felt normal, like a movement I'd done many times before. The whole experience was like a memory. A memory that wasn't mine.

THURSDAY

Chapter 8: Victoria (me)

That night, images of Ana entered my dreams: Ana crying, Ana walking next to me in a park, and the strangest one, Ana snuggled against my chest as she slept. I awoke in the morning feeling strange and agitated, as though Ana's moments were my own. The images were vivid and full of emotion, as though I was living them. Who was this person, and why the hell would she be in my dreams?

I shook the thoughts from my head and got ready for work. Every act of preparation felt like a mistake, as though I was forcing myself to move forward toward doom. After pulling into the parking lot, it was an act of defiance to my body and brain to get out of the car and walk into the building, every footfall filled with dismay. I had arrived a little early and only a few people were settled at their desks as I sat down. Teniese was not yet in. Just as I organized myself and logged in, Franklin's office door opened and he stepped out. He saw me there and gave the same gruff gesture of summons I had received the day before. I felt the usual fear as I rose to comply, but I remembered the voice in my head from the day before: *He is wrong. He is not a good man.*

Sitting down in a chair across from his desk, I tried to make myself as small as I felt. A moment later, Cheryl came through the door, threw me a quick, withering glance, and took the adjacent seat. "Good morning," she said quietly.

Franklin looked up at her and replied, "Cheryl, you may proceed."

She drooped a little, then turned her body so she angled toward us both. "Victoria, Franklin has asked for this meeting to address some concerns he has about your recent performance at work. He has noted some defiance of authority that we need to address today." She opened a slim file folder she'd brought with her. There seemed to only be a single sheet of paper held inside. She consulted it and continued, "Namely, the public questioning of a staffing decision made by the owner of the company…" She gestured slightly toward Franklin without looking up from the paper. "…and several incidents of gossiping during work hours with colleagues." I waited for more, but that was apparently all Cheryl had to say. She reluctantly looked up at me, waiting for a reply. Franklin was staring me down like I was a teenager who had stolen her father's car, and he wanted to know what I had to say for myself.

I looked back and forth between them, not sure how to reply. "Um, I don't really know what you mean by 'gossiping,' and, like I said yesterday…" I inclined my head toward Franklin. "…I was only helping make sure Jeannette was okay."

"You two spoke about this yesterday?" Cheryl demanded, narrowing her eyes at Franklin.

"Calm down, Cheryl. I merely reminded Victoria how important it is for a company that all the employees work together as a team," he said dismissively. "She was in total agreement."

I was beginning to sweat as Cheryl faced me.

"Is that all that was discussed?" she asked, tentatively. I couldn't remember anything else, so I simply nodded. Cheryl let out a small sigh of relief and continued. "Based on Franklin's concerns, we are implementing a review period of four weeks. During this time, your work attitude and performance will be monitored, and you will have the chance to demonstrate the necessary changes."

"I'm sorry," I stammered, "but what exact changes am I supposed to show during this month?"

Franklin chimed in, "You are supposed to demonstrate being a team player and not spreading gossip around the office."

I flushed with heat and humiliation. "I'm sorry, but how can I show change when I have *always* been a team player and would hardly call myself a gossip. I don't even really talk to anyone here except Teniese, and I have been here close to two years without a single complaint." My voice gained strength as I spoke. Dismay was being replaced with anger and indignation. Was all the time before worthless because I decided to speak up this one time? *He is wrong. He is not a good man.*

The voice I heard the day before was back. A deep woman's voice with a slight accent I couldn't place. Why were my thoughts now in a voice that wasn't my own? I put my hands over my eyes and shook my head to clear it. Franklin took this as a sign of my acceptance and despair over being under review.

"Don't worry, Victoria. I'm sure you'll have no problem making the necessary adjustments," he added.

I looked up. How did someone get like him? A new sensation arose, like revulsion. My hands were shaking so I balled them in my lap. I could no longer sit there and nod quietly when someone like him called my character into question.

"I am sorry you feel I have not been a team player, Franklin. You are mistaken. But it doesn't matter anymore. I will not have a 'review period' to prove I don't do things I already don't do. You are wrong. I am a good employee. Or at least I was. I don't need a review period...I quit." I stood up and, without acknowledging their reactions, walked out to pack up my belongings. Teniese took out her earbuds when she saw me return, but I didn't have a chance to speak before Cheryl came over.

"Victoria! Are you really leaving? You don't have to, you know...I'm sure the review month would go without a hitch and the whole matter will be over!" she pleaded with me.

"Cheryl, I can't work for that man anymore. He is not a good person. I shouldn't have to swallow my dignity and self-respect by agreeing to this charade of a 'review period.' His accusations are ridiculous, and I refuse to continue to work for someone who behaves like a petulant child."

Cheryl's eyes darted around nervously, and I became aware my voice had risen as we were speaking. All eyes were on us, and everyone could hear our conversation. Franklin appeared at his doorway, scowling. I was overwhelmed with a desire to run over and hit him. Instead, I laced my fingers together tightly.

"Franklin, you treat people cruelly and disrespectfully. You are not a good person, and as of right now, I no longer work for you. I have wasted far too much time making excuses for your behavior because I was afraid of losing this horrible job. What an idiot I've been." I stuffed my purse with my earbuds, coffee tumbler, and the few other personal items around me. Then I grabbed my coat and, without another glance, I left for good.

THURSDAY

Chapter 9: Victoria (me)

I was exhilarated driving out of the parking lot. Who knew that sticking up for myself could feel this freeing? Then, about halfway home, the enormity of what I'd done settled in. Just as I was starting to panic, my phone rang – it was Teniese.

"Hey," I answered.

"What do you mean, 'Hey'!" responded her hysterical voice. "That was phenomenal! Where are you now? Can you meet me at the Blue Heron?" The Blue Heron was an exceptional coffee shop in town – the kind that roasted its own beans and had nothing on the menu that was poured out of a carafe.

"Don't you have to work?" I replied.

"Girl, I'm done with that place. I'm out. I'll be at the Heron in ten minutes – get your butt there!" she demanded and hung up the phone.

Teniese practically mauled me when I pushed through the door, pulling me into an enormous hug. "I'm so proud of you!" she yelled. "Now what the hell got into you?"

I groaned and slumped into my seat, "I have no idea! I just suddenly… viscerally… couldn't take being there anymore. I reached a breaking point and snapped. I'm not exactly sure what I'm doing."

"Stop right there." Teniese put her hands up in my face. "You have decided to move your life forward – I'm not going to allow you to second-guess the best thing you've done since we met."

"But I have no backup plan! I still have rent and food, though, don't I?" I was starting to spiral.

Teniese was having none of it. "Look at me, Vic," she demanded. "You are not helpless, and this is not the only job you will ever have. You made a brave, positive move. Let yourself feel proud. And, Christ, believe in yourself just a little bit, and you'll be fine. In fact, who knows what amazing changes will come into your life because you've finally decided to live it with intention!"

Bravery wasn't my strong suit, but it helped having someone who spurred me towards it rather than scaring me away from it. I nodded, exhaling my panic.

"Wait, Teniese. What did you do? You said you were 'done with that place'…did you quit, too?"

She waved her hand dismissively. "Franklin blew a gasket with your little speech and started mouthing off about how this was 'his company' and he would not have 'his authority' undermined by anyone, least of all a 'data entry specialist.'" She made air quotes, mimicking him. "I told him, since he felt data entry specialists were the 'least of all,' then he could do without one more, and I grabbed my things and walked out." She snickered, "I think he actually turned purple. That man needed someone to put him in his place – and I'm so glad that someone was you."

I surged with adoration for Teniese.

"Feels good to boldly live your life, doesn't it?" she asked.

It did, and I said as much. "I still need to figure out the job situation, though."

Teniese rolled her eyes. "Vic, you've been unemployed for all of forty-five minutes. You'll be fine, and you are not thinking about this anymore today. You are going to take today to just do whatever the hell you feel like doing." Then as an aside, she added, "And I absolutely forbid you to speak with any member of your family for at least the next twenty-four hours."

I laughed holding up my hand. "Scout's honor. Oh! I almost forgot!" I exclaimed. "Look at this." I pulled the necklace over my head and held it out for her. "I found it in my jacket pocket the other night. It was the necklace that crazy man was trying to give me during the storm. I don't remember taking it from him, but it was in my pocket the next day – so I guess I must have."

"Well, you did get struck by lightning…" Teniese said as she reached across to take the necklace. I hesitated ever so slightly when it left my hand and had to fight the impulse to snatch it right back.

Teniese turned it around and let her fingers trace the images just like I had. "Whoa. This is seriously cool," she said. "Do you think it's real? I mean, valuable? It feels valuable…and really old. I wonder what this symbol means. Scales usually stand for justice, right? And, strangely, the back looks like your lightning scar." She held it up to catch the sunlight from the window adjacent to our table. "It must have been painted at some point…I see little flecks of red on the back here, and maybe some green on the front, unless that's copper oxidation or something." She sighed as she handed it back to me, "I wish I had something like that. Maybe I can borrow it sometime?" She smiled and I turned it around in the light like she had done.

"I actually drove around last night searching for the crazy man to give it back, in case it's a family heirloom or something. But I didn't find him." I flipped the medallion over to look at the etching on the back. "I thought it resembled my scar, too." Sighing happily, I slid the chain over my head. It was cool and comforting on my skin. "I will keep looking for the crazy man – he should have it back."

"For leaving you to your death in the middle of the street in a mad storm? I would call that reparations, my dear. But it might make sense to take it to a jeweler to see if it's even worth anything," she suggested.

"Great idea, maybe that's what I will do with the rest of my wide-open day. How about you, want to come along?" The thought of Teniese and I hanging out all day, shopping, maybe getting lunch, was so appealing I held my breath hoping so hard she'd say yes. I didn't want the elation from the morning to end.

Teniese shook her head. "I would love to, but it's the last night of Diwali and I'm gonna go to my mom's to help her clean. We have to get the dirty evil out to make room for the light." I had no idea what she was talking about and must have looked confused. "It's a Hindu holiday, basically the only one we celebrate. It's five days of parties and lights and food, so you know I'm all in. We pray for a prosperous future, so I'll add an extra little prayer for your unemployed ass tonight." She laughed at her own wittiness.

"Why is it a holiday? Did a prophet die and get resurrected or something?" My ignorance of the world's religions was shameful.

Teniese held up her hand in my face again, "Don't confuse my festival of light with your Christian ghost story. Basically, it's a celebration of the triumph of good over evil and light over darkness. It's fabulous, and we're hosting some cousins tonight. So now I have more time to help my mom get the house up to my grandma's standards. Hey! You want to come? Friends are always welcome, you don't have to be Hindu or anything. The more the merrier. My grandma's making all the sweets, and she's a master."

I froze in the face of the invitation. Social gatherings always made me nervous. There were so many ways I could or would screw it up somehow. And this would be a gathering where I would be the definite odd person out, not knowing anyone. I'd have to make lots of small talk. My palms got clammy just thinking about it.

"Oh thanks, um, I think not tonight. You have fun with your family though, it does sound amazing. Thanks so much for the invitation," I stuttered.

Teniese grinned knowingly. "Yeah, I kinda figured that would be your answer. Your loss, my friend! But do let me know what you find out at the jeweler, okay? And try to remember to have a little fun."

After Teniese left, I sat there for a few more minutes thinking what it would be like to celebrate with lights and food and family. I didn't grow up with any religion, really. We celebrated Christmas and Easter but not with much gusto. My mom's family was pretty reserved – and really boring. Of all the things to celebrate in the world, it would be nice to celebrate good overcoming evil.

I finally got up to go find out more about my necklace. A quick online search turned up a vintage jewelry store downtown, and I headed straight there. Walking through the ornate door, it was as though I'd entered an alternate universe. Elaborately scrolled, wood-carved display cases were positioned throughout the small space, and a giant baroque gold and crystal chandelier hung in the middle of the room, casting a soft glow. A tall, willowy woman with a severe white bob and bright red glasses looked up as I entered.

"Well, hello there, my dear," she offered, emerging from behind a glass display case that ran the length of the wall and seemed to hold nothing but rings. "Welcome to the Golden Scarab. May I help you?"

"Um, yes, thank you," I stammered. "I was wondering if you could tell me if a piece of jewelry is real, er, or valuable I guess, or not. It was given to me, and I don't know if I should get it insured or if it's just costume jewelry." I had practiced my speech on the way over, and it felt foolish and stilted in my mouth. I have always been a terrible liar.

"Of course!" the woman replied. "Let's take a look, shall we? Follow me to this desk here." I handed her the necklace, and she placed it down on a velvet board. She grabbed a magnifying glass from the side of the desk and leaned in closer. Her brow furrowed, and she murmured, "Why is this piece so familiar…? It can't be!" She shot her head up to glare at me and snatched the necklace up again to hold under the desk lamp. "Where did you get this?" she demanded.

"Like I said, it was given to me recently," I answered, confused by her sudden change.

"I have seen this necklace before. Must have been fifty…" She furrowed her brow in concentration. "No, fifty-five years ago now!" She cut her eyes sharply in my direction. "I was just a girl but I never forgot it. A young woman came in, just like you, asking my grandfather to help her find a new chain for her necklace, to replace the one that had been broken. I was about ten years old and was sitting right there reading after school." She pointed to a sumptuous and worn armchair off to the side. Then her attention was back on the necklace, and she lovingly caressed the image of the sword and scales. "I remember he asked me to come look at it, more animated than I had ever seen him. He tried to convince the woman to sell the piece. Well, she became agitated and attempted to grab the necklace back out of my grandfather's hand. What was so alarming was that he wouldn't let go at first. Stood there in a tug of war with the woman, until he realized it might harm the item. It was so out of character. Once my grandfather had let go and it was back in her hand, the woman ran out of the shop. My grandfather actually chased her for a minute, shouting after her to reconsider. Her name was Lydia something or other…Boyd or Blake…something with a B. I remember that because my grandfather tried to locate her after she ran off. It was such a spectacle! And he would ask me from time to time over the years if I remembered 'that necklace with the scales'. " Now she looked back at me, "I have wondered about its fate for years. For it to find its way back to the Golden Scarab after all this time is truly remarkable. I believe I was meant to place this item in the right hands for you!" She smiled brightly.

"Oh, I don't think I want to sell. I just need to know exactly how careful I should be with it," I replied nervously.

The woman gazed intently down at the medallion for a minute. "I believe you should be extremely careful. The medallion is mainly bronze, but do you see the flecks of faint red just here and here?" She took out a magnifying glass, held it over the medallion in the light, and pointed to the edges of the lightning-looking thing on the back. "I believe it was adorned with enamel at some point. It's like a colored glass. And here…" She turned the medallion over again to show the intricate sword and scales. "Here you see little flecks of green in the recesses. It must have been quite spectacular in its prime," she added wistfully. "But the most exciting part of this piece is the fact that it has engravings on both sides. They must have been crafted independently and then melded together once completed, because it's not thick enough to have been able to withstand engraving from both sides. In truth, I'm not sure how it was managed. And see that one lone fleck of yellow in the sword? I believe the front was gilded at one point."

She sighed. "Of course, it's seen centuries of wear and tear by the looks of it."

"Centuries?" *Did I have an artifact of some kind in my possession?* "How old do you think it could be?"

The woman peered down again at the medallion, then shot me a look over the rim of her glasses. "You'd need an historian to tell you for sure, but I'd put my money on somewhere between the twelfth and fourteenth centuries. It's confusing because I have never seen something comparable, but that's my best guess."

My breath caught in my throat. This necklace could potentially be over six hundred years old? "Wow," was all I could muster. I suddenly wanted it back in my hand very badly. "Um, may I see it again?" She grudgingly passed it back. I was now terrified my hands weren't clean enough to hold it. But I took the medallion and turned it back and forth under the light, marveling anew at the colors and intricacy of the design.

"It probably belongs in a museum. If you really aren't interested in selling, I have a friend at the Metropolitan. I would be more than happy to reach out," she added before straightening her back and regarding me.

I couldn't believe what she was telling me. If she was correct, it probably *should* be in a museum. Why would the man just pass it to me in the middle of the street? Obviously, he knew what he had. He had screamed to the sky, "I'm not ready!" before telling me *she* wanted me to have it. *She wants the amulet for herself.* The deep female voice was back. *You must not let her have it.* I shook my head to try to clear it.

The woman took my hesitation as an opening, "But seriously, if you are looking for a merchant for the medallion, the Golden Scarab is really your best option. You won't find a more reputable house for vintage jewelry in the city. I'm willing to offer this." She grabbed a pen and sticky note and scribbled down something quickly before sliding it across the small table. I gasped. It was more than five full years of my salary. I whipped my head up to look at her.

"It's worth that much?" I was floored.

"Actually, I just made you a rather generous offer. I am amazed this medallion found its way back to the shop and it's wonderful to have a chance to lay eyes on it again. It would be a fabulous piece to place in the right buyer's hands. It will have to be formally tested, of course, but I am very confident in my abilities to recognize a real from a fake," she purred.

I took a rather big inhale, then, with my exhale, slowly placed the necklace back over my head, meeting the woman's eyes as I did so. "You are right, that is an incredibly generous offer, and I will have to think long and hard about it. In the meantime, you have been exceedingly helpful and I appreciate your time." I started to back away.

"Wait." She reached under the table. "Take my card. If…please reach out the moment you're ready to sell, Miss…"

I grabbed the card and pivoted quickly toward the door. "Okay, thanks!" I waved behind me as I walked out. There was no way I was giving her my name. I had a feeling the fewer people who knew what I possessed, the better. And the voice had warned me…

THURSDAY + FRIDAY

Chapter 10: Victoria (me)

Once back in my car, I took a moment to study the medallion again. The voice in my head had called it the amulet. Since amulets were believed to protect the wearer against evil and misfortune, it seemed to fit with the images of a sword and lightning. As I looked at them again, the scales extending out from the sword were comforting. I then fingered the little piece of paper that held the massive sum – the offer for selling. I couldn't say I wasn't tempted to run back there and take the deal. It would make this next stage of my life so much easier if I had a cushion like that. I wouldn't have to think about making a decision right away with work. I could take a few weeks, or years, just to relax, read a couple good books...

The amulet is not for sale. You must protect it so it can protect you. The voice snapped me to attention. This was no longer random – this was an alarming intrusion into my mind. I waited quietly in my car, my heart beating out of my chest, for the voice to say more, but it was silent. Looking around to see if anyone was on the sidewalk and might witness an insane lady talking to herself, I spoke up. "Who are you? How do you know what I'm thinking?" I asked the voice, timidly. Instead of an answer, I got a directive. *Be patient and heed my words. You are still adjusting. The time for explanations will come.*

Now I knew I was losing it. I was hallucinating – interacting with a female voice in my head telling me what to do. This was not good. This was hospitalization-level not good.

And to top it off, the voice had been laced with impatience. "Hello?" I whispered. "Are you still there?" I held my breath waiting for a response.

Just at that moment, my phone rang. I jumped and let out a squeal, sending my phone flying out of my hand and into the backseat. Could the voice reach me through my phone, too? I frantically searched around to find where it landed, half expecting the screen to say "Your Conscience" in the caller ID. But it was only my dad. I just missed it. I calmed myself and waited another minute to see if the voice might come back, but it didn't. Once my dad's voicemail was loaded, I played it.

"Hey Vickster, it's Dad. I wanted to see how my lightning girl is doing today…you still feeling alright? Anyway, your brother just let us know he's coming into town this weekend, and I want to have our whole family together. It's been too long. We're having dinner Saturday night and I really want you to be there. Pretty please…for your dear old dad? 6:30 pm. Love you, kiddo!"

Damn. It was Thursday, which meant I only had today and tomorrow to come up with something to tell them about work. Ugh. Could I get out of dinner, somehow? Pretend I was sick? I sighed. Who was I kidding? I wouldn't disappoint my dad and not go. Why couldn't I be a better liar? The excitement over the necklace and the voice was overshadowed by the anxiety of the looming family dinner. I sent my dad a quick text reply saying I'd see him Saturday, then drove home.

All afternoon and evening, I was uneasy, restless. It seemed like my entire life was suddenly in limbo, and I didn't like it. I nervously tried speaking to the voice again, but got no response, which was almost as unsettling as having heard it in the first place. I slept like the dead again, though, and finally lifted my head the next morning to see it was after 10:00 a.m.! I couldn't remember the last time I'd slept that late. Instead of the fatigue I'd been feeling the past few days, I felt invigorated, practically bursting with energy. Before I had a chance to talk myself out of it, my PJs were replaced with baggy sweats, I laced up my sneakers, and I left the house for a run. An actual run…not just ten seconds of jogging in agony followed by thirty minutes of walking and complaining. I was possessed, positively lit from within, and it was as though my feet barely touched the pavement. My movements weren't awkward at all, and without my being aware of it, an hour had passed. I wasn't even winded! When I finally made it back home, instead of feeling exhausted and sore, I buzzed with pleasant energy. Hopping into the shower and soaping up my feet, I froze, confused. My leg was different. There was muscle definition between my ankle and my knee that, before, was more like one continuous soft line. I balanced on my left leg and flexed and straightened my right, amazed to see defined muscles appear with each movement. I had always been fairly thin, but kind of soft around my edges. This change was startling. Could all this really come from just one run? I would have forced myself to do it ages ago!

I moved my hands up and down my new body, feeling unfamiliar angles and firmness. I had abs! Not just one or two, but a whole set that were outlined whenever I contracted them. My forearms were striated with muscle – when I flexed my elbow, there were actual bulges at my biceps. This was incredible! I left the shower to get dressed, but couldn't stop admiring myself. Everywhere, I was firm and lean. I couldn't even pinch an inch at my belly. I had to switch to yoga pants when my jeans wouldn't come above my muscular thighs. I reached to pull a t-shirt down over my head, a move that had bothered my right shoulder since a rollerblading incident several years earlier, and I didn't feel even the slightest twinge. Running was a miracle!

Once dressed, I ate a staggering breakfast of bacon, eggs (over easy, thank you very much) and toast. Twice the amount as usual, but I guess all this muscle needed to be fed. The brilliant sun was calling to me, and I threw on a light jacket and headed out for a drive. I texted Teniese to see if she wanted to meet for lunch – that I had something exciting to share. I was disappointed when she replied she already had lunch plans with her new boyfriend, James. I sat there trying to think of someone else I could call. I was bursting with exhilaration and wanted to share. But there was literally no one, except maybe my dad – but he would most likely be with my mom, so it wasn't worth the risk. I really needed to make more friends.

I drove aimlessly for a while. After living in this town for years, I still hadn't really explored it much. I had always thought the little downtown where my aunt's frozen yogurt shop was located was cute. There were a few small boutiques, a cool independent bookstore and a smattering of cafés and restaurants. Big, old growth trees lined the few main streets and just beyond were large Victorian homes built in the beginning of the century. Behind those streets were more modern, middle-class neighborhoods with mid-sized homes and manicured lawns not unlike the block my parents had moved onto. One street past these small neighborhoods, however, the scene changed dramatically. Lots and homes were tightly packed and more uniform and plain in design. Many had chain link fences or dilapidated wooden ones. The lawns were more weed than grass, and instead of cute shops and restaurants, there were boarded up storefronts and payday lenders. How disheartening it must be to live there. The idea struck me as so sad and unfair, I started tearing up. What was wrong with me today?

I shook my head to clear it and had just started back toward home when I spied some people gathered in a glass-front exercise studio of some kind, tucked into an unassuming strip mall. I was drawn to it and pulled over. The graffiti-esque sign above the windows said "Victory Corner," and I saw men and women engaged in what looked like controlled fighting. Before I knew it, I had jumped out of the car and was walking up to the entrance. Passing through the door, déjà vu hit me like a brick wall. Instinctually, I knew the manager's office was off to the right; Chuck was his name. He was salty and carried a perpetual scowl but could disarm anyone of any weapon before you blinked. *How the hell do I know that?*

Just then, Chuck emerged from the office and noticed me standing in the entrance. "Can I help you?" he scowled.

"Ummm…Chuck?" It made no sense that I should know this. "You're the manager, right?"

He narrowed his eyes. "Yeah, you know who I am, so who the hell are you? I know you don't train here…"

As I took in the surroundings, I was struck with a vision of Chuck attacking me with a stick like the people on the mats were doing. I artfully evaded his attack and disarmed him before picking him up and slamming him down on the mats. The vision was so vivid, so real. For a moment, I actually wondered if I could have been here before. I shook my head – of course I hadn't. Why on earth would I set foot in a place like this? But how did I know this person and the faces of some of the other people training? Could I have seen Chuck somewhere like the grocery store line, and my imagination was just filling in all the rest? Felt pretty real for my imagination. Chuck raised his eyebrows expectantly and crossed his arms over his thick chest. I guess he was waiting for an answer.

"Sorry," I faltered, "I'm Victoria. I don't know…I mean…I must have just heard someone mention you and this place before." I looked around again. Men and women moved around one another in a kind of orchestrated dance. Chuck followed my gaze, then returned his icy stare to me.

"You a lawyer? She send you for more money? I already gave that bitch everything. I'm sleeping in the goddamn office because I can't afford my apartment anymore. So unless she wants the sweat from my damn brow…" he spat, the veins throbbing at his temples.

I held up my hands in surrender. "I'm not here for anyone! I'm not a lawyer. I was just driving by and saw your sign and wanted to check it out." He gave me one more glance before exhaling and lowering his hands.

"Sorry. It's just that my now-ex-wife has decided that she's entitled to every damn penny I make even though I know she's already shacked up with that idiot bartender she left me for. Let him pay for her stupid clothes and salon visits. I am barely staying afloat as it is!" He was getting rankled again and made a motion with his hands like he was throwing away the whole thing. "Anyway – you wanted to know about the gym. We train in various aspects of combat or defensive martial arts including Wing Chun, Jiu-jitsu, and Jeet Kune Do." Seeing my blank expression, he added, "Basically we learn how to attack, and defend against attacks, in scenarios where there are weapons involved, or not." He motioned to the group on the mat. "This class is a Kali class. It's a Filipino style of fighting with bamboo sticks."

It was beautiful to watch, and the clacks of stick hitting stick resounded throughout the gym. Some were moving slowly and coaching each other through the techniques, while other pairs were moving all over the mats, striking and defending with deftness and a sense of calm.

"Is it hard to learn?" I asked, suddenly desperate to hold one of the bamboo sticks in my hand.

"Nah…it's like everything else. If you put the time and effort in, you'll pick it up quickly. Do you train in martial arts?"

"Oh no, never. It feels silly even being here, really. But I've never seen something like this. That couple is moving so beautifully."

"Let's have you give it a go. Omar!" He waved over one of the students. "This is…what's your name again?"

"Victoria, but you don't need to do that." I nervously backed away. Oh God…I was going to make a fool of myself! "I'm really a bit of a klutz when it comes to things like this. I can never seem to get my right and left sides to work together."

Chuck waved his hand dismissively. "Take Victoria here through some basic movements, will you? Here, take this stick." He handed me one of the bamboo sticks. It was smooth and comfortable in my hand, with subtle designs burned into one end. Holding it felt pleasant and natural.

Omar nodded and smiled at me. "Right, so let's start with a basic strike. Bring the stick back a little overhead like you're getting ready to chop something, then step forward with your opposite foot while you arc the stick down across in front of your body."

He did the movement so smoothly, and I attempted to do the same, but stepped with my right foot instead of my left, and it felt weird.

"Try again, opposite foot. Good! Now, I'm going to face you and do the same movement so our sticks can meet at the top."

He turned to face me and raised his stick motioning for me to do the same. My heart beat wildly, and my forehead began tingling. We moved slightly toward one another with our sticks meeting in the middle with barely a whisper.

"Don't worry about hitting my stick, try to give it a little more force," he encouraged.

We resumed our starting positions, and this time, I brought my stick down harder. The sound they made upon connecting was loud, and I felt a jolt. Before I knew what was happening, I had moved in toward Omar, wrapped my left arm around his weapon, brought my stick down hard on his forearm, forcing him to release his own stick. Then I spun around underneath his right arm, bringing it with me so his shoulder locked out and his upper body pitched forward. Kicking his feet back, he fell to the ground and I quickly snaked my body behind his with my own stick positioned at his neck and intertwined with my arms so that I was choking him. All this happened in the blink of an eye and without me knowing what the hell I was doing. It wasn't until I was on the ground with Omar in a chokehold that I snapped to.

"Oh my God, I'm so sorry!" I yelled, instantly releasing him to a coughing fit.

Chuck was on me in a flash. "What the fuck do you think you're doing?!" he screamed, yanking Omar up and away from my stunned form, still on the ground. "You better stay the hell down there!" he demanded, then focused on Omar, still coughing. "Are you okay? Can you breathe?" Omar nodded, doubled over with his hands on his knees for support, and Chuck's fury unleashed in my direction. It was terrifying and I stood up quickly.

"Who the fuck are you to come in here and mess with my students? You think you're some bigshot, need to pretend you know nothing and then hurt people who are trying to help you?"

"I'm sorry!" I stammered again. "I don't know how I did that…"

He yanked the stick out of my hand and shoved me toward the door, "Get out of my gym. I better never lay eyes on you again, you hear me? Get out!" Chuck screamed. I took off running to my car and pulled away as fast as I could.

What the hell just happened? How could I have done what I did to that poor man? How did my body even know what movements to make? And how could I hurt him so easily, without a second thought? This wasn't me. Too many crazy things had happened now, and I was scared. After nearly running a red light from distraction, I pulled over to get a hold of myself. Once parked, I lashed out at the steering wheel in frustration.

"What is happening to me?" I shouted to the air. "How could I do that – what did you do to me? Whatever it is, I don't want it!" I *wanted* the voice to come this time, but I got nothing. What should I do now? I needed to talk to someone. I called Teniese again but just got her voicemail. I needed help. I tried to think but panic made it hard to focus. So much had happened in such a short time. I was doing, eating, and saying things that weren't me. Even my dreams didn't feel like my own. I suddenly remembered Ana, the cashier at the fast food place. I must be connected to her somehow because of the dreams I'd had of her the other night. It was a long shot, but I felt better having something concrete to do. I calmed myself enough to drive, but white knuckles betrayed my agitation.

I was completely deflated when I pushed through the glass door and didn't see Ana working the register. I had convinced myself on the drive over that she would be my connection to answers, and now I wouldn't find any. When the smell of burgers hit my nose, however, my stomach let out a grumble. I got in line and ordered another double cheeseburger and large fries with a diet soda. Even saying the words made my brain shout *no* in rebellion, but it was somehow what my body wanted again, and I wasn't in a mood to argue. The person at the register went to hand me my soda cup as I simultaneously reached forward to grab it, accidentally hitting it out of her hand. I lunged forward to stop it from rolling off the countertop, just as I heard a loud gasp. I glanced up to see Ana standing there, staring at me wide-eyed. Or rather, she was staring at my chest; the amulet had fallen out of my t-shirt. She must have walked in from the back of the restaurant. I straightened up and we locked eyes.

"Oh, I'm so sorry about that! You have really good reflexes!" The cashier said. "Here's the top, they'll bring your order over to the side there."

I flicked her a quick glance and smile and stepped aside before moving my gaze back to Ana and mouthing, "Can we talk?"

She looked anxiously around just as the manager sauntered up behind her. "I am not paying you to stand still," he chided as he brushed past.

"Actually," Ana replied, speaking loudly enough for me to hear, "I need to grab some air. I'm feeling really nauseous all of a sudden. Could I take my fifteen minutes now instead of later?" He rolled his eyes and then nodded in the direction of the back exit. Ana gave me a meaningful look, then headed off toward the door.

"Um, can I change mine to a to-go order?" I asked the person filling the tray with my food and he handed over a couple of greasy bags.

I left out the front door so as not to arouse suspicion, then quickly made my way to the back of the building. Ana was pacing in front of a massive garbage bin and nearly attacked when she saw me approaching.

"Where did you get that necklace?" she demanded.

I wasn't expecting her intensity and retreated backwards. "You recognize the necklace? It was given to me during the storm a few nights ago, by a man I didn't know."

"Given to you? There's no way. What did he look like?" Ana asked.

"He was Asian American, maybe late twenties, early thirties." I offered.

"Andrew. Why would he give it to you? He wouldn't even let me hold it." Jealousy laced her words and she got up in my face. Her aggression caught me off guard. This is not how I expected the conversation to go.

I held up my hands defensively. "He made me take it! He had fallen in the street during the storm, and I stopped to help him. He was acting crazy and I tried to get away from him but he grabbed my arm and wouldn't let go. I assumed he was not right in the head. I have tried looking for him in the days since to give the necklace back, but haven't had any luck."

"There's no way he would just give it to you. You're lying, there has to be something else going on." She pushed me back a little toward the garbage bins. "Tell me."

"I didn't even know his name, I swear. He was lying in the middle of the road – I couldn't just leave him there. I didn't ask for the necklace – he forced it on me. I never met him before that night, and I haven't seen him since. I came here because I need to find him, and something told me you could help. I had a vision or insight or whatever when I saw you and then you clearly recognized the necklace just now. I'm looking for him, that's it. I just need to find him." Words flew out of me as she pushed closer. I had never been physically threatened by anyone, except Philip when we were kids. This woman looked like she was ready to knock me sideways.

"Are you being serious? That's it? You aren't seeing him or something?" I shook my head insistently. She still eyed me suspiciously but backed off a bit. "I haven't seen him or heard from him since the day of that storm. Our last visit didn't go so well. You say you found him in the street? Was he hurt or something?" To my relief, she widened the gap between us.

"Not that I could tell. He had fallen and was just lying there, but when I got to him he started screaming nonsense at me. That I've been chosen and I needed to take the necklace. He tried to force it over my head. He kept yelling he was sorry to the sky. I assumed he was mentally ill. Then lightning struck me and I guess I blacked out because I woke up later in the hospital, with the necklace in my pocket and no sign of the man."

"He wasn't in the hospital with you?"

"I don't think so, or at least if he was I didn't know about it. He was nowhere to be found when the ambulance got to me." It hadn't occurred to me that he could've been found somewhere else and brought in separately.

"And he told you you'd been chosen?" Her voice had gotten quiet, and I could tell she was deep in thought, then she exploded. "Ugh, he's a mental case!" She said to herself, walking in a circle with her head in her hands before exhaling and addressing me again. "Look, I don't think he's been right in the head lately, but something terrible must have happened to him because he told me he would never part with the necklace unless he was forced to."

This was all very confusing, and I needed her to start explaining. "He clearly seemed out of it to me. I need to find him. Things are happening to me I don't understand. If you have any information, I really need you to share it."

She wrung her hands, deciding what to do. Just then a coworker came out to throw a bag in the bin and raised an eyebrow at Ana before heading back inside. As soon as the back door closed, Ana said, "Meet me at the gazebo at Fox Park in twenty minutes. I'll tell them I'm really sick and clock out early. Twenty minutes, okay?"

I nodded and rushed back to my car while Ana went back into the restaurant. It took me all of five minutes to reach the park, and I ate the greasy food while I waited for her to arrive. Thirty minutes later, after I thought she must have stood me up and was about to go back to the restaurant, I saw her walking across the grass from the opposite end of the park.

"Sorry, my manager didn't believe I was sick and wouldn't let me leave. So I had to make myself throw up in the bathroom."

We sat on adjacent benches and appraised each other. Ana was around my age, I guessed. She was Latina with straight, medium brown hair that was gathered up in a high ponytail, and her nails were long and painted a bright shade of blue with little white daisies. She tapped them nervously on the bench next to her.

"So…Andrew? Clearly you two are dating or something?"

Ana nodded. "Yes. Andrew and I are dating. Were dating." She sighed in frustration. "I don't know what we are anymore. I met him through my brother Julian. Or rather, because of Julian." She hesitated, and I could tell she was figuring out how much she wanted to reveal to this stranger who showed up at her work wearing her boyfriend's necklace. "What exactly did he say to you when he gave you the necklace?" Ana asked.

I recapped everything I could remember from my encounter with Andrew that Monday, ending with the lightning strike. Ana furrowed her brow. "Andrew had been struck by lightning before, too. Said it happened when he was a teenager. He even had this scar on his leg."

At the mention of the Lichtenberg Figure, I lifted my pant leg to show Ana my scar. "Did it look like this?"

She gasped, "Yes, so much like that! Holy shit!" She paused to think for just a moment. "Did you say weird things were happening to you? What kind of things?"

I nodded. "It's been so freaky scary. Suddenly, I'm craving foods I have always hated, like fast-food burgers and Reuben sandwiches. Then I'm having memories of places I've never been and people I've never met. That's why I came back to the restaurant today…I saw you a couple days ago and suddenly was having all these visions of you. You walking in the park with me… you at the restaurant. It was like I'd actually been there." Now I was up and pacing. "And this morning I went on a run for an *hour*! Look at these muscles! I was soft and squishy when I went to bed last night!"

Ana stood up too. "We ate at this café in a boring office park a bunch because Andrew loved the Reuben sandwiches so much."

"Could Andrew do martial arts with sticks and weapons and stuff?" I asked frantically, equally desperate and afraid for her answer.

"Yes. He was always at this gym on Rush Street. Victory, something or other."

"I went there this morning and nearly killed someone with movements I have never learned, but could still do. This makes no sense!" Somehow I was remembering things that Andrew knew – not only visual memories, but physical skills too. I was nauseous and sat back down to put my head between my knees. "What is happening to me?" I groaned.

Ana looked stricken. "He tried to tell me this on Monday. God, he was acting so crazy. I thought he'd lost his mind. He asked to meet here actually. He was all jumpy telling me he really tried with Julian but it didn't work."

"Your brother?"

She nodded. "Julian is into some no-good shit. Runs with a gang on the south side of the city." She leaned in toward me and her eyes bored into mine. "He's not a bad person, you understand me? He just got linked up with some bad people and couldn't get out. It's so hard to get free from them once you're in. But Julian wanted to. I know he did. Even if he forgot it himself these last few years.

"Andrew stopped me one night a while back as I left work. He claimed he was part of a secret task force or something looking into the gang's activities. Asked me all sorts of questions about Julian. At first, I told him to fuck off, but he said maybe he could help Julian to get out. He kept pestering me, so finally I agreed to sit down with him. I thought maybe I

could make him see what a good person Julian was deep down.
I knew he was doing bad stuff now, but it wasn't who he truly
was; he was just a product of the situation he was in. Shouldn't
a person's good deeds matter just as much as their bad deeds?"
She looked to me for agreement, and I offered a hasty nod.

"Anyway, Andrew sat there and listened to everything I
said. He told me he'd met many people like Julian in his life.
Most never got out and never changed. But I believe Julian will
– I knew him before all that craziness took over. I tried to
convince Andrew." She ran her hands through her ponytail and
exhaled. "He wanted to know more. Like how Julian got into
the gang in the first place. I told him you get two choices
around here when you're poor: join a gang or become a target
of the gang. He asked about our mom, my job, everything. And,
God help me, I told him whatever he wanted to hear. I didn't
realize how much I wanted to talk about it.

"Our dad ran off on my mom and us about a decade ago,
with a one-line note that said he 'just couldn't do it anymore.'
Julian took it the hardest. He was only fifteen and decided he
needed to be the man of the house. My mom couldn't make
ends meet with her part time job, so when the gangs started
approaching with their new clothes and fancy cars, Julian
agreed to do some small jobs for them. Mostly delivery and
pickup of packages. He figured he could at least get enough
money for us to have consistent food on the table or the electric
bill paid. But with each job, they pulled him further and further
in, until he dropped out of school senior year. I knew he was
dealing drugs by that point, and it broke our mom's heart."

Ana stopped pacing and sat back down. "Andrew listened
to my sob story that first day. Got a real thoughtful look on his
face, thanked me, and asked if we could meet again the next

week. We did, and we met here every week for a month before I realized there was more going on between us than had to do with Julian. That was, well, five months ago, now." Ana took a deep breath and got up to pace again.

"Did Andrew get Julian to stop?" I asked.

"No. He tried. He kept his word and tried to talk to Julian about getting out. He said Julian told him to fuck off. Andrew let me know when we met this past Monday before the storm that just last week he had all this new evidence of big shit that Julian was into. Thefts, extortion, still drugs, but larger scale than he had realized. I guess Julian's gang was hired by a bigger crime ring several weeks ago, and it's bad. I didn't want to believe him. I knew the further Julian got in, the harder it would be to get out."

"That's when Andrew got super weird." Ana put her head in her hands, "Ugh, it's so hard to even repeat. He got all serious and desperate looking, grabbed my hands, and knelt down in front of me here." She motioned at the base of her seat. "He told me he loved me and needed me to know the truth about him. Then he claimed he was a vigilante for a goddess. A goddess of justice." She shot me a look before continuing. "He had been 'chosen' and trained… and had certain powers…God, it was awful. It was like being in a cruise ship of happiness, but then you go below deck and discover the entire first level is already flooded…you're about to drown. He was a complete nutjob!" Ana laughed as though it was a big joke, but I could see she was crying.

Before this week I would have thought he sounded like a nutjob too, but now my mind was racing. There were too many similarities. Seriously though, a goddess? Like in the myths? I *was* hearing a woman's voice in my head…

Ana continued. "Anyway, that was the day of the storm. I screamed at him for leading me on to think he was normal and I could trust him. Then I raged off. I haven't heard from him since. Then you show up saying he gave you his necklace that very night."

"He was not in a good way, like seriously messed up. Maybe it was because of your fight?" I suggested, excited. We were finally getting somewhere.

Ana took a moment before answering. "Julian's crew was attacked that day, and everyone was shot except Julian. He was beaten, but left alive." She dropped herself down on the bench and began crying heavily. "I don't know what to think! We were told my brother was in the hospital, but before we could even get there, he just up and disappeared. I don't know if he's dead or alive, or in trouble…or what, and my mom is so freaked out. And what if Andrew had something to do with it? I'll never forgive him! But I still love him, too…isn't that messed up?" Ana's shoulders slumped, then she looked up at me. "He told me he could never take that necklace off, said it was what protected him. Why would he give it to you?"

"I don't have a clue. Why am I suddenly doing things that Andrew used to do?"

We sat in silence until a thought occurred to Ana. "Do you think you somehow got Andrew's knowledge when he gave you the necklace? Like the powers come from the necklace itself? That would explain why he never let me touch it, right? I mean, I know that sounds ridiculous, but I also know there are things in this world I can't understand. My mom has been going to a psychic medium for years, and they always tell her the craziest shit there's no way they could know if they didn't actually have the magic. Could he really have been telling me the truth about the vigilante nonsense? Even with how stupid it sounds?"

"I have no idea, only that the things that are happening to me are very real. Did he say anything about how he started being this fighter-vigilante person? Like when he got the lightning scar?"

She nodded. "He said his dad had just been murdered. I mean I knew his parents were dead, but he never said how they died before then. I guess the goddess came to him the day his dad was shot by some thug trying to rob their restaurant. He said that was why he chose to be the fighter, because he couldn't imagine going back to life without his father. He was talking so fast about everything. That's all I know."

"He *chose* to be this?" He must have felt he had no options to want his life to be out of his control like this. Maybe having your father murdered was enough?

"That's what he said."

"Why didn't I get a choice? This is happening without me having any control at all." I had an idea. "Wait, if the power actually is in the necklace, I just need to get rid of it and my life will go back to normal, right?" I took the amulet from my neck and held it in my hand, then looked around to figure out what to do with it. My eyes landed on Ana and she backed away.

"I'm not touching that fucking thing!" she shouted.

"Help me find a rock to hit it with. Maybe destroying it would be better than just leaving it somewhere." As the words left my mouth, the booming voice returned to my head. *You will not harm the amulet. You have been chosen, and the amulet is your protection. She is unimportant. Leave her now. Go home and rest. In a few days, your transition will be finished and all will be clear.*

I grabbed the hair at my temples and pulled hard. "Stop doing this to me! I don't want to be the chosen one! Are you turning me into him? Tell me what is happening!" I screamed to the sky above.

Ana crossed herself and regarded me agape. "Are you hearing voices? That's another crazy thing Andrew said on Monday. That the goddess talked to him…in his head."

"Hello?" I yelled to the sky when the voice didn't return. "Dammit! I need to find him, Ana. The voice…this goddess… just said my transition will be complete in a few days…what if I can't remember my own life after that? And if Andrew transferred his memories and powers to me, does that mean he lost them himself?"

Ana put her hand over her mouth. "Could he not know he loved me anymore? Or could he even be dead? If you have his memories and abilities, what if it killed him to pass them to you?!"

"I don't know anything about any of this, but I don't think he's dead because I was alone when the ambulance got to me. I have to try to find him. Will you help me?"

She nodded. "I want to find him, too."

My shoulders dropped with relief. "Okay. Great, thank you. I had no idea where I was going to go from here if you had said no. Do you know where he lives?" She nodded again. "Why don't you visit his house and all the places you know he used to go. I guess I'll just drive around some more? Take my number and keep me posted on what you find out, okay?"

Ana agreed. "I can do this today, but I can't afford to miss work tomorrow, too. Ugh, I wish I knew where Julian was – I feel he has to be connected somehow!" Then she pointed to my fisted hand still clutching the amulet. "What are you going to do with the necklace?"

I uncurled my fingers. "I guess I'll keep it for now. The voice told me it was my protection. I don't know what would happen to me if I damaged it in some way." I didn't mention the relief I experienced as the cool metal slid back down over my collarbone and settled beneath my shirt.

FRIDAY

Chapter 11: Dike

Dike tossed and turned in her bed. For three days, her sleep had been fitful, a difficulty she never suffered before. She missed Andrew. Missed his conversation, his companionship…his adoration. She couldn't wrap her head around what he did. Wasn't she, a goddess, enough for him? Wasn't his life filled with purpose and excitement? Dike had never believed that he was in love with her. Her fighters were not inclined toward those intense feelings anyway – it would interfere with their obligations. And that's not what she wanted from him. But she did expect that he would continue to worship only her. That included doing what he was told.

She hated to admit she'd missed the warning signs the last couple months, little changes Dike hadn't paid much attention to. The excessive reading and the fact that he had been quieter than usual, lost in his own thoughts. And she knew he was spending time with the woman named Ana. Dike wasn't worried, let him have his fun. He continued with work plans, so she didn't have cause for concern. She scorned herself now for being too naïve. She should've looked more closely at what he was reading, should have occupied his thoughts more when he and Ana were together. Should have put a stop to their relationship. He would still be hers.

Dike arose from silken sheets and walked over to her vanity, gloomily grabbing her hairbrush. The more she thought about Andrew, the more forcefully she tugged the bristles through her long black tresses, until finally she threw the brush across the room. "Argh!" This was pointless. She needed to just forget him altogether and move on. She had the new fighter now, Victoria.

At the thought of the woman, Dike grabbed a fistful of hair and yanked in frustration. What a reckless idea that had been, to transfer Andrew's power impulsively to this person she knew nothing about. Of course, it turned out she had a family and friends and a job. Dike had forced the amulet and the power on her, effectively breaking every rule for creating a fighter. She couldn't let Zeus find out. She just had to have faith it would sort itself out well in the end. Dike had never done a transfer of power in such a way, and she didn't know why this woman seemed to be changing erratically. It was unsettling not knowing how she would react, and Dike assumed the full transfer would just take a little more time than usual. As long as the woman rested, she was sure it would take hold.

She had been trying to avoid connecting with Victoria. What little communication they'd had had annoyed Dike. She was too whiny. Too dull. Nothing like Andrew. Hopefully, once the transition was complete, Dike would at least be able to tolerate Victoria as a fighter. Dike was making so many errors in such a short time, but what was done was done. She had to believe it would work, not allowing herself to consider the alternative. Now, in her frustrated state, Dike reluctantly reached out to connect with Victoria's consciousness.

What foolishness was this? Victoria was with Ana and talking of striking the amulet with a rock! The impertinence! She was not changing fast enough and it was infuriating. Dike had already cautioned her about protecting the amulet so it would protect her. She didn't want to be bothered to give this woman an explanation for what was happening to her. Victoria would just have to wait. Dike knew she should be more concerned, more compassionate for what the woman was going through. But she couldn't muster the energy to care. Her empathy was waning. What was happening to her? Gods, she wanted so badly to tell Andrew about Victoria. About how her transition was so different from his. To hear him laugh at her ridiculousness.

Dike struck her pillow hard. Small feathers floated into the air around her and stuck to her hair. She brushed them back and flopped down face first. *Get him out of my head!* she pleaded.

SATURDAY

Chapter 12: Victoria (me)

I woke up the next morning with the same energy as the day before and went out running again. Even if I was able to find a way back to my old self, I would continue running. I couldn't deny its immediate physical result was really gratifying. Ana had gotten nowhere with her search. Andrew's house had been dark and locked. I had struck out checking the streets again, too. Just as I was feeling a bit hopeless I got a text from Teniese asking to meet for coffee at a place I'd never been called Mindy's. She was already sitting down when I walked in. Something was wrong. Teniese was still wearing her sunglasses and gave me a small smile when I got to the table.

"What's going on?" I demanded, concerned.

She discreetly lowered her sunglasses, revealing a black eye and small cut on her eyelid. Seeing my alarm, she said, "I'm good, I'm good. I just ran into a fist-shaped door named James last night." She shook her head. "I sure know how to pick them."

I was enraged. "How could that bastard hit you? I'll kill him!"

Teniese looked around nervously, "Lower your voice!" she hissed at me. "It wasn't all his fault – you know how I like to run my mouth."

"Teniese, what are you talking about? Are you seriously blaming yourself?" I balked.

Teniese closed her eyes and rubbed her temples. "He spends his whole day helping those poor kids deal with all the trauma in their lives, and I have to give him a hard time when he's late to pick me up for dinner." She shook her head.

When they had first begun dating, Teniese bragged incessantly about James. He was a social worker at a nonprofit in the city, helping kids cope with the awful things they experienced day in and day out. He supported them through horrible situations so they could have a chance to lead normal lives. So they could live without the gangs and the detention centers. Her eyes had teared up recounting some of the stories James had shared about the boys' experiences. "He is doing such good work for the world," she had gushed.

But her black eye told an entirely different story, about an entirely different man. "Teniese, he hit you. You can't excuse it because he spends his day helping others. He still hit *you!*"

She weakly dismissed me. "It's not really that bad, and he apologized immediately afterwards, said my nagging was like his own horrible mother, and he just went blind with rage for a second. He felt terrible."

Where was my powerful, confident friend? "Why are you making excuses for him? If it was me coming to you with an eye like this, you'd tell me not only to never see him again, but to slash his tires and egg his house in the meantime. You *know* this is not okay!"

Teniese tucked her chin and began crying quietly, "I really thought he was different. He's such a good person. I've seen him with some of his boys; he's changing their lives for real. He has to listen to their suffering and just tries to tell them to hang in there. To still have hope. It wears him down because at the end of the day they still go home to their awful situations. He just snapped. Most of the time he's loving. One bad reaction shouldn't negate all the good he does for the world."

She was trying to convince herself as much as me. "Teniese," I started gently, swallowing the fury I felt on her behalf, "helping those boys doesn't excuse hitting you. He's easing trauma in one area of life and causing it in another. I don't care that he apologized. He's no good!"

"Don't say that!" she retorted. "Just because he slipped up, it doesn't suddenly make him 'no good.' It's not black and white like that."

"Some things should be black and white, and hitting is one of them. You aren't going to keep seeing him, are you?" I asked.

"I haven't decided yet," she sighed. "Can we please talk about something else now? I really just wanted to see how your newfound freedom was lighting up your soul." She gave me a fragile smile, and I decided to let the matter sit.

I filled Teniese in on everything that had happened in the forty-eight hours since we last spoke. She looked at me side-eyed. "So you really believe this guy's memories are somehow being transferred to you? Perhaps I was wrong, you weren't ready for all this free time. You've gone insane."

"I know how it sounds, but I'm not making it up. Look at my muscles!" I lifted the sleeves of my sweatshirt and showed her my forearms, then did the same with my sweatpants and calf.

She crossed her arms. "Give me that medallion for a while, I want definition like that!" she teased. "I'll admit, the muscle thing is really, freaking strange."

"I need to find him, Teniese. I need to stop whatever is happening to me."

"Have you thought about looking into mental hospitals? Seems to me that someone going around talking about being a hired gun for a goddess might find some resistance from the sane people." She looked at me pointedly.

"Teniese, you're brilliant! I'm going to do that today. You want to help me? I know you don't have work to run off to."

She nodded. "Someone should keep an eye on you now that you've gone all looney tunes. If you show up alone they may just add you to their resident roster."

We headed out to my car. It was a huge relief to have a friend with me. And I didn't want her to be alone after learning what had happened with James. Why did he have to turn into such an asshole? Is it really possible to consider him a good person if he abuses his girlfriend? I didn't think so, but I could tell Teniese wasn't convinced. And from what she'd shared, he painted himself a very pretty picture since they'd started dating. I had very little experience in the dating department, and not much I could call any sort of success, but I always thought I would never stay with someone who hit me. Now, to see Teniese waver, when she was so much stronger than me, was confusing. Shouldn't *some* things be black and white?

Teniese searched for the hospitals in the area, while I called and left a voicemail for Ana, letting her know what we were doing. We were driving to the first hospital when Teniese got very quiet.

"Do you honestly think I shouldn't forgive him? He begged me to. I really felt like I finally found someone perfect."

"I'm so angry that he is making you think like this. Even though he helps others, he was hurtful to *you*. So *you* should not be in his life. Do you really think he'll never do it again? There's no reason you need to settle for abuse. There are other people who don't hit out there in the world for you. People with whom you don't have to weigh the good against the bad." I was surprised to hear the words coming out of my mouth. It's truly what I believed, but I didn't know until the words came out. Since when did I have words of wisdom for anyone?

Teniese and I approached the first psychiatric hospital on the list of three within a fifty-mile radius. It was a beige, blocky cement building that curved around on either side of the main entrance, which stood like the entrance of a cheap hotel. The waiting area was separated from the rest of the building by thick, closed doors with only small rectangular windows at head height. The woman sitting behind the desk wore white scrubs, and as I walked up, I noticed stains on her sleeves and shirt. The whole place felt desperate and sad.

She peered over her reading glasses at us. "May I help you?"

"Oh yes, thanks," I began. "We were checking to see if our friend Andrew might have been placed here recently."

The woman leaned back and crossed her arms. "You know I can't just tell you what patients are in the hospital. You have to be family or a guardian."

"Right. I guess that makes sense. We're worried about him, though. He was hallucinating earlier this week and he's gone missing. We just thought we'd try the hospitals in the area."

"You'll have to have the family contact us if they're looking for him. We can't give out any information to 'friends.'" She made air quotes before going back to the paperwork on her desk, effectively dismissing us.

I made to turn and leave, but Teniese stepped forward. "Look. We know you have all kinds of HIPAA laws and procedures you need to follow; we get that. But our friend is in trouble and doesn't have any family. He's an Asian American male around thirty years old, and he would have arrived sometime between Monday and today. Can't you at least let us know if you have someone fitting that description who showed up this week?"

Now the nurse stood up so she was eye to eye with Teniese. "We get dozens of patients every week – all races, all ages, all stages of mental distress. No way in hell I'm telling you anything about any of them unless you are family or a guardian. Now kindly get out of my waiting room before I decide to call security."

In that moment, the door to the left busted open, and a teenage girl exploded into the waiting room. She had dirty blond hair that flew around as she moved. Her skin was sickly pale, and her limbs were too skinny to be healthy. Seeing us between her and the door, she moved forward and grabbed Teniese, thrusting a ballpoint pen to her throat. "Get out of my way! Let me leave, and I won't stab her," the girl threatened.

Without hesitation, the nurse picked up her phone and shouted, "Code red in the front entrance! I need security immediately!"

The girl got wide-eyed and turned to me, her only barrier to the outside. She pushed the end of the pen further into Teniese's neck and yelled, "Move!"

I stepped aside, clearing the path as the girl and Teniese backed out toward the doors. The moment she reached them, the girl shoved Teniese back into the room and took off. I ran over to Teniese on the floor. "Are you alright? Did she hurt you?" I asked, as the nurse called security again to let them know the girl had made it outside the hospital doors.

Teniese shook her head, "No, I'm good." Then looking at the nurse who had come over to join us, "What was that about?"

The nurse sighed. "Not all the patients here believe they should be patients. It's especially hard on the young ones." She had dropped her guard for a minute, but then stood up and put her hands on her hips. "I apologize that you had to be involved in that, and I'm glad you're alright. Now, I suppose I need to know if you plan on bringing charges against the hospital…" She was cut off by the front doors flying open.

The girl was back, being forcibly led forward by two security guards. Each of them was twice her size, and still they struggled to keep ahold of her as she thrashed about, yelling, "No! I don't belong here! You can't keep me here my whole life, I deserve a life!"

Changing tactics as they neared the door from which she originally erupted, the girl dropped down onto her back on the floor. The sudden shift of weight made the guards holding her lurch forward. She quickly threw her leg up to kick one of the guards hard in the face. He let her go, bringing his hands to his face and yelling, "Bitch!" Then, in a swift retaliation, he began kicking the girl as she was on the ground. He didn't stop until the other guard let her go to forcibly slam him off her against the opposite wall. "What the hell are you doing?" the other guard yelled at him.

The nurse ran over to the girl's side. Blood fell from her nose and mouth, and she was moaning, on the edge of consciousness.

Justice must be served, I thought. The image of an old-fashioned metal scale like the one on the amulet appeared in my mind's eye. I understood immediately the scales were weighing the good versus the evil of the guard and the girl. Yes, the girl had kicked the guard first. Once, and only hard enough to hurt, not to damage. And she had also threatened Teniese with stabbing her in the neck, but knowing her desperate situation and that she was not in her right mind, and that she weighed so little compared to the guard, the scales quickly shifted in her favor. In a flash, the decision had been made. The guard needed to be punished. Justice needed to be served. I ran over and grabbed the innocent guard, throwing him forcefully to the side. Now I had the evil guard against the wall. I grabbed handfuls of his hair and yanked his head hard down into my knee repeatedly. I felt so strong, so in control of my body, so righteous in my actions. When the other guard came back to intervene, I kicked him aside without thinking. It was only when I heard Teniese scream my name that I stopped, releasing the guard, who slumped to the floor whimpering.

The other guard yelled into his walkie-talkie, "We need help in the front entrance! And two stretchers!" I looked down at the guard at my feet, confused and terrified by the destruction I had wrought on his face. As the other guard started to rise, Teniese grabbed me by the arm and pulled me out the door.

"Come on! We have to move, NOW!" she screamed at me. We raced to my car and I peeled out of the parking lot as fast as I could go.

"Oh my God, oh my God…" I was swerving all over the road, and Teniese demanded I pull over so she could take my place and drive.

Once on the road again, she kept checking the rearview mirrors. "What the hell was that? What happened to you in there?"

"It was like before. My body wasn't under my control, it just moved. I can't believe I hurt him like that, I felt like I could have killed him! This idea came into my head that justice needed to be served. Then I saw this scale, just like the one on the necklace. Metal bowls suspended by chains, you know what I mean?" She nodded, not taking her eyes off the road and rearview mirrors. "I saw the scale in my mind's eye, and it was weighing her actions against his. The scale tipped toward the man, and the next thing I knew I was beating the shit out of him." I balled up my hands and tried to breathe.

"That was really scary, Vic, you seriously hurt him!"

"He did it to that poor girl first!"

"So what, it's an 'eye for an eye' or some shit like that? You kicked the other guard, too…did he deserve it?" she yelled.

I moved my fists over my eyes. "I don't know how or why I did it. I don't know why I suddenly hear a voice. I don't know why my thoughts, my memories, and my fucking actions are not mine anymore! And I'm scared, okay? I'm scared as hell and I don't know what to do!"

"Okay, okay. Try to calm down. Christ. We need to think and keep our heads about us." We drove in tense silence for the next several minutes. "Seems to me you need to lay low so you don't find yourself in this kind of scenario again until you get some idea how to control it." She thought for a moment. "Drop me at my car and then go straight to your house. Lock the door and stay there, do you hear me?"

"The only person I need, besides the stupid voice that only talks whenever it feels like talking, is Andrew. I have to find him, and I can't find him if I am laying low." This was so frustrating I wanted to scream.

Teniese nodded. "Yes, we need to find him somehow, *and* you need to stay safe. I'll call the other hospitals on the list, it'll distract me from thinking about James anyway. You try to think calm and sane thoughts…butterflies and kittens and shit. I'll check in with you later and we can make a plan then. Right now, you are too unstable."

Teniese pulled the car up next to her own car, still parked at the coffee shop, and as I switched to the driver's seat, something occurred to me. "Wait! Ana said Andrew had a lightning scar like mine on his leg. Maybe you can ask if they've found anyone like that." She nodded, then made me promise again to stay inside, before I drove away home. I didn't exactly trust myself any more than she did at the moment, and felt the sooner I could get home, the better.

Not five minutes in the door, however, I was already pacing like a caged animal. I kept remembering having the guard's head in my hands and driving it with all my force down into my knee over and over. It was like viewing a movie, but I knew it was me who did that to him. I wanted to throw up. At the same time, I was ashamed to discover a small part of me buzzed with excitement, high by how powerful and strong I had been. I tried to shake that feeling away. If I couldn't control my own body, how could I ever leave my house again? I drew a bath and listened to music as a distraction, but barely noticed when the water turned cold. If it was somehow true that I was given Andrew's memories and abilities, would I keep anything of myself? Teniese called me a little later to say she'd had no luck at the other hospitals. We were no further along. I threw my body down on the bed in frustration and felt it crack under my new weight. Just great.

That night I had incredibly vivid dreams. I crept up a narrow, dank staircase. My clothes were soaked from the hard rains. It was daytime, but felt like night with the darkness of the storm building up speed outside. At the top of the staircase was a closed door, and muffled voices came through. I was holding a gun and readied it, then kicked the door as hard as I could. Cheap wood and locks splintered around me, and I entered the room, shooting the two men seated to my left immediately in the head. The man closest on my right lunged at me, but I was too fast and shot him as well. The remaining four were seated on a couch in front of me. One in the middle stood and drew his gun. I shot it out of his hand before landing bullets in the heads of the three men seated on either side of him. The whole exchange was only a few seconds. My gun had made almost no sound at all.

"Shit, man!" The last one retreated back into the ratty couch, now turning deep red from the blood of his partners. "Don't kill me!"

I yanked him up. Tattoos covered every inch of his body, and the smell of sweat and weed mixed with the metallic smell of the gunshots permeated the air. I lifted him further and slammed his body down hard on the scratched wood floor. Righteousness filled every cell in my body. A voice boomed in my head, *Justice must be served.* I looked down at his pitiful form and aimed my gun. *No.* I countered. *No, I don't want to kill him.* Lightning flashed outside the apartment followed by a huge boom of thunder. *It has been decided, justice must be done.* My hands shook as I took aim again. A battle was waging between my physical body and my mind. "No! let me choose, dammit!" Then turning to the man, "Why the hell couldn't you just listen to me? I tried to help you and you just wouldn't listen! It's only for her that I won't kill you right this very second!" I dropped the gun, straddled his chest, and hit him several times in the face. He tried to fight back, but was no match for my strength. When he stopped fighting, I stood back up and kicked him hard several times in the ribs. "Your sister is the only reason you're still alive. You hear me? She believes there is still good in you, so I'm choosing to let you live. If I hear of you ever doing anything to put her in danger again, I'll come back and kill you without hesitation, do you understand me?" He nodded and curled in a fetal position, groaning, as I picked up my gun and ran back down the stairs and into the driving rain.

"No!" I shot up in my bed, very much awake. "Oh please, no!" I moaned, running into the bathroom to splash cold water on my face. I remembered the weight of the gun in my hand, the feeling of the man's bones under my knuckles as I hit him. I knew immediately it was Julian. It had to be. Ana had told me his gang had been attacked the day of the storm and only Julian had survived, and now I was sure it was Andrew who had done it. Andrew had killed without hesitation. And now I was turning into Andrew.

I ran back into my bedroom and called Ana. A voice thick with sleep answered, "Hello?" I quickly glanced at the clock on my nightstand. Oh, it was 6:06 a.m.

"Ana, It's Victoria. I'm sorry it's so early."

"Jesus. Okay, what's going on?" I could hear her sitting up.

"I'm pretty sure I just dreamed of Julian. Does he have a lot of tattoos? And one of a cross on his neck?" I rubbed my thumb and forefinger hard across my eyebrows, trying to fight the images from my dream.

"Yes! What did you see?"

"It was Andrew. I had to have been reliving one of his memories. Andrew is the one who attacked Julian's group, Ana. He's the one who killed all those men and beat Julian, I'm sure of it." Ana cursed on the other end of the line. "But listen to me. He was supposed to kill Julian, too, and he didn't. The goddess voice was trying to make him, and he somehow resisted. He told Julian the only reason he was leaving him alive was because of you. Because you still believed Julian was a good person. We need to find your brother, Ana."

"My mother and I have tried and gotten nowhere," she cried. "He disappeared from the hospital, and his apartment is a crime scene, so we couldn't get close. The police can't find him, either. They keep coming to us for answers but we know nothing. The rest of the crew are all dead! I have no clue where else to look."

Helplessness was creeping in, and my desire to escape reared its ugly head. I wanted to ignore the problem, let someone else deal with it like I had in my past. In frustration, I realized there would be no running away from this. There was no one else. If I couldn't muster the strength to deal with it, I might not get my life back. I took a deep breath. "We need someone who knows that world. Someone in his gang has to know something. I have an idea, but let me talk to my friend Teniese first. I'll call you later, okay?"

"I have to work, but I'll keep checking my phone throughout the day. Call me the second you learn something."

We hung up and I called Teniese. "What the hell," said the groggy voice on the other end. Shoot, I forgot it was still so early.

"Teniese, it's Victoria. Sorry, but I need to talk to you."

"Vic, are you okay? You didn't leave your house, did you?"

"No, I'm still home. But I have new information and an idea. How soon can you get here?"

TUESDAY

Chapter 13: Andrew

Andrew finally left his bed at 5:30 a.m. Sleep was futile anyway. His mind was hijacked the minute his eyes closed. He needed to think but couldn't concentrate. After a cold shower, he unlocked his office and looked for clues to what he should do next. Photos were plastered against the front wall and told the story of his life over the last six months. Most of the people were now dead. Not Julian. Julian, the one who betrayed and broke his family's heart. Julian, for whom everything in Andrew's life was now upended. Julian, who didn't deserve the ink and photo paper his face now looked out from. The worst humanity had to offer. Was it worth it? Andrew wasn't sure anymore, then he remembered the reason Julian was still alive in the first place. Ana.

He had promised her. And he loved her. He'd never felt so out of control like he did when thinking of her. Thinking of how to change his life to have Ana be a part of it forever. He couldn't remember when he wasn't one hundred percent focused on being a fighter, until Ana. But she had found a way into his heart. At first, he just wanted to get information, but when she started talking, he found he didn't want her to stop. Instead of thinking of her as a tool to get to Julian, she became his ambition. It started that first day they met at the park. Her life became the most interesting story he'd heard in years. The emotions she didn't hesitate to share brought back fuzzy memories of his mom. You never wondered what his mother was thinking because she wore her heart on her sleeve, and Ana was the same. Andrew had pushed the memories of his parents to the recesses of his mind for so many years, he was startled by what remembering felt like. By how intense a flash of emotion could be. Each meeting with Ana released fragments of memories he'd long forgotten. Bits and pieces of his youth. Being a fighter meant never really feeling anything, except maybe purpose and drive. But not the vulnerable emotions of sadness, love, longing. When they returned, even for fleeting moments, Andrew was equally rattled and desperate for more.

He told himself his meetings with Ana were still reconnaissance, but soon he was noticing foolish little things in the world and felt eager to tell her about it. Like how his coffee creamer made the shape of a pirate ship in his coffee cup that morning. Or how his neighbor would sing opera some afternoons with the windows open. He could barely stop himself from reaching out to take her hand when she cried or move a strand of hair from her cheek. Any physical contact at all would leave him shaken and distraught. He'd had sexual partners before. Women with whom he'd found release but no comfort. No ties, no emotions. This was a different beast entirely. His first kiss with Ana left him burning for days. But when he and Ana had finally joined together fully, Andrew knew he was lost.

That was when he started studying free will. He spent every unscheduled moment researching different religions and their beliefs about human will. Even the gods honored it. He had never not followed the rule of justice when it came time to act. Had trusted it was his duty and the right course of action. But as he continued to follow the gang Julian was in, waiting to strike until they'd led him to the bigger fish in this cesspool of a pond, he knew there was no way Julian would make it out alive.

He'd been too bad for too long. Getting kids hooked on heroin, lacing cocaine just for kicks, not caring where it ended up or who it finally killed. Andrew learned about three college kids at a party in the suburbs who died from Julian's doctored drugs. It was their first time getting high, and now they were gone. Andrew had lashed out at Julian after that. Had cornered him walking down the street one night. Julian had faltered for just a split second after hearing what his actions had wrought, then hardened his gaze and told Andrew to fuck off. It wasn't his fault if some shit stupid rich kids didn't know how to "just say no." Andrew almost killed him right there. He didn't want to wager a guess at how many poorer kids succumbed to the same fate but didn't make the front page news. Yes, Julian had tipped the scales, and Andrew wanted to kill him. But he didn't. It wasn't time. He still needed to know the identity of this new henchman they'd started working for. He'd had to wait.

Back in his office, Andrew shook off the memory and moved over to his desk. His phone had been fried by the lightning strike the night before, but he had bugged a couple of the gang member's apartments in the previous weeks and opened his laptop to check in and see if anything was happening. Julian's apartment was still busy with the police and the forensics team, and he could catch bits and pieces of conversation but nothing of use. He switched to another line and was immediately met with two male voices in heated discussion.

"The place is crawling with them. There's no way I can get in there."

"Fuck, this is a fucking disaster. Fucking Samurai. Will they find anything? Was he loyal?"

"They won't find a damn thing, no way Julian was stupid enough to leave shit around the apartment that could lead to us. He was too scared to be that stupid."

"What was he scared of?"

"His sister and mom are still in town. And everyone knows it."

A few seconds of silence followed.

"What hospital did they bring him to?"

"Mercy on the southside."

"Maybe his beating was more severe than the doctors realized. Do you understand what I'm saying? We can't give him the chance to talk to someone. If he's already at death's door, maybe he needs a little push."

"How do I get to him? He's got police protection."

"I don't care how, just handle it. Do you understand me?"

"Yeah, I hear you."

"Let's get the hell out of here."

Andrew took off the headphones and swore. Julian was a sitting duck. Police presence at the hospital was a joke for someone like him. Most wouldn't care if he lived or died. He was the worst of the worst, and Andrew knew cops who had turned a blind eye for better. He had to get there first. He couldn't let Julian get killed, not when he gave Ana his word. Andrew went into the closet to get his gun, then swore again, remembering the metal detectors that adorned every entrance of

Mercy Hospital, located in the roughest part of the city. Instead, he grabbed his laptop and a gear bag and left to retrieve Julian some other way.

SATURDAY

Chapter 14: Victoria (me)

Teniese arrived about an hour after I had woken her with my call, and I brewed us some strong coffee. Once she was convinced I was fine, I told her about my dream.

"So Andrew went against orders, huh? And that's why he had to transfer the necklace to you?"

"That's what I think happened, yes. And we know Julian is still alive, or was, as of a couple days ago. I think if we find him, maybe we'll have more answers. If we can't find Andrew, that is." I wasn't sure how Teniese was going to react to my next idea. "I was thinking we should ask James. He spends all this time helping kids in gang environments, so he's got to know someone who might know something about Julian's whereabouts, don't you think?"

Teniese gave me a pained expression, "You want me to talk to James? I finally decided to end it with him last night. It was messy and terrible and, honestly, I was nervous about how he might react. But I knew it was the right decision and so I did it. And now you want me to call him back up again and say, 'Oh by the way, I know I broke up with you last night, but I could use a little assistance this morning to help my mentally disturbed, possibly deadly friend, find the guy who the person she is turning into decided not to kill after killing all the rest of his gang in a gun rage Monday.' Sound good?"

I winced. "I'm sorry, Teniese. I don't have another idea. Do you know anyone else who might help us?"

She threw up her hands and flopped back on my couch. "No. It's a good idea. That just kinda sucks for me personally right now." Sitting back up, she reached for her phone. "What do you want me to say?"

"Maybe it's better if we meet in person?" I suggested.

"Not a chance, Miss Kicky and Punchy – just because I'm angry he hit me doesn't mean I want you to 'accidentally' kill him." She had a point.

"Okay, don't call him for me – call him for Ana. Tell him her brother has been missing since he disappeared from the hospital Tuesday, and not even the police can find him."

She stood up and went into the bathroom to place the call. I couldn't hear exactly what she was saying, but her voice was raised at one point. A few minutes later she emerged from the bathroom wiping her eyes, and tossed her phone angrily onto the couch. "That was not fun to go through all over again. He'll help. I guilted him into it, because it's not exactly safe for him to be seen asking a lot of questions about gang activity. He's doing it because he thinks maybe it will help me take him back." I went to give her a hug, but she shrugged me off. "Sorry, Vic, just give me a couple minutes okay?" She walked into the bedroom and closed the door.

Teniese emerged a few minutes later and asked me to replay my dream again, thinking maybe there would be another clue, but nothing stood out.

"Maybe we should break into his apartment. I'm sure we could find clues there," I suggested.

"What if we find a dead Andrew?" Teniese shuddered. "We nearly got into a boatload of trouble at the hospital yesterday. I'm not too keen on ending up in jail for breaking and entering or suspected homicide. Having said that, I think you might be right. Dammit. You want to call Ana? We should probably do this after dark."

"She gets off work at 5:30 today. Oh God…I have dinner with my family tonight!"

Teniese narrowed her eyes. "You can't be serious."

"I promised my dad I'd go. And Philip will be there. I want him to look at the amulet. If it's as old as the jewelry lady said, maybe he'll know something about the images. Can we plan to meet back here at 9:30 p.m.? I'll tell Ana."

"I guess being with your family will be safe enough, right?" She sounded unconvinced, then sighed. "Okay – but no drinking…I don't want you punching out your mom because she told you you'll never amount to anything. And come right home afterwards!" she demanded.

"Alright, alright! I'll see you at 9:30 p.m."

Teniese left, I texted Ana our plans to meet at my house that night, and then was back to pacing my floor. Minutes felt like hours, and my mind raced, overwhelmed with thoughts of what might happen before my "transition" was finished – and then what might happen after that. The way things were unfolding thus far, I couldn't imagine any of it would be good. I tried distracting myself with TV, and even spent an agonizing hour playing solitaire without winning one single hand. Sitting back on the couch, I absently fiddled with the amulet, bringing it under the light to inspect it again. The scales were exactly like the ones that had come to my sight right before I attacked the security guard, down to the shape of the chain that joined them. I had no doubt they were directly connected. I planned to show the amulet to Philip tonight at dinner and see if he had any insights into its meaning, since it was apparently a historical artifact. I wasn't sure how that information might help me, but at this point I was willing to follow any lead I could to figure out what was happening to me. I still wasn't sure how to ask for Philip's help without revealing too much about where I got the amulet or what's been going on since. The jeweler's proclamation that it could be centuries old still dumbfounded me. And that she'd remembered seeing it once before, when she was a child. She'd been mystified by her grandfather's behavior trying to find the woman who'd brought it into the shop – Lydia something, something with a B.

I hopped off the couch and ran over to my laptop. The jeweler said it was around fifty-five years ago… I typed "1967 Lydia B Chicago" in the search bar and started scrolling the results. Nothing seemed relevant. I changed it to 1966, 1968, Illinois…tried different last names beginning with "B," Lydia Boyd, Lydia Burke; nothing was coming up. I was about to give up when I had a flash of inspiration. Ana had said Andrew had chosen to change after his father was murdered and he was orphaned. I typed in *murder 1966 1967 Lydia B Chicago*. Nothing. Then, in place of *murder* tried *unsolved murders*, *orphaned*, and *family tragedy*. It was *family tragedy* that finally got me something promising.

At the bottom of the first page of search results was a newspaper clipping from the *Chicago Sun-Times* in 1967 on a website called "Chicago's Cold Case Mysteries." A grainy black-and-white image of a smiling family of four – mom, dad, and two teenage sisters – sat at the top. The headline read, "Family Dies in Fire Tragedy," and the caption beneath the photo listed the family members: M. Boyle, S. Boyle, K. Boyle, and L. Boyle. My pulse quickened. This had to be her! The writer went on to cite the original article stating a fire had swept through a two-flat on the south side of Chicago the previous evening. The cause was undetermined, but the blaze burned with such intensity that they suspected there must have been some accelerant in the house. Only the eldest daughter, Lydia Boyle, survived the event, as she arrived home while the fire was already raging. Neighbors reported seeing her running into the building to try to assist the rest of her family. She was taken to the hospital for severe smoke inhalation and burns on her arms and legs. This is where things got mysterious. According to the writer, Lydia Boyle disappeared from the third floor of the Mercy Hospital ICU two days after the tragedy. Nurses went in and found her room empty with no trace of the girl who had been in and out of consciousness just the day before. There was a search for her within the hospital and throughout the city in the days that followed, but she was never found. The hospital tried to keep it all hush-hush for PR purposes, but for a couple weeks, local speculation of Lydia Boyle's whereabouts ran rampant. The author wrote about different conspiracy theories that were floated about at the time: the hospital was killing orphaned children off for their organs, Lydia was sold to a sex-trafficking ring by a hospital employee, even that Lydia had been one of the "Manson Girls" of Charles Manson's cult because she had recently returned from a trip to California. In any case, it was clear to the author that the girl's disappearance was swept under the rug, and the cause was something nefarious.

I enlarged the happy family picture, where Lydia Boyle's smiling face stared back at the camera. I was sure this was the same girl the jeweler was talking about. For the next hour, I searched for anything else I could about Lydia Boyle and her disappearance, but came up empty. It was like the author of the conspiracy theorist article said, she just vanished into thin air. It didn't help that this was before the Internet. I closed my eyes. Focusing on the search was good for my brain; it made me calmer. I thought again about Andrew and his own family tragedy, maybe there was some clue to be found there. I texted Ana quickly *Where was Andrew from, and what was his last name? How long ago did he say he became the vigilante?*

Ana texted back a few minutes later *Somewhere in California. fifteen years ago maybe? Last name Liu. Find something?*

I texted back no, but that I was trying to, then quickly searched for *Andrew Liu California tragedy* 2006. The first couple pages of results weren't relevant, but on the top of the third page a headline from the *Los Angeles Daily News* read, "Restaurateur Shot; Son Missing." The article said on the afternoon of Friday, May 13, 2006, a man entered a Chinese restaurant owned by Mr. Zhang Liu and shot him before running away. The motive for the murder was unclear, as no money was taken or damage done to the establishment. Witnesses saw Liu's son, Andrew, running after a man dressed in all black and yelling for help. The son was never seen again. Help was sought locating him in what was believed to be a possible double homicide. A phone number was provided for people to call if they had any information on the disappearance.

I sat back in my chair. Two young people, both orphaned, both vanished into thin air after tragedy robbed them of their families. Something struck me about both of those situations. In the fire, Lydia was seen running into the house to try to save her family. Then Andrew was seen running after his father's murderer. What courage it must have taken for the teenagers to do those things rather than just falling apart or collapsing in fear. I didn't think I would have courage like that. Scratch that, I knew I wouldn't. What must it feel like to be that brave?

I checked the time. Darn it. 6:15 p.m. I had to go to dinner. Reluctantly, I tucked the amulet into my shirt and headed to my parents' house, butterflies in my stomach.

SATURDAY

Chapter 15: Victoria (me)

My brother's car was in the driveway when I arrived, and I opened the front door to the sound of him and my mother laughing hysterically at something. My stomach knotted up and I paused on the threshold. *Come on, Victoria, you're too old to be jealous.* I scolded myself and headed in to join the merriment. They were perched shoulder to shoulder at the kitchen table and glanced up, smiling at my arrival.

"Oh Victoria, perfect! Come join us. Your brother was just telling me about the funniest antics of one of his students, what's his name again?" My mother opened her arms in a welcoming gesture, and I headed over to hug them each hello and sit at the table, a rare, warm feeling of belonging inside.

"Salvador. He likes to play practical jokes on his teachers and some of the other students." Philip shifted his hips to lean forward and continued his story. "Last week we had an assembly, and he managed to airdrop a picture of the chess club members superimposed on the bodies of a Victoria's Secret ad. It was hilarious. I mean, he will totally be suspended for a couple days, but what a prank! Here, look." Philip held up his phone for my mother and me to see. The image was indeed the bodies of beautiful models striking various poses, their faces replaced with the faces of the students. They were not flattering headshots, and looked as though they must have been taken without the kids' knowledge. Underneath each body image was a name crafted to insult and embarrass: "Alec Cysticacne,"

"Melanie Buckteeth." I felt sorry for those kids. My mom laughed out loud at the image. I just gave a little smile, nothing more. My brother picked up on my lack of exuberance. "What, you don't think that's hysterical?"

"I don't know, it seems really mean to me. He airdropped this to the whole student body? Those poor chess club kids were probably horribly embarrassed." Both my mother and Philip looked at me like I was crazy.

"It's just a silly prank! Those kids could stand to lighten up a bit anyway," Philip responded, pulling his phone back and sticking it in his pocket.

"Like our Victoria, here. Never could take a joke." My mother rolled her eyes just as my dad walked in the front door.

"Well! I was about to send out a search party! What took you so long?" my mother shot at him as she walked over to the stove.

"I'm sorry everyone, you know I hate to be late…especially to a dinner I planned in the first place. I just had some business to check on. We've had some trouble with a few of our trucks lately, and I needed to talk to the drivers. Nothing serious, just took a little longer than I anticipated," he apologized.

"Dad, you're walking so much better now. That's great!" I told him.

"Oh yeah, you don't know how relieved I am, too. This bout of back pain was a doozy. I'm right as rain now, though. So where are my hugs from my children!?" He walked over, arms spread wide, and I ran to get enveloped in them. I could've cried for the comfort his arms gave me in that moment, after all that had been going on. Philip rose to hug him as well, though it seemed reluctant. "Marcia, it smells absolutely dreamy in here." He walked over to embrace my mom and planted a kiss on her head.

"You sure everything is okay?" she asked quietly.

"Right as rain, love. Right as rain." He smiled at her, and her shoulders relaxed a little. I wondered what that was all about.

A short while later, we were all gathered around the dinner table, and my dad raised his water glass to toast. "It does my heart good to have you two here with us. We sure miss you at home, but we know you're out living wonderful, exciting lives. Philip, your new book is outstanding. Truly, I couldn't put it down. And, Vic, here, plotting her rise up the corporate ladder! We couldn't be prouder of you both," he gushed.

I felt ill as we clinked glasses. Philip grimaced. "I'm glad you're reading the book. Could you tell a few thousand of your friends about it for me?"

"It's not selling well?" my dad asked.

"It's a freaking joke. You know, I get about two dollars per sale, and my advance from the publisher for this book was next to nothing. It's a rigged system. I complained that they should be doing a better job of getting the book out in the world, and they gave me some excuse about demand for the subject matter, and then blamed staffing shortages and the fact that they're a smaller publishing house with only a two-person marketing team. Then they even suggested I might try marketing the book myself as well! How can I possibly have a full time teaching job, write two complete novels, and handle my own marketing?"

My mother looked pained. "That's absolutely ridiculous, Philip. They should be knocking down your door, your book is that good. And to tell you to do your own marketing? That's preposterous!"

"I know! And some jerk left a terrible review the other day, calling it, and I quote, 'an absolute slog.' Obviously, he's a moron who probably reads graphic novels and is clueless to how impactful that part of history was!" He threw up his hands. "Nobody wants to learn anything these days. It's all about easy money and no work. People spend all day getting high, scrolling YouTube videos of the most ridiculous stuff, and complaining loudly and anonymously online about it. I just underestimated what little value people now have for learning. If it means you have to work, no one has a need for it anymore."

"That's why what you're doing is so important, Philip," my dad countered. "The young minds you're helping to sculpt can change the future of this country."

Philip snorted. "Yeah, right. I make less than sixty thousand dollars with a master's degree and spend fifty-plus hours a week 'sculpting the future of this country,' as you say." He gestured grumpily at our father. "Do you know the teenage drug dealer in my building is driving around in a Lexus? Turns out that's the future of our country right there."

My father frowned. "People find their own ways to succeed in a capitalist society. I agree this modern world has set honest people up to fail." He cleared his throat. "But those who can work legitimately, should. Do you need a little temporary money help?"

Philip raised his eyebrows. "No. Thanks, Dad. I have something in the works."

"Another book already?" I asked.

"No, something different. Don't worry about it. And then soon I won't have to deal with those awful teenagers anymore. God, they're so whiny." He took a long swig of his wine.

"You're thinking about giving up teaching, Philip?" My dad furrowed his brow. "But I thought you loved being at the school. I'm surprised you would leave it."

"I did love it…for maybe the first year. I had all these grand ideas around being a teacher. But the reality is the hours are terrible, the kids are spoiled and act like it all day long, and the pay is despicable. I'm done with working my butt off and being broke. Teachers get no respect from anyone, not the students, administration…not even other teachers. It's so cutthroat and petty and bureaucratic. I'm sick of it. And don't get me started on the parents. I have one student this term who never turns in homework and got a C on our latest unit exam. This kid spends the day either sleeping at his desk or disrupting my class. The progress reports just went out and it shows he's currently getting a D. His mother demanded a meeting with me and basically berated me for not giving her son a better grade! When I told her he has only turned in three assignments out of twelve this whole term, you know what she said? That I should just take the average of those three assignments and grade him on that. How are people like that even allowed to procreate?"

"How did you respond to her?" I asked, thinking I'd be the worst teacher in the world if I had to deal with people attacking me all the time. I'd probably just hide under my desk all day.

"I said 'I'm sorry, but each kid knows the expectations of the class and is measured on the same rubric.' I reminded her that her son could always come in before or after school for some help, and I even said he could turn in the last unit's missing work for half credit, and it could raise his grade to a passing C. She stormed off, yelling at how the elitist liberals are ruining our education system with their unfair demands on poor students who are already stressed out enough. Then she complained about me to the principal, with whom I now have a meeting on Monday." He shook his head in disgust.

"I thought the books would make enough money for me to leave and become a full-time writer. But that's just another disappointment." He downed his wine and reached for the bottle to refill his glass. "Don't worry, though, I won't be a peon forever. I'm just not going to play by the rules anymore."

"I didn't know it had gotten so difficult. Can you at least tell us if this new endeavor of yours is still in academia or if you're planning something completely different?" My dad looked crestfallen. He was so proud of his son making a positive difference in the lives of children, and the disappointment in hearing the way Philip spoke now was written all over his face.

Philip shook his head. "Don't worry about it, Dad. I won't give up my day job until I know where I stand with everything."

"You know you can always come to us for money help if you need to." My mother patted his knee.

"You guys need to be saving for your retirement and not thinking about your grown-up children anymore. You've had a rough few years, too." Philip answered, spreading a thick smear of butter on a roll and shoveling it into his mouth.

I was taken aback. "I didn't know you've had a rough few years." I looked between them. "Has the trucking business been struggling?"

My mom answered first. "You might've known if you were here more often. But your father has everything figured out now, and we're doing just fine. You kids don't need to worry about us. Focus on getting yourselves straight instead." She looked pointedly in my direction.

"Yeah, what about you, Vic? I'm impressed you're still at that job. I thought you'd have died of boredom after six months in data entry," Philip chuckled.

My dad answered for me. "Vic's putting her time in, right? Gotta pay the dues in the beginning to reap the reward later on. Our Vickster has a healthy dose of stick-to-it-ness. Gets that from me." He winked at my mom, who just rolled her eyes and began eating.

I took a bite of food, but it sat like a lump in my throat. This was torture. "Um, thanks, Dad, but actually I left my job a couple days ago. It was time." I kept my eyes down at my plate and tried to keep my voice nice and even, like what I said was no big deal.

My mother chimed in first. "Did you say you left or you were fired?"

"I wasn't fired, Mom. I quit. It wasn't a good working environment anymore. The owner was not a good person, and I just felt it was time to go, that's all."

"Do you have another job lined up to take the place of this one you could no longer tolerate?" She raised her eyebrows at me and put her fork down.

I sighed, "I'm going to take a few days to figure out what kind of company I'd like to work for first, then I'll start applying to jobs next week. Maybe I could even drive one of Dad's trucks for a short bit." I gave my dad a half smile. He gave me an uncertain smile in return.

"Ha! Not likely you'd enjoy *that* job!" my mom snorted, then sighed. "Honestly, Victoria, it's extremely irresponsible to just quit a job because you don't like the boss and not to have even begun trying to find other jobs. Just like Philip said he won't leave teaching until he has his next move decided. You have bills to pay! You're an adult now! It's time you grew up."

Why did I open my big mouth? She sat silently, even offering money, when Philip talked about leaving teaching. But I leave meaningless data entry, and it's all about how irresponsible I am. Her attacks usually left me sinking quietly into myself and just letting her rant, because that was easier. But not this time. I flushed with anger. Looking at my mother, I wracked my brain trying to remember a time, any time, she had supported me. Or taken my side. Nothing came to mind.

"Actually, Mother, since I know you are *so* concerned for my well-being that you meant to ask questions before just making assumptions about my level of responsibility, I quit because my boss was insulting my dignity, just as he had a coworker of mine the day before. He is not a good person. I was standing up for her, and for myself, for once. I don't expect you to care that I was disrespected, but I did. I spent enough of my childhood being made to feel worthless. I don't feel the need to continue throughout my adulthood, too."

Her mouth dropped wide open. "What nonsense is this? You feel like having a little pity party tonight or something? You have no idea how good your childhood was! How easy you had it!"

"You're right, I had food on the table and clothes on my back and a roof over my head and books to read, and for all of that, I'm grateful. I just could have done without the incessant criticism and lack of any encouragement from you in any form. As for finding another job, I will just have to believe that I am capable and skilled enough to make that happen. Again, something I wouldn't expect you to imagine possible from your deadbeat and disappointing daughter."

"Vic..." my father started.

"How dare you talk to me like this?" my mother roared back. "After everything I've done for you?"

I was too far in to back down now. "Everything you've done for me? Are you joking? What you've done for me was teach me to believe I would never be good at anything, that I was an idiot and a complete disappointment to you. I have lived my life afraid of doing *anything* because of everything you've done for me! And I don't know why! What was so horrible about me?"

My mother drew back like she'd been slapped. I stared her down while my brother and father just sat silent and wide-mouthed at my outburst. She looked at them, waiting for one of her men to come to her aid, but Philip only gave a little shrug, and my father shook his head gently side to side. She set her jaw and focused back on me.

"You don't know what you're talking about. My whole life has been about you kids. And I will not sit here and be assaulted like this!" She pushed her chair back violently and turned to my father. "Thanks a lot for your help, Arthur. I can always count on you!" she snarked before storming away. I stared her down as she went. I didn't even feel guilty. What a revelation!

My father exhaled and turned to me. "That was a little harsh, don't you think? Your mother has had to suffer through a lot."

"What, Dad? What has she had to suffer through? I'm tired of being her doormat. Everything I do is wrong or not good enough," I whined.

"That's not true, Vic," Philip chimed in.

"What would you know about it, Philip?" I returned. "You're the golden child who can do no wrong. You don't know what it was like for me."

"Okay, try to calm down," my dad said. "Your mother has dealt with more than you kids know. I'm going to go check on her. See if you can find it in your heart to see how she's loved you and the good she's done for you over the years." He got up and walked off.

Philip turned to me, and I held out my hand to stop him, "Don't start, Philip. I don't want to hear it's my fault again. That I'm imagining it or I just need to lighten up. I'm not the same as you two, but that doesn't mean I should just sit and take her criticisms. It's not fair, and I can't stomach it anymore. I am a decent, intelligent person, but if I listen to her, I'll never believe myself capable of anything!"

"I was only going to say that it was nice to see you have a spine, actually," Philip replied. "I think it's a long time coming. And she'll get over it, though I wonder if you needed to be quite so severe. You know she loves you. She just worries about you."

"She has a terrible way of showing it." I sank back in my chair, deflated. "What is it about me that's so awful, Philip?"

"Nothing about you is awful, Vic. But, man, you are wound pretty tightly. And, Dad's right, she's been through a lot over the years."

"Like what? Getting third place instead of first for her quilt at the fair?" I sounded as salty as I felt.

"Like Dad sleeping around and gambling away all their money, that's what," he shot back.

I couldn't have heard him right. "What the hell are you talking about?" I crossed my arms over my chest. There's no way my dad would do that.

"Why do you think he agreed to move back here? He never liked Mom's family. He screwed up everything. Mom told me all of it. The cheating when we were little, the gambling losses. He really messed her up – she almost left him. She told him the only reason she'd stay married to him was if they moved back close to her family, so she'd have support nearby if he ever put her through that again."

"Put her through what exactly? An affair?" My head was spinning.

"Not an affair, a prostitute. It was when we were kids. Dad had started staying out late and drinking a lot."

"Dad doesn't drink," I interrupted.

"This is why, genius. He drank when we were little. He had lost his job but was afraid of telling Mom about it. So he would get dressed and leave the house like he was going to work, but head to the casino to try to win them quick money instead. Problem was he ended up losing all their money. Then one night, he didn't come home. Mom freaked out and called the office but everyone had left for the day. In the middle of the night, a car pulls up to the house and Mom sees this woman trying to help Dad out of the back of her car. He was stumbling and barely conscious. Mom was mortified and heartbroken because it turned out the woman was a prostitute and Dad had passed out drunk in her apartment." Philip looked at me wide-eyed for effect. "Can you imagine? Mom had to help this woman drag Dad into the house. She was furious, but devastated too. The next morning, he confessed to everything. Losing his job, losing their money. He said that night he was so drunk he didn't even remember going to the prostitute." Philip shook his head. "What a bastard. Then he did it again a few years ago. Not the prostitute thing, but the 'gambling away all their money' thing."

"I can't believe that's true, Philip. Did you talk to Dad about it?" My head was spinning.

"Mom made me promise not to let on that I knew anything. She's never even told her sisters the whole story because she was too embarrassed. And she says she still loves him."

"How did none of this ever come out? I can't remember ever really hearing them actually fight about anything." Just my mom picking at my dad and him silently taking it.

"They had a good marriage in the start. When things changed, they just kept it from us. I'm sure that wasn't easy either, and she built up a hefty resentment over the years. I think she's been pretty freaking lonely. As for Dad, he's been trying to make it up to her since they moved here."

The idea of my mom keeping a secret like that seemed completely out of character. Not when it would have bought her a lifetime of sympathy from everyone around her.

"Why wouldn't she tell me, too, if this were true?" It'd be more likely to me if my mother made up the whole thing so Philip would feel sorry for her and be even more her devoted fan. I wouldn't put it past her.

Philip looked at me like I was an idiot. "Are you serious? Why would she tell you, who worships the ground Dad walks on? You'd be devastated and probably find some way to blame it all on her." He had me there. "Be a grown-up, Vic, and look around you. Not everything is as black and white as you think it is."

Why did people keep saying this to me? And what the hell was it supposed to mean, anyway? Had I been blind to everything or was this just a joke? Could I really believe my father capable of cheating? Maybe, knowing the way my mother constantly picked at him – which I was now to believe was all his fault in the first place?

"What happened with the gambling the second time?"

Philip had just taken a large bite of his potato and pieces of it fell out of his mouth as he spoke. "The year before they moved here, Mom found out Dad had lost their money again betting online when she went to pay for something and discovered her card was frozen. Dad broke down again when she confronted him and promised to replace all that he'd lost and more. And agreed to her ultimatum to move here and get counseling for gambling addiction. She told me everything one night just before they moved here. I was down her neck about the move, saying it was selfish of them to do that to you, since you were just starting college. That's the only reason she told me, so I would understand she was trying to survive it the best way she knew how. Why do you think I never came home that first year they came here? I couldn't stand to be in the same room with him, I was so angry."

Philip was right about one thing – this news was completely devastating. I couldn't reconcile the man I knew so well with this new and disturbing version. Voices wafted over from my parents' room and brought me back to reality. I suddenly needed to get out of there – the walls were closing in. Did my mother really not deserve all the anger and resentment I'd felt for her for years? Could I really let all that go and accept there might be another version of reality, and that I was the one who was wrong? But she was still awful to me…just because she might have had a reason didn't change that fact, right? I was suddenly panicky.

"Look, I need to process all of this – I don't know what the hell to say. If what you're telling me is true, then everything I thought was reality growing up is wrong…or at least massively skewed. I need time to think about it. I'm gonna head out so you guys can finish your dinner in peace. I don't think I could just pretend I'm okay with everything right now." I got up to leave, then remembered the amulet. "Oh, wait. I forgot I wanted you to look at something for me. A friend gave me this necklace, and it's quite old…I think the symbols are historical in nature. If anyone could recognize it, I figured it would be you." I pulled the amulet out from under my shirt but left the chain around my neck, leaning forward for him to look.

"Huh, looks like a sword but this lighting is not so great. Could you take it off? It'd be easier to see under the lamp." Reluctantly, I looped the chain over my neck and held it out. Philip took it and moved over to hold under the lamp. "Whoa, where the hell did you get this?"

"Like I said, it was a gift."

"It feels really old." He turned it around in his fingers. "I have the notion that I've seen this image before somewhere. It's really familiar, but I can't think from where."

Anxiety crept over me, along with a need to have the amulet back in my possession. "Let me see it again, quick." I pulled it away from Philip's fingers abruptly, surprising him with the roughness.

Just then, my father walked back into the room. "I'm afraid she won't be joining us for the rest of dinner. So much for our lovely family gathering." I took in my father, my savior and favorite person in the world. How could I connect what I'd just learned with the man I knew so well? Or *thought* I knew so well. "What are you two looking at?"

"You have to check out Vic's necklace, Dad. It's one of the coolest things I've ever seen." Philip forcefully yanked the necklace out of my palm again. *He is not a good person. He does not deserve your respect.* Suddenly, the female voice was back in my head. I whipped my head up to look at my brother, once again fingering the medallion on the chain.

My father leaned over to get a closer look. "Where did you get this, Vic?"

"A friend gave it to me." I didn't take my eyes off Philip. Why was the voice targeting him?

"I was telling her I think I've seen the image before…." I got up and moved over to my brother with my palm out for him to hand it back. "Just a second." Keeping the amulet in his hand, Philip went over to grab his phone.

"Seems like an awfully nice thing for a friend to give you. How well do you know this person?" my dad asked.

Leave it to my dad to want to know about my love life. "Just a friend, Dad. He didn't want it anymore so he gave it to me. I'm sure it's just costume jewelry, nothing valuable." My father regarded me quizzically. I moved closer to Philip, not wanting to let him or my amulet out of my sight. The voice spoke again. *He is succumbing to evil. He has begun tipping the scales the wrong way in his life.* Oh no, not now. I needed to get out of there. No way I wanted to lose control and hurt my brother in some way.

Philip held up his phone in one hand and the medallion in another. "I knew it! Look." On the screen was the image of a painting of a girl sitting atop a white horse, one arm holding a banner while the other pointed forward, leading the dozens of men in armor on horses behind her toward battle. Around her neck was a medallion. My medallion.

"Who is this?" I enlarged the image to look more closely. It was the front with the sword flanked by scales of justice and encircled. "Why would she have this necklace?"

"Joan of Arc, of course. Are you sure you graduated university? We did a class a couple years ago on the Hundred Years War in a medieval Europe unit, and I remember seeing this image when I was putting slides together."

"Why would Joan of Arc wear a medallion like this? What would a sword and scales mean to her?" I nearly failed European history in high school. I loved the stories but could never keep the names and dates straight.

"Don't you remember her story? She claimed to hear the voice of God when she was just thirteen years old. She said God sent her on a mission to save France by fighting its enemies and helping Charles of Valois reclaim the throne. She was later captured by the Anglo-Burgundians and burned at the stake for her crimes, not the least of which was dressing like a man and claiming to be a voice of God. Maybe the scales are a nod to her seeking to tip the scales of justice in the war, and the sword for the fact that she was waging war on behalf of God." He looked up at me triumphantly. I was so grateful I didn't even mind his smugness. "Do you know where your friend got his necklace? I would love one designed for me, but instead of the sword with scales, I would have the outline of a Templar Knight in armor kneeling with the sword in front of him. Now, that would be sweet."

"Um, he didn't tell me where he got it. I'll have to ask him next time I see him." If I ever found him.

I held my palm open to my brother again. He slowly handed the amulet over, only letting go after I yanked it away. I quickly had it over my head and tucked under my shirt. Now I could breathe a little easier. *Be more careful. You are still vulnerable until the transition is completed. Do not part from the amulet.* This was the most the voice had ever spoken to me, and my whole body tensed. I looked over at my large, but out of shape, academic brother with suspicion.

"What are you doing with the knife?" Philip asked.

He and my father were gazing at my hand, now firmly grasping one of the steak knives from the dinner table. I had no recollection of picking it up, but now it sat in my iron fist, ready to strike. I dropped it as though it had burned me. *Holy shit! Was I about to stab my brother?* I needed to get out of there now.

"Um, thanks for your help, Philip. I'm going to go now. That way Mom can come enjoy dinner with you both without my presence souring the experience." I quickly grabbed my bag and coat and moved toward the door, terrified to spend another moment there.

"You don't have to leave, Vic. Why don't you just apologize for what you said and we can all have more time together?" my dad suggested.

"You really think she's going to forgive me for talking back to her? Besides, I'm not wrong here. I am allowed to defend myself against injustice." *Where the hell did that come from?* "I mean, I just think it's time I stop being her punching bag. Anyway – bye." I maneuvered away from my dad's attempt at a hug and made a hasty escape before I could say anything more. I was too conflicted by what Philip had told me to accept a hug from him.

I began hyperventilating in the car on the way home. My only concern was getting inside and locking the door. What if I had stabbed Philip? What if I had hurt my dad if he tried to protect Philip like the guard at the hospital had done? I wanted answers. I ran inside my apartment and screamed at the air, "Tell me what you want! Why would you make me hurt people? Tell me why you're doing this!" I waited, but nothing came. My frustration and anxiety were so intense, my body shook. My thoughts turned to everything Philip revealed about my parents' relationship. I struggled to believe my father would do the things Philip said, but once I began reviewing my life with this new information, pieces started falling into place. Like why my dad would always back down in any argument with my mother, as though he was afraid of upsetting her. It would infuriate me that he let her walk all over him, but was it because he was so guilty for having cheated? For losing their money? And damn if I hated her for being angry all the time, but was it because she was suffering so much? *What the hell do I do now?* I wondered. My pride wouldn't let me accept I could be wrong about everything.

"I just want to know why this is happening to me!" I screamed and threw a pillow from my couch across the room. "Why me?" This time I got an answer.

He betrayed his mission. You showed your goodness and stopped to help him, so I chose you to have the honor of serving in his place and wielding the amulet. It is not a usual transfer of power, so be patient. If you keep the amulet with you, all will be well. Once the transition is complete, you will be at ease with your mission and all will be understood. You must rest, for that is when the changes take hold. Have faith that you are being called to fight for a higher purpose.

"Stabbing someone is a higher purpose?" I yelled back. "And why didn't I lose control like before if he had truly tipped the scales like you say? Why didn't the scales flash?"

Some humans are more susceptible to evil than others. The scales of justice determine when evil has overtaken the good, and punishment is warranted. You have not fully reached your potential. Rest now. In a couple days all will be known to you.

"I want to know now! I don't want to be someone who hurts others! I don't like to fight – not even for myself. Please choose someone else!" My yells were met with silence. "Did you hear me, goddammit?" Nothing. I punched my fists hard into my couch and cried my eyes out until I collapsed with exhaustion.

SATURDAY

Chapter 16: Victoria (me)

The doorbell woke me with a start. I had fallen asleep with my upper body draped over the couch and my legs on the ground, a pillow still clutched in my fist. I jumped up and ran to the door, where someone was now banging. Teniese was mid-knock when I pulled the door open.

"Christ! What took you so long!? I worried something happened and you never made it home!" She and Ana pushed through the door.

"I fell asleep on the couch. Your knocking woke me up. Sorry." I said.

"We've been here for five minutes, ringing the bell, banging on your door, calling your phone. You must have been out like a light," she responded.

"Wow. I heard nothing till just now." Was there something I was supposed to remember about sleep? Teniese collapsed on my couch, and Ana slid a chair over from the kitchen table. I hovered, trying to shake the dread I was suddenly feeling. Like I'd done something wrong. "Ana, this is Teniese. Teniese, this is Ana."

"We got acquainted outside your front door there," Teniese said, nodding in Ana's general direction.

"I went to Andrew's house after work again tonight. Figured I should see if he's home before we go trying to bust in. It's still dark and he's still not answering the door." Ana added with a troubled sigh.

"Thanks for thinking of that," I said. "Would have been pretty embarrassing if we went over there to bust in and he was sitting on the couch watching TV."

"How was dinner?" Teniese asked. I filled them in on everything, leaving out the part about the prostitute in the night – I was ashamed even voicing it. "You had a damn knife in your hand and didn't even realize it?"

"But you wouldn't have actually hurt your brother, would you?" Ana asked timidly.

"I wouldn't do anything to hurt him consciously, but these things are happening without my control. It's like I enter another state of being or something. This is why I'm so scared. But thank God the scales of justice didn't show up. I think if that had happened, I would have been uncontrollable. I asked her about that, but she just told me I hadn't yet reached my potential…so I think things are a little unpredictable until that happens. And I only have a couple days left before the transition is done. That's what the voice said when I screamed at her." Now I remembered what was important about sleep. "Shit! She said it's during rest that the changes take hold. I can't believe I let myself fall asleep just now! No wonder it was so deep."

"Okay – so looks like we need to keep you awake as long as we can to buy us more time." Teniese moved into my kitchen, Ana and me at her heels. "Where's that froufrou coffee you keep in here?" She rummaged in my corner cabinet, pulling out bags of various sizes and colors. "How many types of coffee can one person living alone really need? Look at this, dark roast, pumpkin spice, half-caf, espresso, vanilla bean…you know this much caffeine will stunt your growth, right? How do you even choose?"

I grabbed the dark roast and thrust it at her. "Just use this." I paced the kitchen. "The craziest part is that Philip pulled up this image on his phone of Joan of Arc going into battle with what looked like this exact amulet on her breastplate. I mean, the jeweler said it was really old. Like centuries old. Could it actually be the same one? Maybe they get reassigned to new fighters after an old fighter dies?"

"What are you talking about? Joan of Arc? That makes no sense." Teniese crossed her arms. I searched out the image Philip found and held out my phone.

Teniese snatched it out of my hand while Ana looked over her shoulder. "That's crazy!"

Ana furrowed her brow. "Andrew had said he wasn't the only one. He said there have always been humans who helped the goddess stop the spread of evil on earth and maintain justice. Maybe Joan of Arc was one of them? I mean, she heard voices telling her what to do, right? She said it was God's voice." Ana had a point. If that was true, I was in the same category as a famous badass woman from history. It wasn't so bad to think I could be a hero like Joan of Arc.

"Um, can we remember she was burned at the stake for being a witch and cross-dresser?" Leave it to Teniese to bring a heavy dose of reality to the conversation. "And are you saying that there are people all around us with an overwhelming urge to kill people? Great, I feel better about this whole scene already." She rolled her eyes.

"Guys, I did find out something else earlier today. Listen to this, the woman at the Golden Scarab jewelry store said she remembered the amulet from when she was a girl and her grandfather owned the shop. Her grandfather had made a huge deal about it for some reason, and the woman who'd brought it in fled, but the jeweler remembered her name was Lydia B…something. So I did some searching and found this article about a mysterious house fire in Chicago in 1967. The daughter and lone survivor, Lydia Boyle, was admitted to the hospital in pretty rough shape. Then she went missing two days later, just vanished from the hospital. So I then did a similar search on the information from Andrew's father's murder, and found one short article from 2006 about a man entering a Chinese restaurant, shooting the owner, and then his son Andrew being seen chasing after the gunman. That article said Andrew was listed as missing after that and they were seeking any information on his disappearance." I looked at them both expectantly, but they just frowned at me. I huffed and crossed my arms, "If Andrew is a fighter, I think this Lydia Boyle must have been, too. She had the same amulet as Andrew, and she also went missing after a tragedy left her orphaned. Doesn't it sound like there has to be a connection? Maybe there are a lot of these fighters living all around us, and we just don't know they exist?"

We sat in silent musing for a minute, then Ana spoke up. "Maybe the lightning mark shows who has been chosen. You and Andrew both have the mark, and it was after being struck by lightning when you started changing, right? Same for him."

It was a good point. I grabbed my laptop off the desk and plopped it down on the kitchen table, just as Teniese served up hot mugs of coffee.

I typed "People who have been struck by lightning" into the search bar. "This says that up to five hundred people globally get struck by lightning every year…that doesn't seem like a high number of vigilantes roaming around the whole world if two of them overlapped right here in Chicago, does it? And many of them are severely injured for life. I barely felt a thing and actually got stronger."

"Does everyone who gets struck by lightning get a mark like you and Andrew have?" Teniese asked.

I did another search. "This says Lichtenberg Figures are pretty rare…and typically disappear after a few days…"

"Andrew's had his since he was a teenager," Ana interrupted.

"…and usually show up on arms, necks, or torsos…not a lot of legs. I don't know, most of these people talk about pain. Did Andrew talk about his hurting?" Ana shook her head. "This feels like a dead end and I'm not sure it makes any difference anyway. I don't want to find more people like that – I want to stay away from them. And I sure as hell don't want to become one of them." An unpleasant thought occurred to me. "Wait a second. If Joan of Arc had the amulet, shouldn't she have been protected? The voice said it was my protection…"

The other two just shrugged. "Maybe it can be taken away from you? She was young and small, maybe they just took it," Teniese suggested.

I nodded. "It did show up in my jacket pocket without me actually putting it there…so I guess it was taken from Andrew." I needed to do something helpful instead of sitting and musing about what might have been, getting more stressed out. I needed to find Andrew. "We need more information. Are you guys ready to go to Andrew's house?" Caffeine had hit my system, and I was eager to move.

"Yes, but I don't know the first thing about breaking into a place, do either of you?" Teniese pulled my laptop over to where she was sitting and started typing in "how to break into a locked house." I stopped her before she hit Enter.

"If we get caught and they go through my laptop, they'll see I just searched how to break open a locked door. It shows premeditation. I'd rather say it was desperation in our search for Ana's missing lover that made us do it. I figured we could break a window. I saw this movie a few weeks ago, and the person took a rock and wrapped it in fabric to dampen the sound while she broke the window. That's where I thought we could start. I have a hammer, and we can wrap it into this sweatshirt. What do you think?" Personally, I thought my idea was pretty ingenious.

"I think we're screwed," Teniese replied. "Can we at least check if any of the windows are unlocked before we bust up the glass?"

I looked at the clock, it was almost 10:30 p.m., late enough to give it a go, so we headed out.

The air in my car was thick with fear and anticipation as Ana directed us to Andrew's house. It was a small two-bedroom with a weedy, unkempt yard in one of the more rundown parts of town I had driven through the other day. I didn't stop at the house, but drove past, and we parked in the alley behind an adjacent, abandoned apartment building. Looking around, I was seriously rethinking this idea. What if someone saw us? The houses were close together here, which was good on the one hand for decreasing our visibility, but on the other hand, it meant more people around to hear us. I experienced a wave of guilt for bringing Teniese and Ana into this precarious scenario. Ana quickly put my misgivings to rest, however.

"Let's go. If Andrew's dead or hurt in there, I need to know." Her fierceness gave Teniese and me strength to swallow our fear and get focused on the task at hand. We moved as quietly as possible through the alley, keeping close to the edge of the abandoned building, then scurrying like rats from that building to the back of Andrew's fence. His house was still dark, so we hustled through the fence and crouched low to creep alongside the small shed in his backyard. It was dark enough in the yard, as many of the streetlights were out, but the night was cloudless, and the moon lit up our faces. There was a door at the base of a small set of stairs leading to Andrew's basement. Ana suggested this would be the best place to start since we'd be somewhat hidden in the stairwell. I could see now that the door had no window, though, so I wasn't sure how we were going to get in. The three of us covered the fifteen feet between the shed and the stairwell as fast as we could, then paused to listen for sounds of anyone who might have seen us. My heart was beating out of my chest – I had never felt this scared before. But strangely, I had never felt this alive either.

Ana tried the door just in case we were lucky enough to find it unlocked. Nope. Then, using the metal nail file she'd brought based on something she'd seen on TV once, she tried to shimmy the lock open. I will say that it didn't seem all that sturdy of a lock or door, but she wasn't able to budge it. After the nail file failed, she tried a credit card, also to no avail. We looked around at the small basement windows closest to us. Unfortunately, they were the thick block glass variety. I didn't see how we could break in without whacking the hell out of it, and that would make a lot of noise. Ana left the stairwell and slid along the brick of the first floor wall. The windows were all just slightly above her reach, so she ran back to the stairwell.

"I don't know how to do this without being out in the open," she said. "I didn't remember all the first floor windows being so high up. But I guess I only entered from the front porch, before. Do we dare go up on the porch?" We had been relieved thus far to let Ana take the lead, and now that she was stumped, Teniese and I weren't sure how to proceed.

The dream I'd had of Andrew attacking Julian's gang came to mind, and I recalled the swift kick that had sent that door flying open. I was not Andrew, but I was transitioning to have his knowledge and abilities, right? "What if I just kicked it open?" I asked them.

Teniese eyed me up and down, "What, all 120 pounds of you? What makes you think you could do that instead of just breaking your foot and making us have to carry your butt back to the car?" She had a point.

"It felt real when I had the vision of Andrew doing it, I think it's worth a shot. I'm just worried it will make a lot of noise." I worried about a lot more than that, actually, but somehow I believed I could do it.

Teniese shook her head at the stupidity of the idea, but said, "I guess you should at least try. Lord knows I've been alarmed more than once over the last twenty-four hours by your actions. Maybe if we hold the sweatshirt against the door and you kick it, it will help muffle the sound a bit?" We had no clue what we were doing.

Teniese held the sweatshirt gingerly over the door frame, closed her eyes, and turned away, "Try not to kick my hands!" she squeaked.

I closed my eyes, put one hand on the amulet, and remembered the sensation of the movement from my dream. I was there again in the dark stairwell, hearing the muffled voices within. I took a deep breath and launched my foot into the door with my entire body, opening my eyes at the very last second. The door cracked apart on the outside of the knob and lock hardware, leaving them attached to the outer door frame, and swung open.

The sound was not small, and we all ducked down into the darkness, holding our breath for someone to respond. After a minute that felt like an hour, we quickly moved in through the busted door, closing it again as best as possible behind us.

"Holy shit!" Ana exclaimed. "I can't believe you did that!"

"Do you really think no one heard it? It was pretty damn loud from where we were standing," asked Teniese

I had never felt so powerful before. It was incredible. But now we were in the creepy, dark basement, and the uncertainty of what we might find loomed large. "I have no idea, but we shouldn't stay here long." We moved to the basement steps leading to the house interior. I went first, thinking it was only right since I was the one to get us into this mess in the first place. It was really dark, so I turned on my flashlight. It felt like we were walking into a scene in a horror movie. At the top of the stairs, I slowly turned the doorknob and opened the door leading into the main level of the house. Nothing jumped out at me, and I could see more clearly as the light from the street and the moon shone through the windows. I quickly swept my flashlight around, keeping it lower than the windows, and was relieved not to find any dead bodies. I shut off my light and moved into the room. The basement door had deposited us into the side of the kitchen. Teniese and Ana crept in after me and we looked around. Though it was dark, I could see the kitchen was neat and orderly. There were no dirty dishes on countertops, no clutter anywhere. The only evidence that anyone lived there was a calendar on the wall close to the refrigerator. I moved over to see it, and it was the right month, October, but nothing was written on any of the dates.

"This guy is a neat freak!" Teniese whispered, opening a cabinet and finding glasses and mugs arranged in perfect order on the shelf. "Or completely OCD."

We moved into the living area where a small couch and coffee table faced out toward the front window, and a round table stood with four chairs, all pushed in and in place.

"Are you sure he lived here at all?" Teniese asked Ana.

She nodded. "Yes, he made me dinner once. It was this neat then, too. It was super irritating."

The bathroom had signs of life – there was a toothbrush in a holder on the sink, and a towel hung on a hook next to the shower. The first room on the right was locked with a bolt, so we went to the left.

"This is his bedroom," Ana said, her voice heavy with trepidation. She moved over to be the first to enter. Slowly, she pushed open the door and turned her flashlight on, then exhaled loudly with relief. "He's not here."

We moved into the room. Even though his bed was made up perfectly, his closet door was open and a lot of clothes were still hanging from the rod. "He hasn't left for good, look at all the clothes still here," I said, moving over to the closet. "Ana, see what you can find in his nightstand, and Teniese, you look through his drawers."

The one window in the room had heavy curtains drawn closed, so we used our flashlights liberally. I rummaged between clothes and around the base of the closet. There were shoeboxes lined neatly along the back of the closet floor. I opened them one by one. The first two just held shoes, and I was beginning to think this guy was a psychopath for how organized it was. But when I opened the third shoebox and felt inside a pair of slippers, my hand met metal. I pulled out a gun. It was small and black, and the moment I held it, my vision flashed to myself working at the kitchen table, removing the silencer from the front end of the gun and wiping both down with a damp cloth. Then I saw myself walking to the bedroom to remove the slipper box and stick the gun inside. The silencer went into a sneaker in the next box, and the magazine went into the cutout soles of those same sneakers. I put them back in their place in the closet and closed the door.

Returning to reality, I stared at the gun in my hand. Immediately, I moved to open the next shoebox and quickly found the silencer and hidden magazine in the sole. "Look, you guys, he left his gun here. Do you think that's a good sign or a bad sign?"

Teniese watched me intensely as I efficiently inserted the magazine and attached the silencer, then calmly held the gun against my thigh.

"Where did you learn how to do that?" she asked tentatively.

"I touched the gun and had a vision of Andrew putting it away. I guess I know how to use a gun now, too."

"Well, I got nothing in the dresser," Teniese sighed, shaking her head at me.

Ana was sitting on the edge of the bed holding a sheet of paper and hadn't responded.

"Did you find something that can help us?" I asked her, walking over. Then I stopped when I noticed she was crying.

"It's a letter to me. He wrote it after the meeting where I called him a lunatic and stormed off." She wiped her eyes. "He says he's not going to kill Julian. He doesn't know what will happen to him, but he will always love me." Ana crumpled on the bed. "Oh God, I treated him so badly that day! I was so hurt, I wanted him to suffer, too. What if I never get to see him again and that's how he remembers me?" Her eyes implored us to offer her something to hold on to.

Teniese went over and put her arm around Ana until she calmed down. "We don't know anything yet. Let's not lose hope, okay?" Ana nodded, folded up the letter and put it in her pocket.

"That's all I found in the side table. Nothing like a gun." She sniffled and wiped her nose on her sleeve.

"So I guess that leaves door number two. Are you feeling like kicking again?" Teniese asked me. I looked across the hallway. The door to the second room was much more substantial than the others in the house, and there was a deadbolt added to the regular lock.

I walked over and knocked on the thick wood, and was met with a muffled thud. "This isn't a hollow door like the basement one. I don't think me kicking it is going to do a thing. Let's try using the tools again." Teniese tried the metal nail file but it just broke off in the keyhole. One look at the thickness of the deadbolt and we knew the credit card would be useless. Now what?

"Maybe I can hammer the hinges out?" I suggested, putting the gun down and pulling the hammer out of my jacket. But I couldn't even get the hammer head in far enough to touch the hardware.

"What if we used that?" Ana said, pointing to the gun on the floor. "I mean, it has a silencer, right? So it shouldn't be too loud?"

I looked down at it. Yes, the gun felt comfortable and familiar in my hands, but I had never fired one before. A shiver ran through me. This gun had killed many people, and I swallowed down my revulsion. When I picked it up again, it seemed a little heavier.

"You guys get back, I don't know what my aim will be like and I don't want a bullet to bounce off the bolt and hit one of you." Was that even possible? I knew nothing about guns, and frankly never wanted to. But if it could help us tonight, I would try to be brave.

I positioned the gun about a foot and a half from the bolt and couldn't help turning my head away and shutting my eyes just as I squeezed the trigger. My arm jerked back and a dampened bang and slightly metallic smell filled the air around us. Lowering my arms, I leaned in to see how I did. I missed the bolt by about an inch, and now the thick door had a hole in it. A faint light shone through on the other side, and I panicked and dropped to the floor.

Ana, bolder than me, positioned her eye at the hole to look through. "You guys, this is crazy!"

Teniese and I moved over and took turns peering in. From what I could see, the inside of this room was as cluttered and messy as the rest of the house was clean and bare.

"Try it again, Vic. It might help if you keep your eyes open this time," Teniese chided.

I steadied myself and aimed again. *I know how to do this.* Then I took a deep breath and fired three more rounds into the door. Two went clean through the deadbolt and the third through the door knob latch. Perfect shots. I pushed the door open and walked through, keeping the gun out in front of me.

"Okay, so that was a little better," Teniese said as she brushed past me. "What the hell was he doing in here?"

The walls were covered with papers, photographs, and a large whiteboard filled with writing. None of it made much sense. A desk sat in front of the wall, and a standard office chair accompanied it. The rest of the small room was cluttered with books and papers and two duffel bags filled with who knows what. This was obviously his workroom, and it seemed he'd left it intact since the last time he was here. I didn't know if that signaled he would be back soon, or if he had no chance to come back because he was dead. If Andrew was dead, then I would really be screwed. I kept my worries to myself as the three of us surveyed the room.

"Julian is in these pictures." Ana raced over to one section of the covered wall, and Teniese followed her. I moved instinctually to the desk. Addresses and dates were hastily written in a small notebook to the left, and a cord for a laptop sat on the right. Books were piled haphazardly on the far right corner. I put the gun down on the desk and flipped through the titles: *The Complex Human Morality*, *Violence and Humanity*, *Justice in Mythology*. Picking up this last one and leafing through, I saw writing in the margins and several page markers. I turned to one of the markers and found a passage underlined: "Humans became selfish and turned on one another, creating chaos and violence where once there was peace and equity."

I turned to the next page marker, and the highlighted section read, "The gods made justice for the earthly sinners swift."

"Looks like he was really into mythology," I called over my shoulder.

Ana joined me and looked at the books, "He talked about how the gods were still with us, invoking their influence on the earth. I teased him and told him I only knew of one God, and *that* God had given us free will to determine our destinies." She got thoughtful. "It was the only time he got upset with me. Told me I shouldn't believe everything I am taught at face value, that there is always more to the stories written by man."

"Look at these underlined areas." I shifted through the stack of books again. "It feels like he was doing research." I showed Ana and Teniese the words I'd read. "What do you make of it?"

"Well, he was doing the work of a goddess, right? Maybe he was just trying to learn more about his boss?" Teniese offered.

"This feels specific, though. You know the scales of justice I saw before I attacked the guard? Andrew must have seen them, too, right? A quick measurement of a person's goodness." I closed the last book reluctantly and moved over to the photos. "What was he doing, anyway?"

"He was tracking the gang's movements," explained Ana. "Andrew told me they'd gotten involved with another organization and were doing bigger jobs – he didn't go into details. All these guys here, all except Julian that is, were killed on Monday," She pointed to a handful of photos surrounding Julian, swallowing hard.

I scanned the photos. Julian and Ana looked alike – he had the same dimple under his left eye. Ana traced his face with her finger.

"We'll find him, Ana," I said, not knowing if it was even a remote possibility. Then my eye caught something familiar. I leaned in to look closely at another photo. Three men stood in front of the back door of a shipping truck. Just barely visible on the side of the truck were the first five letters of a logo I knew well: Esteemed Trucking. "Wait a second. This is one of my dad's trucks."

"What do you mean?" Teniese asked.

"My dad owns a small logistics trucking company called Esteemed Trucking. This is one of his trucks. He was late to dinner tonight because he was meeting with one of his drivers. Apparently, the trucks have been having some trouble lately. Now, looking at this, I'm guessing Julian's gang had something to do with it. He brushed it off as nothing serious, but he must have been trying not to worry my mom. I'll have to ask him next time I see him." Though I wasn't sure how I would explain knowing a thing like that.

"That's a weird small world," Teniese moved in to look more closely at the photo.

"Hey, you guys, look at this!" Ana was back over at the desk and turned to hold up the business card of a hotel downtown. "Do you think he could have gone here?"

Teniese and I walked back to look. "It's worth a shot," Teniese answered. "And what do you think these other addresses are? They're not all local, these two are from other states."

There were dates next to the addresses. Most had already passed, but one was tomorrow at 9:00 a.m. at an address in the warehouse district. Teniese took a picture of the document with her phone.

"Good idea," I told her. She tapped her index finger to her temple.

I moved over to a duffel bag on the floor and found a change of clothes and a long-lens camera. On the floor, partially hidden by the bag, was another book. This one was tattered and falling apart, as though it had been leafed through a hundred times; the cover said it was a translation of *Works and Days* by Hesiod. I paged through it, and it appeared to be a short book of prose. A small string peeked out of one page, and I flipped to it and read the underlined passage:

"You princes, mark well this punishment you also; for the deathless gods are near among men and mark all those who oppress their fellows with crooked judgments, and reck not the anger of the gods. For upon the bounteous earth Zeus has thrice ten thousand spirits, watchers of mortal men, and these keep watch on judgments and deeds of wrong as they roam, clothed in mist, all over the earth. And there is virgin Justice, the daughter of Zeus, who is honoured and reverenced among the gods who dwell on Olympus, and whenever anyone hurts her with lying slander, she sits beside her father, Zeus, the son of Cronos, and tells him of men's wicked heart, until the people pay for the mad folly of their princes who, evilly minded, pervert judgement and give sentence crookedly. Keep watch against this, you princes, and make straight your judgments, you who devour bribes; put crooked judgments altogether from your thoughts."

I closed the book, "Have you ever heard of this author? Hesiod?" They both shook their heads. My eyes fluttered back to the wall and a clock hanging amid the words and images.

"Oh man, we've already been here for over thirty minutes, we need to wrap it up. What do we have so far?"

"The hotel card and the date and location from the paper on the desk, that seems about it," Ana replied.

"Teniese, can you take pictures of the walls in here? Might help us if we had more time to analyze them." Teniese methodically went section by section, then took a picture of the desk contents, while Ana and I arranged the books and papers back like we'd found them. We left the light on and filed out of the room. As I pulled the door shut behind us, I groaned looking at the bullet holes and busted locks. "Well we certainly weren't subtle."

"Desperate times…" Teniese replied, then we all jumped as there was a sound of footsteps on the front porch. In the moonlight, we could see the shape of a body approaching the front door.

"Go!" whispered Teniese, motioning to the basement. We ran down the steps and only paused a brief moment to peek out the outside door to see if anyone waited there. Seeing no one, we flew out the back to the darkness beside the shed. Then we dashed to the car and drove away into the night, barely breathing from fright.

SATURDAY

Chapter 17: Victoria (me)

"We should have stayed!" Ana yelled from the back seat once we were a half mile from the house. "What if it was Andrew?"

"Even if it was Andrew, how do you think he'd react to meeting us that way? Your boyfriend ran with really scary people. Something tells me he wouldn't be happy we busted into his house and messed with his things," Teniese suggested.

The reality of how close we came to being discovered was terrifying, and adrenaline and fear coursed through me. "This isn't fair. I tried to help him cross the street, that's all! It was a good deed. And now I've been struck by lightning, my brain has been fried and wired to someone else's, I'm hurting people I don't even know, and I'm putting us all in danger. I want to know why this is happening to me!" A rumble echoed across the sky as I screamed, but there was not a cloud to be seen. "I don't care if you're mad!" I yelled to the sky. "You had no right to do this to me!"

In answer to my anger, the voice returned. *You have been chosen to serve the gods. There is no greater honor. Your insolence is futile and childish. Soon you will understand your worth as a servant of the gods.*

"What does that even mean? Why can't you just tell me everything instead of making me wait? And who the hell are you anyway?"

Another rumble of thunder and the voice boomed, *ENOUGH!* Then it was silent.

"Hello?" I tried again and was met with silence. "Dammit!"

SATURDAY

Chapter 18: Dike

Dike unleashed fury into the air around her. What insolence! What disrespect! This woman didn't know what she was being given – how dare she scream at Dike! Dike kicked at the dirt and stomped her feet like a toddler in the middle of a tantrum, the irony of her actions entirely lost on her. She grabbed at her long, black hair. Things were getting out of control so quickly. In truth, she was as surprised as the woman by how the transition was taking place. There was no precedent – she had never taken a fighter like this. Dike had, in fact, never acted so impulsively in her long life. She was breaking so many rules, and while that nagged at her, she mostly just seethed with anger at Andrew for putting her in this position.

Once before, centuries earlier – in human time, Dike had lost a young fighter. A preteen daughter of farmers who suffered terrible mental afflictions. Dike had found her on the cusp of taking her own life. She convinced the girl to become a fighter instead, to act on behalf of the gods to influence the war in Europe. To have purpose in life. She was the most charismatic of all Dike's chosen warriors, using mental manipulation to change the course of the war and esteem herself to the king. Dike had broken her own rule about recruiting only those with no earthly ties, which she justified by the fact that the girl would be dead if not for her interventions.

Unfortunately, this girl's mental troubles still lingered even after Dike enlisted her and presented her with an amulet.

Her actions became more and more clouded by paranoia. She hallucinated often, and her mental demons conflicted with the guidance Dike herself was giving.

The girl should never have been in the middle of a physical war – Dike had only meant for her to influence the balance of power through words and persuasion. Alas, her psychosis convinced her that her powers would be null if she wasn't present at the battle, if she wasn't actively fighting. Then, predictably, she was thrown from her horse during a conflict. In a panic, she tossed the amulet away, thinking it would expose her if discovered. Instead, she allowed herself to be taken captive, tortured, and killed. Dike was unable to save her. She became collateral damage.

Dike shuddered, remembering what that young girl endured following her capture. Dike knew she was responsible for her death and swore never to choose a human as a fighter who wasn't also alone in the world and of sound mind. She also decided to imbue future amulets with intense attraction for their fighters. They would feel so incomplete without the cool metal around their necks that they would endeavor to keep them close above all else. Dike was determined to never place her fighters in such peril again. Their safety was paramount. And she would not let Zeus know what had happened. Because she would make certain nothing like that would ever happen again.

And nothing had, until now. Dike had taken this woman and forced her to become a fighter without free will. She was so furious with Andrew that she didn't even consider her actions. If Zeus learned what was transpiring, Dike knew he would be outraged and withdraw the power he'd entrusted her with so long ago. She must not allow that to happen.

The most confusing problem was that Dike had no idea how this woman, Victoria, would react to suddenly having Andrew's powers coursing through her. She had never stolen powers from one to force onto another. This was unknown territory. And instead of immediately being available as Dike had hoped, it seemed the powers were coming to her in random spurts. She was aware of what happened at the mental institution and knew the woman, Victoria, was scared. It was surprising how soon the scales had appeared to her and compelled her to action without thought – it was not the same with any other fighter she'd recruited, and it was worrying.

Dike decided she could wait it out over the next couple days and assume everything would be complete. Whatever happened between now and then would no longer matter once the woman was fully a fighter. She knew she should care more that the woman was upset, but Dike couldn't think straight enough to deal with it. She just hoped the transition would be finished in a couple days and she would no longer have to be faced with the uncertainty of what she'd done. She could just move on with this woman as the new fighter, and put Andrew "out to pasture," as the humans said.

She just needed to be patient and wait.

SATURDAY

Chapter 19: Victoria (me)

Teniese, Ana, and I drove back to my apartment to regroup after our visit to Andrew's house, which hadn't given us as much information as we'd hoped. I was too agitated to sit still. I didn't feel any nearer to understanding what was happening to me, but after seeing what Andrew was doing in his office, it was even clearer that I didn't want any part of it.

"Okay, okay." I shook myself. "We need to focus. What did we learn?"

"Andrew was deeply involved in the movements of this gang," Teniese began. "And he loved Ana." She gave Ana a small smile.

"And I know from my vision that he was the one who attacked the gang Monday and left Julian alive," I said, clenching my eyes shut to block out the brutality of the night.

"Right. And that he was tracking something with all the dates and times he'd written down. And we have the name and address of a hotel in the city nearby," Ana added.

"You guys, every minute that passes I'm closer to this transition taking hold. I'm afraid to go to sleep. I know it's late, but I say we try the hotel tonight." I needed action desperately. I feared if I didn't keep moving I'd unravel…or worse, fall asleep.

Ana nodded, "I'm off the next two days, and if we have any lead at all to finding Andrew or Julian, I want to take it."

"Vic, do you really think you should come?" Teniese stared me down hard. I knew what she was alluding to, and I was as worried about it as she was, but I couldn't sit alone in my apartment waiting while Ana and Teniese put themselves in danger. After all, I was the one who now knew how to fight. And, selfishly, I couldn't imagine staying still while the ticking time bomb of change was nipping at my heels. Then there was the nagging sensation I'd felt at Andrew's house while kicking one door and shooting the other…power. I liked it, and part of me wondered what else I was capable of.

"I hear you, Teniese, but I'm not sitting it out. I'll need your help if I start to go down that road, because your voice pulled me out of it when it happened before with the guard, but I'm coming with you."

She held my gaze a moment more before giving a slight nod. "So where is this hotel then? I'm assuming we don't just show up at the front desk and ask if they've had any Andrews checking in recently," she added sarcastically. We had learned our lesson at the mental health facility. Gathering our things, we headed out the door.

In the car on the way to the hotel, we came up with the only plan that seemed to make any sense at all. We'd get there and scope things out. Teniese found out there was a bar within the hotel, so we planned to go sit in the bar with drinks and decide what to do next. As plans go, it wasn't a very good one, but it at least kept us moving forward toward something. Doing nothing was torture. The hotel was thirty minutes away, and Teniese drove my car. Neither she nor Ana felt safe with me beating the steering wheel and talking to gods while on the highway.

The streets became denser with traffic the closer we got. At one point, as a motorcycle zoomed past us, weaving in and between cars and nearly causing an accident. The scales of justice flashed quickly in my mind's eye, then were gone. I threw my fists up to push against my eyelids. Thankfully – I don't think I could've acted on that judgment, anyway.

We pulled up to the front of the hotel, nearly hidden by the high-rises flanking it. The entrance was on the ground floor, but it recessed back and morphed into a twenty-two-story, glass and steel, modern-looking structure. We parked on the street nearby and hastily walked the two blocks back to the hotel. Pushing through a set of rotating glass doors, we found ourselves in a lobby filled with neutral colors and clean, modern furniture. It felt cold and unwelcoming to me, but many people milled about even at this late hour, so apparently it was a popular place to stay. We skirted the front desk and popped into the main level bar, trying not to be seen in the lobby. The less we were noticed the better. We sat at a table that granted us a partial view of the lobby, while keeping us mostly out of the light, and a waitress quickly took our drink orders. The bar was hopping, and for a moment I imagined I was just there for a night out with my friends. Once this was sorted out and I was no longer ruled by a goddess intent on vengeance, we would have to come back here.

I took a couple fast sips of my drink. "Okay – what next?"

"I need this liquid courage right now." Ana downed her drink in one gulp.

Teniese smacked us both, "Do I have to be the only grown-up? Do you not remember what we've been doing all evening? We can't have our judgment impaired, keep it together!" she scolded. She was right, of course, but Ana scolded back.

"It's because of my nerves that I needed that drink. One won't cloud my judgment but it may help me calm down enough to keep going, so back off!" She leaned back in her chair and folded her arms across her chest. It was a strange awakening to the reality that we may be in this intense situation together now, but we only just met Ana, and she didn't have to trust us any more than we had to trust her.

Teniese regarded her with amusement. She appreciated someone who could show a little gumption. "So long as you don't go making a fool of yourself or us," she relented. "I think we need to call the front desk from here and ask to speak to him. Ana – you should do it."

She took out her phone and the hotel's business card, and dialed the main number. "Oh, good evening, yes, I'm hoping you could connect me with your guest Andrew Liu, please. L-I-U." She used a fake accent as she spoke to the man at the desk, who was within our line of sight. "Ah, I see. Thank you so much." She put down her phone and turned to us shaking her head. "They have no record of an Andrew Liu staying here. He's probably using a fake name."

"Could we just take the elevator and randomly walk halls or something?"

"Vic, there are twenty-two floors to this hotel, and only three of us. And I doubt if he's using a fake name that he'd be out in the hallway."

I took another absentminded sip from my cocktail, then quickly set it down when I realized what I was doing. "Sorry…I'm anxious."

Ana abruptly shot forward in her chair, knocking the rest of my drink over. "Emilio's!" She sprang out of her seat and ran toward the hotel lobby again before turning back to us, "Come *on*!"

We caught up to her in the lobby and followed as she quickly walked to the elevators. A delivery man had just stepped into an elevator and the door was starting to close, so Ana ran for it and threw her arm between the doors.

"Sorry, can we join you?" she asked the startled man. He wore a bright red shirt with Emilio's Pizza emblazoned on the front, and the smell of pizza and meatballs filled the elevator. My mouth watered as I walked in and stood behind Ana. It occurred to me I never ended up eating at my parents' house, and it had been hours since lunch. My stomach audibly growled.

"What floor?" the man asked, raising a finger to the panel.

Ana looked at the buttons and saw "11" was already illuminated. "Oh! We're going to eleven, too. How lucky!" When the doors opened again, Ana got out first and then exclaimed, "Oh darn, I think I forgot the room key in the car. Can you guys check if you have yours?" We moved off to the side and pretended to check our purses while we instead watched to see which door the delivery man went to. He stopped at a room four doors down on the left, and we peeked a sidelong glance to see who would open the door, but whoever it was never crossed the threshold.

As the delivery man turned to come back to the elevator, Teniese said, "Here's my keycard!" and then walked off to the right with us following. We pretended to chat about dinner while walking slowly away from the elevators, until he was gone. Ana immediately pivoted to walk back when Teniese stopped her. "Ana, what are we doing? What's important about pizza?"

"It's Julian's favorite pizza place from the south side. Their meatball pie will change your life. I'll bet you anything he's in that room!" She ran to the door and knocked before Teniese and I had even caught up. At first nothing happened, then Ana blurted out, "Julian! Are you in there? It's Ana!"

The door cracked an inch, then flew open fully and a man stood on the threshold staring us down. He had a bruised up face and his arm in a sling, but I could tell it was the same man from the photos on the wall in Andrew's house. Ana's brother, Julian.

Ana threw herself at him. "Oh my God, I can't believe we found you! We've been so worried. Why the hell didn't you tell us you were okay? Or at least alive!"

Julian moaned in pain under the attack, and Ana quickly let go. His breathing was ragged, and when he moved back, he swayed a little before finding his balance. He looked at us with confusion. "Ana? Why are you here? Who are these two?"

Before Ana could answer we heard a door opening nearby and Julian's eyes widened.

"Get in the room, quick," he said before looking down the hallway and closing the door behind us. "How the hell did you find me here? Did Andrew tell you where I was?" I could tell Julian was hurt the way he carefully shuffled forward, leaning on a chair to sit on one of the two beds in the room. His eyes darted around, and the cadence with which he spoke was off. This man was definitely high on something.

"Andrew disappeared. I haven't heard from him." Ana noticed her brother struggling, too. "You're badly hurt, aren't you?" Then she looked more closely at his face. "Are you stoned?"

Julian pointed to a pill bottle on the night table adjacent to his bed. "Mercy Hospital's finest painkillers, courtesy of your boyfriend. Tell me how you found me, Ana." His eyes swept over Teniese and me again. "And who the *fuck* are these two?"

Ana peacocked with pride, "We broke into Andrew's house and found the card for this hotel on the floor, then we were sitting downstairs thinking we'd find Andrew, until I saw the Emilio's pizza guy walk past! I knew it *had* to be you!" She was so impressed with herself, but Julian didn't seem pleased.

"You went to his house? Did anyone see you? Could you have been followed here?" He stood up and swayed again.

"I don't think so, no. This guy came to his house as we left out the back, but no one saw us." She looked to me for support. I nodded, but it honestly hadn't occurred to me that someone might consider following us, so now I worried we could have easily missed it.

"Who the fuck are these people, Ana?" Julian demanded again and I wondered if he remembered he had just asked that question. He seemed really out of it.

"Relax, Jesus! This is Teniese and this is Victoria," Ana introduced us. "They're the reason we found you. Vic has Andrew's necklace and was looking for him when she found me at work. And Teniese is her friend who's been helping us track you and Andrew down."

Julian whipped his head around to me, and frantically crawled, slid away from me on the bed. "You're the one? Ana, how could you bring her here? She'll...she'll kill me!"

"No, I won't!" I stepped back.

"Julian, what are you talking about?" Ana asked.

"She has the amulet, she's the fighter now. Andrew only spared me because of you, Ana. He was supposed to kill me, that's why the goddess made him give it to her. Do you have any idea how dangerous she is?" he whined. "Andrew said she'll pick up where he left off. And killing me would probably be first on her agenda!"

I shook my head. "I won't! Or, at least I'll try not to." I looked warily between Teniese and Ana for encouragement, but both looked as unsure as I felt.

Ana then came to my aid. "She hasn't completely changed yet – the goddess said it would be a couple days. Until then, she's still herself mostly. We need to find Andrew. He's the only one who can help her."

"Andrew is the one who busted me out of the hospital and brought me here. He was sure that you," he flailed an arm in my general direction, "would now be trying to kill me. And he heard street noise that I was a target. The police found out about some of the shit we were doing in my apartment after the attack, and I was a…a talk risk. I was better off dead." He eyed me suspiciously. "That dude is seriously messed up in the head, the things he says. And I think he may be suffering some kind of mental breakdown. But he is dangerous as hell, so I'm inclined to believe and do what he tells me. And if he says you're a threat, then you being here is a big problem. You sure you don't want to kill me?" He squinted and pointed a finger at me.

The scales of justice and the voice of the goddess hadn't yet made an appearance. "I don't want to kill you. Things have been happening to me that are out of my control, but for now I think we're safe." I got up and moved to the far end of the room by the door anyway, just to make everyone feel a little better. I looked around the hotel room. There were two beds: the one where Julian sat was unkempt and had clothes haphazardly thrown over it, and the other had been neatly made, with a small pile of folded clothing atop the coverlet. That had to be Andrew's bed. "Andrew is staying here with you, right?" I said. "So he'll be back soon?"

"He went home. Needed to get some things and wasn't sure he'd be back before tomorrow, or tonight. I don't fucking remember. He was too afraid to go right after he busted me out of the hospital because he's no longer protected or some shit like that." Julian paused to take a breath. He looked like he was concentrating very hard on his thoughts. "He's got a plan or some shit for us to get out of town, but he needed something from his house first. He left a few hours ago. Fucker told me not to make any noise, not to do anything at all. Just to sit here and be grateful I was still alive." He frowned and looked around the room again, eyes landing on the neglected pizza sitting on the desk off to the side closer to me. Seeing the pizza, he awkwardly made his way over to the box. "But I was fucking hungry, and I figured if I was really gonna die, my last meal should be that meatball pizza." He opened the box and pulled out a large slice, spilling tomato sauce on the desk. "He's gonna be so fucking pissed," he chuckled.

"Oh my God, that *was* Andrew who came to the door while we were there. I knew we should have stayed!" Ana lamented.

"Sounds like Andrew might have been ready to pull his trigger if he saw Victoria now that we know he thinks you're going to kill him, so it's a good thing we didn't stick around to find out," Teniese replied.

Julian took a bite of his slice that looked like it had an entire meatball in it. "How's Mama doing?" he asked Ana through stuffed cheeks.

"She's terrible. She hasn't been sleeping and I hardly see her eat. It was bad enough that we knew some of the shit you were doing, but not to know whether you were dead or alive was torture. You have been putting us through hell." The words were harsh.

Julian's shoulders slumped and, alarmingly, he started crying. "I know. Everything got so messed up and out of control. He should have killed me along with everyone else. I

don't deserve to be alive. I never wanted to end up like this."
He dramatically flung his good arm over his head while he
wept, forgetting he still held the slice of pizza. The toppings
began sliding down toward the floor. Just before they fell,
however, Julian seemed to revive and bring the slice back down
to his mouth for another bite between sobs.

"Christ, how fucked up are you?" Ana moved over to the
bedside table to grab the pill bottle. "Oxycontin? Seriously?
How much of this did you take?"

Julian moved over and grabbed the bottle from Ana's
hand. "Stop fussing, I took one…look." He held the bottle up to
her face and pointed at the label. "One tablet every twelve hours
as needed. Andrew broke my ribs and my arm and screwed up
my face…so yeah, I got some meds."

Ana squinted at the label, "Who the hell is Emilia
Gutierrez?"

Julian moved in ridiculously close to look at the fine print
of the bottle, then shrugged. "Andrew must have stolen them
when he took me from the hospital."

"What time did you take it then?" Ana crossed her arms
over her chest.

"When the alarm went off I took it, I don't fucking know
what time it was. Dude set me an alarm so I wouldn't overdose
and die on his watch. He's real clear I can't die. So I just take it
when the alarm goes off."

Ana looked at Teniese and me. "Is it supposed to make
someone this messed up?"

Teniese moved over and knelt down by the floor next to the nightstand. "I have a feeling these might have helped him along." She held up four empty mini-fridge alcohol bottles.

"You idiot!" Ana looked furious at her brother. "Do you *want* to die? You're not supposed to mix these things!"

Julian just shrugged and took another bite of pizza before plopping himself back on his bed. "I'm good, Ana. Stop fussing."

"The least you could do is try to stay alive for Mama."

At the reminder of his mom, Julian resumed his pitiful crying. "I'm no good, Ana. Tell Mama I'm sorry."

Ana wrapped her arms around him. "There's still time to change. Andrew's given you a second chance to be a better person."

Julian took a minute to compose himself and control his breath. Then I could see his body shift and stiffen against Ana's touch. He clumsily pushed himself out of her embrace. "I think it's too late for that. I don't know how to live any other way, and they'd never let me escape anyway, despite what your boyfriend says. Probably better for you and Mama if you treat me like I died in that apartment. Move on. 'Cause I don't see this ending any other way."

Ana fixed a hard, hurt stare at Julian, then punched him in his good shoulder. "You fucking asshole. You don't get off that easy. Andrew saved you because of me and now you're going to get your shit together, so help me God. I'm not playing around, Julian. This shit ends now."

A low rumble from the sky interrupted them. "That's weird, the sky was completely clear a moment ago," Ana mused, looking out the window.

I followed her gaze with a sense of dread, and Teniese whipped her head to me. "Time to go, I think," she said, staring me down.

Julian looked wide-eyed between us. "What's happening?"

I nodded nervously and moved toward the door. "Ana – I need to go. Like, right now. Are you coming?"

"You're going to try to kill me, aren't you? I knew I shouldn't have trusted you!" Julian cried.

Ana shook her head, "I want to stay here. I can stay with Julian and wait for Andrew. Can you come back? I mean… once it's safe?"

Teniese followed me to the door. "I don't know. I still need to find out how to stop it in the first place!"

There was another thunderous rumble, and Teniese pushed me through the door just as the voice was back in my head. *Justice must be served.*

I crouched in the hotel hallway and put my hands over my ears, trying to shut her out. "No! I don't want to!" The scales flashed before my eyes again, and this time they lingered long enough to render judgement. Julian was found guilty. Without further confusion or hesitation, I bounded up off the floor and positioned myself back in front of the hotel room door, then stepped back and threw a hard kick. The door was too sturdy. I kicked again and again in blind fury. My efforts made a dent, but that was it. Looking down the hall, I spied a fire extinguisher in a glass case. I sprinted over and elbowed the case to grab it, broken glass littered the carpet, but not a single shard touched me. Then I ran back and swung the canister at the door with the sound of splintering wood and the dent got larger. One more hit and I would be through. Just as I readied the extinguisher to strike the door one last time, I heard a small voice. I paused and it got louder.

"Vic, stop! You don't have to do this! This isn't you, come back! You are Victoria, not a fighter, just a normal, boring person! You are not a fighter!" Teniese was pleading with me from a cowering position halfway down the hall. I snapped back to myself, noticed the canister in my hand, the terror on Teniese's face, and the dent in the door. No more than ten seconds could have passed, but I understood how much damage I had inflicted in such a short time. I stood there trying to get my head sorted. The thunder rumbled one more time but the voice didn't come.

"Oh God, oh no. Not again!" I moaned, dropping the fire extinguisher to the floor and running to Teniese. "Did I hurt you? Are you okay?"

Teniese was trembling, "No, I'm good. I'm okay. Shit, Vic, that was some scary shit."

I reached a tentative hand out and rested it on her arm. "Teniese, I'm so sorry." I moaned, fighting to calm myself down. "Thank you for bringing me back." The desire to punish Julian was so intense. I felt driven without reason. Was this what her fighters were like? Bloodthirsty robots? Composing myself, I went back over to the mangled door. "I'm so sorry," I said through the dented wood. "It's over. This episode is over. Please, can we come back in?" A couple heads had begun peeking out from their hotel rooms to see what the commotion was. We were too exposed.

"No way in hell!" came Julian's voice. "Get the fuck out of here!"

"Vic, we have to go. And they can't stay here, security is probably already on their way." Teniese rose to her feet.

"Ana, listen to me. You guys have to leave the room now – take the stairs to the basement parking level and meet us at the car." I hissed through the door. "Security will be here soon."

"Come on, we can't wait," said Teniese, pulling me to the elevators. We didn't speak, walking out of the hotel as quickly and casually as we could manage. I barely kept it together until we were back in my car. Once inside, Teniese's fear took over and she started shaking again. I put my hand on her shoulder but she shrugged me off. "I'm okay, it's okay…just a little shock, I think. I'll be okay. I don't like to be touched when I'm dealing with something. Just give me a minute and it will pass."

I sat silently stewing in my own panic until she was able to calm herself enough to recover her breath. "I'm so sorry, Teniese," I said miserably, then jumped as my cell dinged. "It's Ana. She says Julian is refusing to come to the car."

"Dammit, they can't stay here. Tell them to take an Uber to my apartment. You know the address, right? The code to the door keypad is 80435. They can stay there till we figure out what the hell to do next," Teniese offered, and I texted the info to Ana. She responded she'd find a way to make him go, and we drove off, weaving aimlessly through the city streets and trying to regroup.

"Okay," Teniese said, after several minutes of wandering. "Okay, what now?"

I didn't have an immediate answer. I wasn't sure what should come next. It was the middle of the night at this point, and I knew I couldn't let myself sleep. But Teniese looked completely spent from the hotel trauma. "Let's go back to my house for now," I said. "Would you stay with me tonight? I'm afraid to be alone. You can sleep, I'll just feel better having you there. You haven't murdered anyone, or stolen someone's life savings or anything like that, have you? No skeletons in your closet that I should know about?" I was trying to make light, but if Teniese was going to stay with me, I needed to be sure she would be safe.

Teniese grasped what I was getting at and shook her head. "I stole sparkly nail stickers from Target when I was in the sixth grade. They were the envy of all my girlfriends, but I felt so guilty about it. I went back a week later and left the $3.79 on the shelf in front of the packages. I think I'm pretty good." She turned the car around and headed back toward home. Then after a few minutes she added with a wry smile, "I can't believe how good it was to get that off my chest."

We drove the rest of the way in silence. When we walked through my apartment door, my mind was still racing, but my body was beyond fatigued. Ana texted that they had made it to Teniese's apartment and asked what they should do now. I told her they should sleep – I didn't know what tomorrow would bring, but the craziness of the day was too much for any of us. Teniese stifled a yawn and I saw the heaviness in her eyes.

"You go to sleep for a little while. I'll wake you if I need you. I'm going to just try to work out a plan for what's next."

Teniese took off her coat and pulled out her cell. "Oh! I missed a call from James." She listened to the voicemail, then turned to me. "He didn't find out much. He says all he could get out of anyone was that an Asian American guy nicknamed 'The Samurai' has been causing hell."

"Andrew's parents were Chinese, not Japanese," I interrupted, and Teniese squinted at me.

"Well let's be sure to correct the nice gang members when we see them again, shall we?" She shook her head. "James said he got that nickname because he's a fierce warrior that no one can get near. He's rumored to be invincible."

"That's it? He didn't say anything else?"

She gave me a side glance. "Only that he hopes we can meet for dinner this week. I need sleep. Wake me in a few hours or if anything happens." Without another word, Teniese went into the bedroom, but left the door open a sliver. She must have been worried she wouldn't hear me if the door was latched.

I was a terrible person for making her connect with James. I guess I would just have to add it to the list of other awful things I'd put her through over the last couple days. Grabbing a pen and piece of scratch paper from the printer drawer, I set myself down at the kitchen table to work through everything that had happened since the storm. The act of writing thoughts down has always helped me make sense of problems in the past. Once I'd gotten everything I could think of down on the paper, I went through all the pictures from Andrew's office that Teniese had taken and shared with me.

When I saw the one of his desktop, I understood what our next
move should be. There in the picture was the paper with
addresses, dates and times hastily scribbled on it, and I focused
my attention on the one that hadn't passed yet. The one
scheduled for 9:00 a.m. today. I didn't know what the places
and dates referred to, but it was the only thing we had to go on.
I looked at the clock: 2:12 a.m. I was so very tired.

Standing and stretching my stiff back, I moved into the
living room and turned the TV on low. Figuring an action
movie would keep me engaged enough not to succumb to sleep,
I found one of the Jason Bourne trilogy. *Perfect*, I thought. *This
guy can't remember why he knows how to fight either*. But the
first action scene reminded me of the security guard at the
mental health facility, and I felt sick again. I switched it to a
comedy and made more coffee.

WEDNESDAY

Chapter 20: Andrew

Andrew wanted to throttle Julian. What a waste of airspace that man was. He'd finally managed to get him out of the hospital by convincing him the alternative was being killed. It took some stealthy slipping of activated charcoal and ipecac syrup into a cafeteria caffe mocha, with fake sugar to mask the taste and increase the reaction time of the charcoal, then getting the coffee delivered to the officer on duty. He had waited fifteen minutes for the officer to run off in the direction of the bathroom, then slipped into Julian's hospital room without much trouble. It was convincing Julian to trust him that proved the most difficult. Thankfully, he was too weak and sedated to put up much of a fight. Andrew awkwardly changed Julian into the clothes he'd brought for him, then practically had to carry him out of the hospital room. Andrew almost got caught when the officer turned the corner to resume his post before he'd gotten Julian all the way down the hall. But they quickly ducked around a corner and watched as the officer sat back down in the chair without a single glance in the room. Andrew smirked – yeah, Julian's safety here was of minimal concern.

The hotel seemed the easiest place to stay hidden. It was trendy and expensive, and way too exposed for people like Julian to want to frequent, which suited Andrew just fine. He would have to physically support Julian the whole way up to the room – thank God, he knew enough to leave Julian in the car while he checked in, handcuffed to the steering wheel, of course. Andrew was just returning to the car when it must have occurred to Julian to start hitting the car horn. What fool draws attention to himself when people are actively looking to kill him? Andrew reached him after the first long beep and politely pushed a finger into his broken ribs. Julian yelled out, but no one seemed to be in the garage with them to hear. Andrew got him to cooperate with the promise of pain medication once they got to the room, and Julian barely made it.

They spent the next hour with Andrew pacing the floor, asking Julian about Ana, and Julian just flopped on his bed moaning for painkillers. Andrew gave him one pill from the prescription he'd stolen at the hospital and told him to shut up. Unfortunately, Julian did just that and fell asleep without telling Andrew anything useful. Now he was trying to figure out what the hell to do next. Andrew hated this uncertainty and self-doubt. He'd had nothing but complete confidence in his decisions and movements his entire adult life, and now he was questioning every move. He absently passed the bottle of pills from hand to hand then stopped and looked down at the bottle…wouldn't that be the easiest thing to do? Just take them all and let Julian fend for himself? Rot in hell with the rest of them? He was pretty sure Ana wouldn't come back to him now anyway. Not after Monday. She had known him as steady and stable, someone she could rely on. Now what was he? Lost in every way. And every moment he stopped thinking about Julian, or stopped physically moving, he was flooded with images of all the people he'd sent to the underworld. He imagined most of them would have ended up being sent to Tartarus for everlasting punishment. Andrew paused – could that end up being his fate, too? Oh no, he couldn't die just yet, not when that was a possibility. If only he could think!

THURSDAY

Chapter 21: Andrew

Andrew sighed. It was late, he was exhausted in every way, and Julian's snoring form made Andrew long for sleep. He didn't bother taking his clothes off, but lay down on the other bed and let the darkness take him. Only a few hours later, however, he woke choking with a memory: the first time he'd exacted justice as a fighter.

It was only six months after his father's murder and his decision to accept the goddess's offer. With the goddess's help, he had left everything behind in California and taken a fifteen-hour bus ride to a small town in western Colorado. She guided him on what to say to the motel manager, and when he reached into his pocket, he had found cash, a credit card, and an ID. The ID had his name but a different birth date and home address somewhere in Colorado. He'd slept for two days in that motel, only rousing to satisfy his crazy thirst. After the second day, he'd awoken feeling different. Renewed, clean. Energized and clear-headed. He could still conjure up the idea of his father, but in a detached way, so the thoughts held no weight anymore. It was a relief.

From there, the goddess directed him to find an apartment in a suburb of Denver. It was at this location Andrew spent the next several months reading books on American and foreign history, learning about different weapons, and training in martial arts. When he wasn't studying or training, he was scouring the news for information on the cornucopia of terrible things happening in the world. By that time, he had gotten used to the information that had begun flooding his brain. Andrew could walk into a room and know instantly how many people were there, how long it would take him to get from wherever he was to the nearest exit, and what items in the room he might be able to use as makeshift weapons.

All these changes Andrew had taken in stride, and then the day came to perform the duty he'd been preparing for. The goddess hadn't given him the scales of justice until she was sure he was ready, and now he was.

She had instructed Andrew to go into the city so he would be among groups of people. He went to the busiest pedestrian shopping district in downtown Denver and sat at an outdoor café with a cup of coffee that he never touched. As strangers passed him unaware, Andrew was singularly focused on whether or not the scales would show. Time passed with no incident, and Andrew had switched from his café lookout to wandering the streets. He wasn't tired – even after hours, he still felt focused on his task. Close to midnight, the goddess had told Andrew to head for home and rest, for he would repeat the experiment the next day.

But as he had rounded a corner heading back home, his shoulder bumped a man going the opposite direction. Instantly, the scales appeared to his mind's eye, and this man was on the losing end. Surprised, Andrew's head shot up, and he watched the man walk away from him. Then Andrew began following, staying a good enough distance behind so as not to arouse suspicion. The man walked into an apartment building to the left. When Andrew got there, he found the outer door locked, but he could see an elevator through the glass in the door. It looked to be stopped on the third floor. Andrew calmly reached into his pocket and took out a small tool kit for various locks. Checking his surroundings first to make sure no one passed by, he got to work and quickly sprung the lock on the outer door.

He moved into the building, pushing the elevator button. Before the elevator arrived, the stairwell door opened and a woman walked out. Andrew met her eyes and smiled. She was young and attractive and smiled back at him.

"You might want a sandwich while you wait for that beast to finally show up. Stairs are always faster," she said flirtatiously. "Are you here for Malcolm's party? I'm just grabbing some more tequila for it now."

"Oh, awesome." Andrew stood taller to make himself seem older, though he needn't have bothered - he was already taller and stronger thanks to the goddess's magic. "Maybe we can have a drink when you get back? Only I am embarrassed to say I don't remember what floor he's on."

"Number 210...and I'll see you up there."

"Thanks for the tip about the stairs, too," Andrew replied, gesturing to the elevator that still hadn't arrived.

She winked and headed out while Andrew slunk into the stairwell. Bypassing the second floor where he could hear music pumping through the walls, he continued on to the third. Peeking out the stairwell and seeing no one, he slowly walked down the hall, his hand raised to sense the energy close to each door, and eyes closed to focus on the sounds inside. At the third door on the left, 310, just above the party apartment, Andrew had paused. Something felt off. He leaned his head closer and the air around the door held a faint rancid scent. Andrew knew this was it. He casually knocked on the door three times before stepping to the side just beyond the door viewer. Andrew calmed his breathing and placed his hand loosely over the outside door handle; he hadn't expected to feel this excited. After a few moments, he heard movement by the door, then the slow turning of the knob, and the door cracked open two inches. Andrew swiftly closed his hand and yanked back hard on the doorknob, pulling the man's arm and jerking his body forward, then, just as fast he slammed the door back again against the man's head. The man flew back into his apartment and Andrew quickly followed, quietly closing the door behind them both. The scales flashed again.

"What the fuck," started the man, bringing a hand up to his bruising forehead. Andrew didn't let him finish but kneed him hard in the mouth. Then he grabbed a handkerchief from his other pocket and quickly wrapped it around the man's mouth so he couldn't yell. He needn't have bothered – the man was unconscious. Andrew quickly moved through the apartment. The bass beat from the party below gently shook the floor. Room to room Andrew went, opening doors and looking in closets. It was in the last closet off the kitchen where he found what he was looking for. As Andrew opened the door, a woman's arm fell forward and hit his face. The rest of her was suspended like a coat along the back of the closet wall. The smell was extreme, and Andrew assumed she'd been dead at least a couple days. He turned on the light overhead and saw she was not the only body taking up space. Another woman slumped on the floor of the closet. Both were naked and the deep bruising on their necks suggested they'd been strangled.

Andrew heard a groan from the other room and abandoned the women where they were. Their souls had already left those physical shells, and Andrew wasted no concern for them. He moved back over to deal with the man, who had managed to get to his knees. Not wanting to make any more noise than necessary, Andrew grabbed a chef's knife from the knife block in the kitchen on his way, then spied a kitchen towel and grabbed that as well. Holding the towel in front of the knife, he quickly plunged the blade into the man's neck. The towel collected most of the blood spray and Andrew jumped back to avoid any other contamination. Then swiftly and cat-like, and with one quick look out the door viewer, Andrew slipped out of the apartment and back through the hall to the stairwell. Just as he reached the bottom level, the stairwell door opened in front of him. The woman from earlier in the night stood there, this time a plastic bag dangling from her arm.

"Hi again!" She exclaimed. Then realizing that Andrew was heading down, she added, "You're not leaving are you? I thought we were going to have a drink." She raised her eyebrows.

Andrew felt the adrenaline moving through his body, but it didn't overtake him. He didn't sweat, his eyes didn't dart around – he had a feeling of justice and righteousness swimming around his chest. He liked it. But he knew he couldn't go to a party where the host would clearly know he wasn't supposed to be there.

"It wasn't my scene." Andrew leaned in closer to the woman. "But maybe we could go have a drink at my place instead?"

She wrinkled her nose and backed up. "Yeah, I'm not quite that easy, asshole." She moved out of the stairwell and gave him lots of room to pass. Andrew shrugged and laughed at himself before walking out into the night, high on life. He had been only seventeen years old.

The memory of that day was so detailed: the colors of the bruising on the women's skin in the closet, the weight of the knife in his hand. The elation of serving the goddess. At the time, Andrew had only felt pride and virtue for ridding the world of someone so vile, and certainly the goddess had praised him for doing just that. But now, he felt nauseous. Ill from what he had seen, how easy it had been to kill another human, and how he'd been ready to celebrate after it was done. He got up and paced the room. Julian still snored away in the bed next to him. At the time, he had put all thought of who he was before his father's death out of his mind. But as he wore a path on the hotel floor, he remembered there had been a girl, Amber, whom he had just started dating back then. Amber was short with long dark hair, not so different from the woman in the stairwell, and a laugh that made his insides flip. They'd been on two dates, and she'd let him kiss her. Then he disappeared. Andrew knew he had chosen to become the fighter, that it was his doing, but now, with their connection severed, he felt rage at what the goddess took from him. What she made him become. And deep shame at how much he craved it all back.

Andrew checked the time – it was barely 4:00 a.m.. He jostled Julian awake.

Julian startled and cried out. Andrew put his hand over his mouth. "Remember me asshole? Look around, you're in the hotel, remember? We left the hospital where people were trying to kill you. You remember?" Julian's eyes swept the room then returned to Andrew. He nodded slowly. "Good. I am going out. Stay in this room. You will be killed if you leave, you understand? When the alarm goes off on your phone, take one of these pills." Andrew handed Julian the bottle. "I'll be back and then we'll get out of this place to somewhere safer, okay?"

Julian nodded again and Andrew let him drop back on the bed. Then he grabbed his keys and coat and headed out the door to get some air.

SATURDAY

Chapter 22: Dike

Dike walked back and forth in the soft grass in front of a little known tributary of the river Lethe that extended beyond the borders of the underworld. It was tucked into a corner of Olympus few of her fellow gods ever visited. Most didn't even know it existed. Dike had been coming to its shore for centuries to escape the evils that filled her days and find respite in its beauty and tranquility. Swift-flowing and steady as always, it had an inviting turquoise patina that drew mortals in to forget their failings in one life and restore them fresh for the next. The sunlight sparkled like diamonds on its surface, and Dike was drawn ever closer to the water's edge. She understood the river was designed to be this beautiful, this inviting, to compel the mortal to drink and forget. Dike felt feverish and desperate as she scanned the shoreline for signs of life. Trees of full leaves and fragrant flowers lined her view, and she relaxed ever so slightly. She knelt down by the water and let her hand dip into the cool, silkiness of it. In a flash of impulsiveness, she cupped her hand full of the elixir and drank greedily. In that moment, nothing mattered more than forgetting. Forgetting his betrayal. Forgetting his love for another. Forgetting these mortal feelings that now flowed unchecked within her.

Zeus had warned her centuries ago that the link she created between herself and her human fighters would threaten to change her. That she would be susceptible to their fragilities and emotional weaknesses. She had scoffed then and carried out her program of justice without much trouble. Then she chose him. Right away, something was different. Right away, she spent more time in his consciousness than all the others. More time training him, instructing him, making him reliant – no, dependent – on her. His neediness of her attentions filled her with a desire for more and more. She knew immediately, deep down, this obsession was folly, but for the first time since her creation, she overruled her own intuition and knowledge. Dike conveniently pushed it aside and made excuses for her behavior, and her feelings, just like she'd seen the humans do for millennia. She could rationally see the trouble she was in, but she couldn't seem to stop its momentum. It was maddening.

How did the humans live like this? The internal pain affected everything. Her thoughts were muddled and distorted, and she found herself desperately focused on one concept alone: Andrew was hers, and he had betrayed her.

Dike was ill with the human emotion she had always hated most: jealousy.

She shook her head violently to rid it of his face, his words, his actions. When it did nothing to abate the fire that threatened to consume her, Dike refilled her hand and drank once more. She sat still to see if anything would happen. A twinkle of a laugh emerged from the river and cut through her thoughts like a serrated knife.

"Oh my dear Dike," the voice began smugly. "The water cannot affect the minds of the gods. It is only for the soft spirits and minds of the mortals." Lethe, goddess of the river that shares her name, then laughed heartily at Dike's predicament. "You have allowed yourself to be poisoned by them. You deserve to experience their pain as punishment for your idiocy. My water will not aid you. Seek your sustenance elsewhere."

Dike's anger flared, and she experienced acutely yet another of the human conditions that led to countless problems on Earth: shame. Moving away from the water's edge, Dike walked through Olympus until she became weary with the task. She knew she had gone too far. Lethe was right: she had become too intertwined with the humans so that her godly mind was confused by what she actually desired. She understood she could stop the pain in an instant if she cut herself off from her fighters, returned Zeus's power, and restored the original order of things. But that would mean letting Andrew go for good.

Yes she had broken her connection with him days earlier, but she had been so angry at the time. Dike knew she had the option of transferring his powers back if she decided that was what she wanted. If she missed him enough. But she also wanted him to be punished for how he disobeyed her. And, admittedly, Dike knew Zeus would be even more aware something was wrong the more she threw her borrowed powers around at will. Then she would no longer have a choice. Zeus would definitely make her give up her fighters. And that would include Andrew, and would be final. The idea of it filled her with anguish. She would rather kill the whole lot of them than be without that one.

Dike stopped where she stood. Is that really what she just thought? That she was ready to wipe out all of humanity if she couldn't have the one she coveted? That all of the world would suffer for her pain? Was that what it was really like to be a human? Dike had never fully understood how humans behaved the way they did. Now, she stood stunned at the reality of that loss of control, loss of rational thought. No wonder humans were always at war. Always behaving like monsters. Dike found that in her meandering, she had arrived back at the willow tree. Parting the branches to enter the magical den inside, Dike moved to sit on her marble bench. When had she last been here to witness the ails of man? She saw her blindfold, given to her by Zeus to exact justice in a world that she now more deeply understood existed on a razor's edge between calm and chaos.

The blindfold sat on the bench, unmoving, awaiting her patiently. Dike picked up the cloth and gasped at the realization that she hadn't done so since the first day she'd made Andrew a fighter. Though a speck of time in her immortal existence, it must be fifteen or sixteen years in the human realm. Had she truly neglected her duties so fully? Had his appearance in her life altered her so completely that she had forgotten her purpose?

She sat down and affixed the soft linen around her eyes. Immediately, as since the dawn of mankind, images of the wrongs of humans filled her vision. Dike had always kept a grand eye on the world as a whole, while her fighters helped manage smaller evils, but what Dike saw now filled her with sadness. Wars were being waged on multiple continents, mass murders, genocide, pestilence, all at once in every corner of the globe. While she had been neglecting her purpose, the world suffered more than usual. She ripped the linen away and saw that the soil was thick where her eyes had seen the darkness.

She sat in stillness, absorbing what she'd witnessed and steadying her breath. He had distracted her. He had infected her with his weak, human emotions. Andrew was to blame for her mistakes! Anger seethed in her belly as her thoughts returned to his face, his betrayal. She should just kill him. Then she'd be free.

Before she had her next thought, the sky around Olympus thundered and the ground shook mightily. Dike knew immediately.

She was being summoned.

SUNDAY

Chapter 23: Victoria (me)

I awoke in a panic. I must have dozed off because the movie I was watching was no longer on, it was just the home screen. Dammit! I grabbed my phone off the coffee table and frantically checked the time. 6:07 a.m. The last time I remembered checking the clock it had been 4:15 a.m., so I must have fallen asleep soon after that. That would mean I slept close to two hours. I had dreamed again, as vividly as before, and tried to recall the pieces of it now.

In the dream, I was crouched between the wheels under the bed of a medium shipping truck. My gaze was trained on another truck parked off to the right about three car lengths away. It was still dark, but I wore some kind of glasses that allowed me to see like it was daylight; everything had a green tinge to it. Some movement caught my attention, and I watched as two men moved from around the front of the truck to the back and raised the door. It was too far to see the inside from where I was crouched, but I pulled a long camera lens out of my duffel bag and zoomed in on the men. One wore glasses and the other had a scraggly beard, and both had tattoos peeking out from their sleeves and collars. They entered the truck and pulled out a large crate of some kind. They placed it between them just as the back of a third man moved directly in front of my line of sight. He was bigger and wore work gloves and a baseball cap, so I couldn't make out any tattoos and he didn't turn his face to me. He bent down to seemingly look into the crate, then gestured into the truck and walked out of sight again. I tried to follow him with the lens but never got a good enough look before he moved out of view. Frustratingly, that was where the dream had ended for me. Now, as I thought about that third, bigger man, I had a nagging sensation that he was familiar somehow.

Checking the clock again, I got up to wake Teniese. She startled up in my bed as I opened the door and the light from the living room hit her face. "What happened? Are you okay?" she blurted out.

"It's fine, everything is fine. It's just time to wake up."

"What time is it?" she asked.

"6:15 a.m.. I fell asleep, but only for a little bit. I'll tell you when you're ready to come out." I left her to get herself roused and set to making yet another pot of coffee. Once fully awake, I told her about my dream, and the meeting time this morning that I thought should be our next attempt at finding Andrew.

She nodded along, then narrowed her eyes. "Wait, wait. Do you hear what we're talking about doing? Andrew was following a crime ring. People have been beaten and murdered, and we are gleefully discussing crashing their party. Have we completely lost our minds?"

She had a point. "You're right. I was so focused on just having a way forward and finding Andrew that I didn't think about what else we might end up finding." I paused, realizing that I couldn't put her in that kind of danger, but I was still desperate to stop what was happening to me. "I will go – I have to. We don't have any other leads at this point, and I can't just wait for this thing to take me over completely. We'll drive by

211

and check it out first, and then find a place for you to park a safe distance away, but not too far that I can't get to you if I need to. If I run into trouble, you can be my backup. I'm protected by the amulet, you're not. I'll go and see if Andrew is there, or if I can learn anything else. Then maybe we'll know what to do next." I could tell Teniese was about to argue, and I held up my hand to stop her. "I'm going, and you're not. End of discussion. I have a little more ability to be foolish than you do, Teniese." I didn't add that my skin prickled with goosebumps of anticipation.

She set her jaw and sighed, "Fine. How far away from here is this place?"

"Looks like it's going to take half an hour or so. See if you can find us anything to eat for breakfast, and I'll let Ana know what we're doing." Teniese rooted around in the fridge while I texted Ana our plan. At around 7:30 a.m., we got in the car and headed out. Andrew's meeting time was 9:00 a.m., and we needed to be there early to stake it out first and see where Teniese could wait for me safely. We still hadn't heard back from Ana.

The address Andrew had written down turned out to be an abandoned bottling plant. The driveway into the gated property had more potholes and broken asphalt than road, and it led up to a dilapidated brick building. We didn't turn in, though, because two cars were already parked in front of the building. That was all that was visible from the road, as wooded areas surrounded the plant from the east and west. We drove a quarter-mile further and saw a dirt access road mostly overgrown and tucked off at the edge of the woods. This would be a perfect place for Teniese to wait for me, as it was secluded and close by. We decided we'd double back a bit and Teniese would drop me off along the wooded area where the fence had seemed scalable, then I'd be mostly hidden while I approached. I didn't have a strong camera lens like Andrew did in my dream, but I had my cell and would zoom as best as I could with that. I would keep Teniese up to date on everything so she didn't lose her mind with worry, and if I needed her I'd run back through the woods to the drive or she'd call the police for me. Teniese watched until I cleared the chain-link fence and entered the woods before she turned the car around and headed back to the dirt road.

As I left the car, Teniese's parting words were, "Don't die, Victoria. I mean it."

It was a cold fall day, and wind whipped around the trees. This was good for masking the sound of my feet crunching dead leaves as I made my way toward the building. Just as I caught a glimpse of the parking area ahead, my phone dinged loudly. *Shit!* I had forgotten to put it on silent mode. I crouched down and frantically looked around to see if anything shifted in response to the noise. When it seemed clear, I looked at the message that had come through. It was from Ana and it read: *DO NOT GO TO THAT MEETING! JULIAN SAYS THEY'LL KILL U IF THEY SEE U! LEAVE THERE NOW! HE SAYS IT'S A MASSIVE DRUG DEAL!!!*

Almost immediately after I read the text my phone rang. "Shit!" I hissed.

It was Teniese, who spoke before I had a chance to say anything. "You saw Ana's text? You need to come back, now!"

I sat immobile in my crouched position, considering the options before me. I was nearly to the bottling plant already, and I was too scared to return to the hotel and wait to see if

Andrew would return, because they most likely had my door-busting incident on video. I had no other idea than this to try to find Andrew and stop the transition from happening. I couldn't turn back without at least trying to see if he was here. My heart beat wildly. I had taken the gun with me, but it only had a handful of bullets left, and I had to imagine everyone here would be heavily armed.

Teniese's voice broke through my thoughts. "Hello? Vic, did you hear what I said? You need to come back now. Abort mission or whatever the hell they say! It's too dangerous!"

"I can't. I know what Ana said but I don't have any other ideas and I'm running out of time. I'll just go right to the edge of the woods and see what I can see. I won't engage. I'll stay quiet and invisible, but I still need to go." I had made up my mind. "If you're in any trouble at all, call 911 and get the hell out of here, okay? No hesitating."

Teniese swore under her breath, "Oh my God, oh my God…don't fucking die!" Then, as she was about to hang up, she added, "Wait! What if you become the fighter again? You'll be in the presence of all those bad people. What if you lose it and can't control yourself?"

She was right, that would be pretty bad. "I don't know what to say, I have to try. Just remember to get out the minute you sense something is off. And, Teniese? Thank you for being my friend." I heard her curse in the background as I hung up.

I made sure my phone was silent before carefully creeping the rest of the way forward, making as little noise as possible. As I got within ten feet of the edge of the woods, my visibility opened up. I could see three cars parked off to the right and the hulking frame of the bottling plant about forty yards off to the left. A large, white truck was parked with its back to the building and two men were at the back door moving in and out of the cargo area. I was too far away to see their features. Suddenly, a car door opened to my right and another man exited one of the parked vehicles only twenty feet from me. He was dressed in all black like the two men at the back of the truck, and before he slid his black hat over his head, I could see he was completely bald. He lit a cigarette as he made his way toward the two men at the truck. I glanced at my phone; it read 8:42 a.m. There were still more than fifteen minutes until the scheduled time Andrew had written on his paper in the office.

A heavy gust of wind interrupted the steady breeze, and yellow and brown leaves fell around me. I zipped my jacket tighter against the cold just as a black SUV came down the drive and entered the parking lot. It backed up along the opposite side of the white truck, so that its tail was hidden from my view. A large man wearing a winter knit cap and sunglasses got out and moved to the front of the SUV, put his hands on his hips, and looked straight at the woods where I stood. I panicked and dropped to the ground behind a felled log. Did he see me? He seemed to be looking right at me. My heart beat hard, but I mustered the courage to peek around the side of the log. He had already moved out of view. I shook my head at my jumpiness. If they were far enough that I couldn't make out their faces, chances are they wouldn't be able to see me at all unless I moved to the clearing's edge. I needed to calm down. Panic would not help me here.

None of the men I had seen so far looked like they could have been Andrew, and I doubted he would make himself visible. I had a sudden thought that he might be here, in the same woods as me, trying to assess the scene in front of him. I whipped my head in all directions, but only saw trees and dying brush on the brown, autumn ground. I probably wouldn't see him until he was right on top of me anyway, the way my observation skills were.

More activity drew my attention back to the bottling plant as a second white truck entered the parking lot and backed into the space next to the truck closest to me. Three SUVs pulled in and parked in a semi-circle around the front of the trucks so that my vision was even more obscured than before. Bodies exited the cars and, if I counted correctly, we were now up to a dozen people. This new group seemed more like an organized unit than the first group of men, and even from this distance, I could see a couple had large guns slung over their backs.

Jesus, why the hell had I been so excited to come here? If they see me, I am dead, no question. I just needed to know if Andrew was here, and then I would head back to Teniese and we'd bolt. I remembered my dream from last night when I was spying on people from underneath the carriage of a truck, so I knelt down further to peer under the cars closest to me on the right, but I didn't find Andrew crouching there. Some cars had now assembled along the building to the left and out of the way of the trucks and SUVs, but they were too far for me to get a good look at them. A clanging brought my attention back to the trucks. The back door on the second truck, now closest to me, had been thrown open with a loud, metallic sound. Men stood in an arc around the activity so that I couldn't clearly see what was happening. The two men who met at the truck's end were the large man who had looked into the woods and another who came with the second white truck. For a moment, the bodies moved just enough for me to see the large man on his own. I could tell it was the same man who looked so familiar from my dream last night. How would I possibly know this person, though? I tried to zoom my phone camera on him, but as soon as I set it up, the bodies of other men were again impeding my view. I snapped a few pictures of the whole scene since I had my camera out anyway. As I went to put my phone back in my pocket, my brain was unexpectedly flooded with figures and measurements.

Suddenly I knew that the building was exactly ten feet from the back of the trucks, and eight feet from the first person. There were thirteen men, eight of whom wore the same clothing, like a uniform, and carried an estimated total of eleven firearms. The five additional men were less organized but still armed, and I assumed each carried at least one firearm making it a total of sixteen weapons in view. The driveway and only escape route for the vehicles was forty yards from the front of the trucks and would take a large truck like that nearly six seconds from starting the engine to reaching the road.

I noted six broken window panes on the building within close range of the gathering and two others closer to the woods and hidden enough to grant me access to the building without being seen or heard. Examining the parking lot, I noted that the car closest to me still had keys in the ignition, and I could get there and drive the car out to the road before the group had time to get more than a few rounds off at my back. I gauged there were two bosses of the transaction and each had one man who stood closest, who must be their personal bodyguards. If the first truck was filled with drugs and the second truck was empty, it would take the men approximately thirty minutes to move the cargo from one truck to the other if all of them helped.

Thirty-five minutes if the two bodyguards didn't move cargo and instead stayed close to their bosses. These thoughts were coming fast and furious, and I didn't understand how I knew what I suddenly knew. I had mentally entered a zone. I was gathering details I could never have known before, and my brain was processing information at a rate I'd never experienced.

Just then, a powerful force hit me from my right rear, and I went flying down into the dirt and leaves. Before I could react, a man was on top of me with one hand over my mouth and the other forcing my arms down and pinning them under his knees.

Andrew.

Though the man hovering over me now was different from the man in the street Monday evening. Same crazy eyes, but the rest of him was completely disheveled and unkempt, as though his appearance finally caught up with the craziness of his words and actions. I was stunned from the blow but not hurt. The information and statistics that had consumed my mind from a moment ago were gone as quickly as they'd come.

"If you make a sound, we're both dead," Andrew hissed at me. "I'm taking the amulet back, don't resist me!" He snaked his free hand around behind my neck and fumbled for the chain, but it was under too many layers of clothes. Andrew swore and looked wildly at me. I tried to remain calm and get him to settle down, too. He seemed as terrified as he was determined. I shook my head and spoke but it just came out as nonsensical sounds. "I said be quiet!" He looked frantically over the log we'd fallen alongside. It mostly covered us by sight, but the activity of a fight in all these dry leaves and twigs would definitely give us away.

I pulled my right hand hard to the right along the ground and out from under Andrew's knee. He pitched to the right just enough for me to know he'd lost balance, and I used that distraction to hit his other hand hard away from my mouth. Before he had a chance to recover, I whispered, "Andrew, stop. I'm not going to fight you!"

Andrew's face contorted, and he paused just a moment, trying to decide what he should do. I knew he thought I would hurt him if I got the chance, so I tried to remain as still as possible and held my hands out in front of my body. After a minute that felt like an eternity, he moved off me and let me sit up. I thought for sure I'd be sore from where he had kicked me, but it was as though it hadn't even happened. Andrew, on the other hand, winced when he put his hand down on the ground to slide his body apart from mine. "Are you injured?" I whispered.

He ignored my question. "You need to give me back the amulet." His voice had a frantic edge to it and he held out his hand.

"I never wanted it in the first place!" I whispered back at him. "If I give it back to you, will everything go back to normal?" I asked, moving another foot or two away from Andrew.

"Yes, I think so." He replied carefully, reaching his hand out further. I slowly freed the necklace out from under my coat. Before I had the chain looped over my head, though, the now familiar dread washed over me and I hesitated. My body fought the idea of taking it off again, even more than last night at dinner when Philip held it. Andrew looked at me expectantly, a tremor in his hand betrayed the effort it took for him to stand there and wait instead of just ripping my head off to get to it faster. Before I decided what to do, a shout erupted from the parking lot. We both turned and ducked farther beneath the log to see what was happening, and I let the amulet fall back down around my neck. The arc of men had moved in closer and several of them had their guns drawn on the others, while the two men in the middle shouted and gestured at each other. We were too far away to make out what they were saying, but the scene was incredibly tense.

Forgetting the amulet for the moment, Andrew grabbed a long-lens camera from the duffel he had at his side and pointed it at the group. "What can you see?" I whispered to him, but he gestured for me to be quiet, so I turned back and strained my eyes to try to see what was going on.

All of a sudden it was mayhem. I couldn't tell what was happening, but I saw at least one man fire his gun at another who fell to the ground, and the rest of them went scurrying in all directions like mice, yelling and shouting. The bald man took off across the parking lot toward us and his waiting car, but was shot down before he could get there, only about thirty feet from our hiding place behind the weathered log.

Andrew shoved his camera back into his bag and turned to run toward the back of the bottling plant. "We need to go now!" he said.

"Wait!" I cried, no longer concerned I'd be heard over the melee transpiring by the trucks and screeching tires of SUVs driving away. "This way! I have a friend waiting to drive us!" I started running deeper into the woods and farther from the fighting and could hear the sounds of crunching branches and leaves of Andrew running behind me. We didn't stop until we broke through the clearing and were right upon Teniese's car. She jumped and screamed as I erupted from the woods.

"Holy shit! You scared the hell out of me! What's happening?" Then she yelled, "Look out!" as Andrew emerged a moment later.

"It's Andrew! Teniese, we have to go now!" I turned to him. "Get in!"

Just as Teniese turned the key and was about to drive off, one of the SUVs from the parking area screamed past, followed closely by one of the white trucks. We collectively ducked down in our seats, though I didn't think they noticed us. They were going so fast, and our car was tucked off of the road in the shade of the trees. Once they'd passed and nothing else happened, Teniese yelled, "Will there be more of them? What should I do?"

Andrew answered her, "This is a service road, follow it."

"How do you know? What if we trap ourselves?" I countered.

"There are a bunch of them back here that crisscross through the woods. I used a different one to get to the plant, but I'm pretty sure they all converge. I looked at an aerial map of the roads a week or so ago. I believe I can still figure it out."

Teniese put the car in drive and whipped around quickly.

"Slow down!" Andrew yelled from the backseat. "You're kicking up dust and you'll draw their attention!" It felt like torture, but Teniese slowly rolled us along the service road. I didn't breathe until the road was further into the woods and shielded us on both sides by trees. It was probably only five seconds, but felt like an eternity.

Once we were no longer visible, Teniese said, "What happened? Why were they speeding off like that? And why did you run back without letting me know you were coming? Did they see you? I mean, were you being chased? Did they have guns? I mean, that's probably the stupidest question in the world because it was a fucking drug deal, but were they shooting their guns? And how the hell did you find *him*?" She was rambling and getting more frenzied by the second.

"Teniese, take a breath," I yelled. "They just started shooting and freaking out. It became absolute mayhem in one second flat. I have no idea what happened."

Andrew leaned forward from the back seat. "They were short. I heard them talking about it the other night. Two bundles of cocaine have gone missing. They were going to try to just let it slip by in the deal and hope the buyers didn't notice because of the volume. I guess they noticed." Andrew added angrily, "Fucking idiots. I knew this would happen. At least they exacted justice on each other since I wasn't able to." He was really agitated now, and he turned to me. "Give me the amulet."

I bristled. "You're the one who forced it on me in the first place! Isn't it linked to me now? I was ready to give it to you in the woods in exchange for answers. I need to know what's happening to me."

"I had no choice, she made me. But I need it back now. How the hell did you even end up at the bottling plant, anyway?"

"We've been looking for you. We broke into your house last night."

"That was you?" He threw an angry fist into the back of Teniese's seat.

"Hey! Trying to drive here!" Teniese swerved slightly with the surprise of the hit.

"How did you even know where I lived?" He ignored Teniese and stared me down hard.

"I found Ana, and she brought us to your house. She was worried you were dead."

"Ana?" He gasped. "You found Ana? How?" he asked, perplexed, then abruptly lunged toward me and yelled, "You better not have touched a hair on her head!" I recoiled away from him toward the front of the car.

"We're on the same team, here, okay?" Teniese yelled back. "She's having your freaking memories, that's how she found Ana. Ana has been helping us. She's how we found your apartment. She was with us when we broke in and saw the details of this meeting scribbled on a paper on your desk and the card for the hotel where you were hiding Julian—"

"You found Julian, too? How can that be? I used an alias for the booking. Did you hurt him?" he interrupted, looking ready to smash the seat again.

"No, you covered that just fine yourself." I shot back. "*I* didn't hurt him." I left out the part about desperately wanting to and busting up the hotel door in his place. "Ana is with him now at Teniese's apartment. And as far as she's concerned, he's never doing another bad thing for the rest of his life, or *she'll* kill him. He's safe for now. Look, I need to stop this transition before I turn into some version of you, and I think I only have a day or two left."

"Maybe you can start by giving me the amulet. I don't know what she did to you to make you have my memories, but I don't care. Your life isn't my main concern right now." He held out his hand again for the amulet.

"I was struck by lightning, remember? I only stopped in that freaking storm to help you! You forced the amulet on me, then abandoned me in the middle of the—"

"What's your name?" He interrupted.

"Victoria."

"Great. Victoria, here's the deal. You are a threat to me and Julian and the faster I can get away from you the greater chance I have to survive. So maybe we can talk *after* I have the amulet back." He pushed his hand further forward.

What an asshole. "Tell you what, *Andrew*. I'll give you the amulet when you give me some answers and I stop turning into you."

He regarded me with fury and ran a rough hand through his wild hair, then turned to Teniese. "Turn right at the fork here, I think it'll bring us out to a larger road south of the plant." We exited the woods a moment later. "Right. My car is parked a mile west of here." Andrew looked at me, this time more desperate. "Look, I don't know what to do—since the storm, everything is a mess. I can't even think straight anymore! I don't know why you haven't tried to kill me yet, but I can't trust that you won't no matter what you say. You want answers and I want my life back." We had pulled up alongside his car, and he got out and slammed the door, then stood unmoving, figuring out what to do next. A car turned the corner and made toward us. Teniese and I slunk down and Andrew dropped to the ground by the car. It just continued on without giving us any notice.

Once it passed, Andrew leapt up and made for his car. I opened the window. "Wait! What should we do?"

He turned back and paused with his hand on his car door. "Go to the hotel."

"Not a good idea," Teniese answered him. "She tried to bust down the room door to get to Julian when the crazy set in. Pretty sure people saw her."

"Fuck!" Andrew kicked his car's tire hard and clenched his fists at his sides. "Fine. Go to my house since you know where it is. Tell Ana to meet us there. You said Julian is at your house? Have him stay there—he's mostly out of it anyway, the fucking cockup. Maybe she doesn't want me dead yet," he gestured in my direction, "but I know *she* wants the job finished." He pointed up to the sky. "Park in the back and don't let anyone see you." Then he got into his car and peeled off, not bothering to worry about the cloud of dust trailing behind him.

SUNDAY

Chapter 24: Victoria (me)

Teniese and I texted Ana to bring her up to speed and then headed to Teniese's house to pick her up. When we entered, we were greeted by the smell of pancakes and an older woman standing at Teniese's stove with a black apron covered in little red flowers wrapped around her waist.

"What the hell?" Teniese started just as Ana walked into the kitchen from the other direction. "That's my apron!"

Seeing our expressions, Ana got between us and the older woman with her hands raised. "Wait, relax, this is just my mom. When I told her we found Julian she insisted on coming. Mamá, estas son mis amigas, Victoria y Teniese." The older woman nodded at us and gave a shy smile. "I wasn't sure how you'd feel about us using your kitchen, and your food…so I made her stick with pancakes. When I woke up this morning she had pulled out your entire fridge, ready to cook everything in it. I think it's a miracle I got her to stick with the pancakes. Is it okay if she stays here, Teniese? Just for now, to take care of Julian while we're out? I promise she'll clean up. And, frankly, I don't think I could get her to leave if I tried. Julian is still knocked out on the couch from his drugs and alcohol binge so won't easily be going anywhere anyway. He hasn't even woken up yet since she arrived. He's going to get an earful when he does."

Teniese walked over and gave Ana's mom a hug. "Mi casa es su casa. Tell her she can cook whatever she wants as long as she saves me some." Ana's mom smiled and hugged Teniese back. Then Ana said goodbye to her mom and shepherded us out.

"Come on, I need to see Andrew."

Once we were suitably parked back at the abandoned apartment building near Andrew's house, she bolted from the car and ran through the basement door, which was still hanging on its hinges. We followed at her heels and caught up just in time to see her launch herself across the room at Andrew's startled form.

Andrew faltered backwards under the assault, then regained his balance and held her tightly. They stayed that way for several seconds, just holding each other. Finally Ana broke the embrace and pushed back enough to look Andrew in the face. "I'm so sorry, Andrew. I thought you had lost your mind," she started.

He shook his head. "No, *I'm* sorry. Sorry that I dragged you into all this, Ana. Sorry I couldn't be normal. But I didn't kill him. I kept my promise."

"I know. I know you did. Why didn't you call me or answer any of my texts? I've been imagining you dead all week!"

"The lightning fried my phone on Monday. And I didn't think you'd want to hear from me anyway. Not after I screwed everything up."

"Well, I'm still trying to get my head around it all. You know how crazy it sounded, right? But then Victoria found me and had your necklace on and started telling me about all these experiences she was having that were like yours. It was harder not to believe at least something bizarre was happening. By the way, I found my letter here."

"I didn't know what she would do to me when I didn't kill Julian. I had never gone against the scales before. I figured I should tell you how I felt in case that was it for me." He suddenly noticed Teniese and I standing there and moved protectively in front of Ana.

"Just us," Teniese said, seeing his guardedness. "Vic hasn't managed to kill anyone yet, so I think we're all still on the 'good' side of things." Though still really clean, there were dishes on the counter and in the sink, and a jacket was slung on the back of one of the kitchen chairs. The house wasn't so perfect now that it looked like someone actually lived here. Much less creepy this way.

Andrew motioned for us to sit around the kitchen table. "Thanks for busting up my doors, by the way." He directed his words sarcastically at me. "And I want my gun back."

"It's in the car, safe and sound," I replied. I had considered keeping it in my purse or back waistband like they do in the movies, but was too nervous I'd have an episode like at the hotel and shoot someone. In the car it stayed.

"I brought them here, looking for you," Ana interjected. "Once Vic met me at the restaurant, and you didn't answer your phone, and with all the craziness with Julian, I thought you could be here hurt or dead."

Andrew turned to Ana. "You've seen how Julian is, right?"

"Yeah, he's in pretty rough shape but still well enough to be the same smartass brother I used to know."

"I did that to him, Ana. I was able to resist killing him, but I was the one who hurt him like that. You need to understand who I am. Or…who I was, anyway." He swung a hand in my direction.

Ana nodded, "You didn't really have a choice, right? To do those things, I mean? You were controlled by…that goddess?"

"For a long time, it simply *was* my choice, and I wasn't looking to stop, anyway. I was proud of ridding the world of the worst mankind has to offer. You have to understand this has been my life since I was a teenager. Meeting you was the first time I ever considered what it was I was doing. And even then only because my lifestyle didn't really lend itself to 'happily ever after.' As a fighter, you're compelled to seek justice. That's how it's supposed to work." He replied, rubbing eyes that were hollow and dark. It was clear Andrew hadn't done much sleeping this week. "There's no remorse, no guilt…just power and satisfaction that you're working for a higher good. But that's all you need, really. Everything else seems superfluous so you don't waste your time worrying about it. You still feel, but it's like the depth of emotion is shallower." Andrew paused and took a deep breath. "I don't know if I'm making any sense."

"And now?" I leaned forward, "Do you still feel that way?"

He turned to me coldly. "Now I am trapped under the weight of a waterfall of emotions. My brain is overwhelmed with the pain and constant flow of them. Ask me your questions."

I'd been so desperate to find Andrew I wasn't sure how to begin now that I actually had him in front of me. "What exactly is happening to me?" was all I could think to say.

"I assume she is turning you into one of her fighters," he answered plainly.

"What does that even mean?" I hit the table exasperated. "Does it mean I'll be living the rest of my life going around killing people? Did you just wake up one day and start changing like this?"

"Okay, okay, calm down. No. She offered the choice to me when I was sixteen and my father had just been murdered. She told me I was worthy because I had a strong sense of justice and had been orphaned. I was given the amulet and enhanced strength and analytical skills. Then I trained in martial arts and reconnaissance, and learned everything I could about the underground world where the worst of humanity usually resides. It was at least six months before I was ready to act as a fighter."

Teniese chimed in. "You keep saying 'she.' Who is this goddess?"

"Dike," he said. I gave him a blank look. "You know, Greek goddess of justice?" I shrugged my shoulders. "You need to read more." Andrew shook his head.

"So wait – if you're saying Dike is actually real…does that mean we are to believe Zeus and Hades and the rest of them are real, too?" Teniese cut in.

"Well, I've heard of Zeus!" I added. Andrew rolled his eyes and ignored me.

"Yes. Dike, Zeus, Hades…they all exist and still influence human existence. Dike's role is judging and then meting out justice for those who have succumbed so far to evil forces that they don't deserve another chance. She maintains some balance between good and evil among humans. She monitors the wrongs of man on a large scale while her fighters help on the ground." He spoke matter-of-factly, as though describing his job as an electrician.

"Do you know any other fighters like you?" Teniese asked.

"No, It's not like we have a club and a Facebook group and get together for potlucks once a quarter. I understand they exist, but I don't think there are so many that we would run across each other. And Dike has her fighters spread out around the world to cover different areas. Too much visibility and it would be harder to stay in the shadows."

"We found another fighter who was here in Chicago. In the 1960s. Lydia Boyle. Have you heard of her?" I asked.

"No, how do you know she was a fighter?" he replied.

"She had this amulet. Or at least one just like it. I took it to a jeweler in the city who remembered Lydia bringing it in decades ago. I guess she'd be quite old by now, but maybe you walked by her on the street and didn't even know."

Andrew brooded for a moment. "There was one time I thought maybe I'd encountered another fighter. I had just carried out justice on a serial killer in the Ozarks. Her cabin was deep in the forest and completely isolated, which is how she was able to keep killing undiscovered for so long. Young runaways she'd pick up along the road. I was leaving the cabin at dusk and caught a glimpse of a man watching me from a copse of trees a short distance away. He just stood there and stared at me as though confused. He held a gun in his hand the same as me, but it rested easily against his leg and he made no move to raise it. After a minute of us staring each other down, the man said, 'So it's done then? You took care of her?'. I answered that I had, and the man nodded once then turned and walked away into the woods."

"How do you know it wasn't another fighter?" Teniese asked.

"I asked Dike. She told me he was just a local man who had figured out what was going on and decided to kill her himself." Andrew shrugged. "I was surprised to feel a moment of disappointment that he wasn't like me. But then I put him out of my head and left the woods. Like I said, it wouldn't make sense for fighters to occupy the same space. For lots of reasons."

"It must have been really lonely," Ana mused, gently placing her hand on his shoulder. "And I imagine you missed your parents terribly."

"Not really, no. I didn't need anyone. And Dike was with me daily, so I didn't feel alone. I barely even thought about my parents once I became the fighter – which seems terrible to say out loud now, but what good would it be for Dike to have her fighters dwelling on the past? We need to be precise and focused and reliable."

"Like robots," I mumbled.

"Like soldiers, choosing to do good for their country. In my case, for my world," Andrew shot back.

"But you're killing people! Basically hunting them down. How can that be considered 'doing good for the world'?"

"Killing the worst of humanity so they can't infect more people!" Andrew yelled. "Do you have any idea how many forces of evil are at work constantly trying to make humans fall? It's like a game to some gods and goddesses, they don't care for humankind in the least. Some who have succumbed must become collateral damage in order to protect the majority. This is how it's been since the dawn of time."

"So, wait, are you saying anyone who does anything bad could randomly be chosen to get killed by one of these fighters?" Ana asked, wide-eyed.

"No, all of us have a balance of good and evil. We are constantly, and mostly unknowingly, fighting against invisible forces, demons and other gods who are trying to create chaos on Earth. Spread evil. Dike monitors this with the scales of justice. When the evil outweighs the good in a person's life, that's when the scales tip and justice must be brought to them."

I couldn't believe what I was hearing. "So you're telling me that we're being watched constantly, and if we do more bad than good we could be struck down by someone like you? That doesn't make any sense! There are so many horrible people who live really long lives. What about them?" I asked. "And why is our prison system overflowing with murderers? Aren't they the worst of humanity? Why don't they get struck down, too?"

"The idea isn't to eradicate all evil on Earth. That's impossible. The idea is just to keep evil from overtaking good as a whole. To maintain balance on a grand scale. And there are too many humans on the earth to possibly deal with each one individually. Dike's not that powerful. That's why she started her army of fighters in the first place. To help her keep up." Andrew got up and started pacing the kitchen tile.

"Wait." I put my hands up, confused, "You said you trained for months before you knew anything. So why do I know how to do things so quickly? And why am I remembering things that are yours?"

"Yeah, explain what you mean by that, 'remembering things that are mine.'"

"Like Ana…Reuben sandwiches! I choked this guy Omar out at the martial arts gym where you trained because I had a flash and suddenly knew how to kill someone with those stick things. You think *your* brain is messed up!"

"You hurt Omar?" Andrew thundered.

I backed away and threw my hands up defensively. "It's not like I wanted to, I just did it! Same with a security guard at a mental hospital, same with the hotel room door. I see an image of these scales and my body does whatever the hell it wants. How do I make it stop?"

Andrew shook his head. "I don't know why, that's not how it happens for me. But I angered her when I didn't honor the scales and kill Julian. She was punishing me by taking the amulet away and giving it to you. And stripping me of my power and protection. Maybe she figured it would be easier just to give you what I'd learned? Is that why I feel so damn clumsy and dumb now? Nothing is working the way it's supposed to anymore. And my scar is gone." Andrew lifted his pant leg and showed nothing but smooth skin.

Teniese had been anxiously biting her cuticles and staring hard at a scratch on the table, deep in thought. "What if someone spends most of their time doing good in the world, but then some of their time doing bad. Do they just never tip the scales enough?" she asked quietly. I knew her mind must be on James. Would hitting your girlfriend be enough to tip the scales?

"There are levels to all good and evil. It's gray, not black and white. And fighters can't be everywhere at once. Same with Dike. Like I said – we're keeping the balance, not ridding the world of evil."

"Was Julian really that bad? So bad he deserved to die?" Ana stood and faced Andrew.

Andrew softened his gaze, "He's spent the last several years dealing drugs to kids on school playgrounds, terrorizing business owners, and putting people in the hospital. I know you still see him as your big brother, but he was the worst of all of them. Yes, he deserved to die. And I should have killed him." Andrew held her gaze until Ana turned away.

"Okay, okay…so stopping this transition? Any ideas?" I steered the conversation back.

Andrew reluctantly looked back in my direction. "I have no idea. Maybe you can start by giving me the amulet, like I said before."

I fingered the heavy metal settled on my chest. He noticed and gave me a wry smile. "I know that feeling. Once you have the amulet, every cell in your body screams for you to protect it as it protects you. And you distrust everyone who sees it."

"What does 'protection' even mean? What does it do for you when you have it?" Teniese leaned closer to me to examine it again, this small metallic disc that held so much power.

"A fighter who wears the amulet cannot be hurt or killed," Andrew said flatly, and we all stared back at him slack-jawed.

"It makes you immortal?" This was inconceivable.

"You'll eventually die of old age, but you can't be hurt. A knife will not reach you. A bullet flies around you. You can get pushed and punched but will hardly feel a thing."

No wonder I wasn't hurt when Andrew kicked me in the woods earlier. Visions of jumping off buildings and landing on my feet or diving into deep shark-infested waters without even a scratch flooded my head. If I had the amulet, it meant I was basically invincible. What a life I could live with a gift like this! No wonder I didn't want anyone else to hold it. And no wonder Andrew wanted it back so badly. I had a sudden flash of ill will toward him. He was a threat.

"No wonder you want it back so badly." Teniese voiced what I was thinking.

Ana whipped her head around to face him. "Is that true? You don't actually want to be this fighter person again, do you? Hunting and killing people?"

Andrew ran a hand through his hair and walked angrily over to the cabinet to get a glass of water. "Yes, I am craving it back. I don't want to be her fighter anymore, and I am desperate to be her fighter again in equal measure. I can't think clearly and it's making me insane!" he exclaimed with frustration. "Logically, I don't want to be that person anymore. But I literally can't imagine my life as anything else. I have done nothing but her bidding for fifteen years, Ana. I have known nothing else. Was always guided, always righteous in my role. Now what?" He threw up his arms. "I don't think I could just wake up tomorrow morning and decide I want to be an accountant or farmer or something like that. I literally know nothing but profiling people, judging them, and executing that justice. And my body itches for that purpose again! As vile as it sounds to you, I was serving the gods, for fuck's sake! What could be more important than that?"

"But you had no life…and you're a murderer!" Ana replied. "You have nothing but anger, evil, danger, death. You're a human…with no human life! What about love? Family? Friendships?"

He roared back in pain, "I've known nothing of that in fifteen years! She hijacked my brain, my emotions. You don't understand! It feels like exacting justice is the only desire in your soul. Those other things creep in now and again – but they're fleeting and gone the minute the scales appear. You don't want for anything else. You are content to be in that life." He wrapped his arms around his chest. "I know nothing different, Ana. I love you, that I believe with every fiber of my being. But now that it's been taken away, I can't even envision how a different life could look."

"You guys, what he's talking about is *happening to me*!" I turned to Andrew. "The immortal thing is pretty enticing, I won't lie, but every other word out of your mouth is terrifying. I'm sorry you're going through an existential crisis, but help me! How do I stop it?"

"I was hoping to finish the assignment this morning at the deal…thinking maybe that would make her change her mind. I used to know exactly what to do in every situation, and now I can barely remember how to hold my gun. Kicking you, this morning, hurt me." He shook his head. "I thought if I could get the amulet back and finish the assignment then she would forgive me for Julian and transfer everything back to me from you."

"No!" Ana stood and got in Andrew's face. "Andrew, you can't be that person anymore. What about us?"

He looked miserably back at her. "What the hell can I do for you, Ana, when I am no longer myself?"

I had an insight. "You said you are compelled to mete out justice. How did you deny it with Julian?"

"Free will. The one universal gift for mankind."

"That's it?" That was anticlimactic.

"I studied all I could about Dike and justice and the will of man. I read old texts and listened to lectures by storied professors trying to figure out what I could do to keep from killing Julian…but it was a Christian pamphlet that gave me the answer. I was sitting at a bench in this random park, trying to figure out how I could have allowed myself to fall in love, when the wind blew a dirty pamphlet at my feet. The front page was a cartoon drawing of a man standing at a crossroads, and the title said, 'Man's Free Will.' A light bulb went off and suddenly I was looking up everything I could find on free will. Every religion makes mention that we humans have the ability to choose for ourselves, even in the most fraught circumstances. From there I knew I would spare Julian for Ana. I would trust that she could bring him back to good, and I would use my free will to do it."

Finally, something that sounded promising. "So I can just choose *not* to obey the scales? How? I had no control when they flashed."

He shook his head. "It's not that simple. I had to practice. Every time the scales flashed, I needed to make it about my choice, not my commanded duty. I would silently affirm, 'This is my will' before each and every little choice I made for weeks. About everything from what to eat for breakfast to how I brought justice down on someone. The first time I tried with the scales, it didn't work. I wasn't able to do it." He hugged his hands to his head, his disheveled hair poking through his fingers. "I made the decision I wasn't going to shoot Julian at his apartment Monday, but the scales were so demanding and I started beating him instead. It was me screaming in my head that I choose to let him live, that I was going to stop before I'd gone too far. Luckily, I was able to pull myself away and leave so I wouldn't be tempted to finish the job."

Ana chimed in, "When the goddess made Vic the fighter, did you lose your ability to see the scales?"

Andrew nodded. "I lost everything it seems."

I started pacing too, so that now Andrew and I were like rival tigers sharing a cage. I wanted to give him the amulet to see if it would make things change, but my body started sweating in protest. "Andrew, if I give you the amulet, do you really think there's a chance we will change back?"

He stopped, and regarded me intently, bringing his hand forward, betraying the desperation he felt. "I have no idea. But don't you think we should try?"

I tried to steady my breath as I reached for the chain. Slowly, I pulled it over my head and held it out for Andrew, my arm shaking.

He snatched it quickly and threw it over his head. I stood perfectly still and paid attention to my body. Had anything changed? Did I feel any different? "I can't tell if anything is different. Can you?"

Andrew paused a little longer, and I could tell he was concentrating like I had been to see if he felt any change. "I don't know. I just don't know. Nothing has happened yet."

A thought occurred to me. "Wait – this morning you could have been killed at that deal, right? Why take that chance? I mean everyone there had a gun and went crazy shooting."

"I have been invincible for the last fifteen years. Old habits die hard." He sighed and held up his water glass. "I need something stronger than this. I've got whisky in my office. Won't take me but a minute since I don't have any locks to worry about." Andrew walked down the hall.

"There better be enough for all of us!" Teniese called after him. "Well – all except you." She pressed her index finger to my forehead and suddenly images of the morning flashed through my mind at lightning speed. I could see it all in striking detail. The trucks, the groups of men dressed in black, the factory with the broken windows. My mind was running through it all as if I was watching it on a movie screen, but with so much more information. I had missed the slight sound of a twig snapping right before Andrew kicked me in the woods. Just before the bald man left his car and walked toward the truck, he sniffed something from a packet in his lap and wiped his nose. And the large man in the center of the gathering that seemed so familiar to me was…

"Philip!" I exclaimed, scaring everyone at the table. "Oh my God—it has to be Philip! Philip was the man in the circle— the drug dealer!" I turned wide-eyed to Teniese. "I knew that man from this morning was familiar to me somehow! Philip said he was working on something to make more money at dinner and then I heard the voice and had the knife in my hand, remember?"

Teniese nodded uncertainly. "You really believe your boring brother was part of a well-orchestrated drug deal that ended in bloodshed? Nothing you've ever told me about him sounds like that. This doesn't compute," she rationalized.

"But Dike told me he wasn't a good man at dinner when he had the amulet, remember? Oh God, this must be why he really came into town this weekend. I need to warn my parents! He's staying with them. What if one of the rival gang members follows him or tracks him down or whatever to kill him, and my parents get hurt, too?"

"Who are you talking about?" Andrew came back into the room, but I was already on the move.

I ran out of the house to the car, ignoring Teniese yelling after me to stop. My only thought was that I needed to warn my mom and dad that Philip was dangerous. Or at least that he had a lot of dangerous friends. I panicked that they might already be in trouble and increased my speed.

SUNDAY

Chapter 25: Dike

Dike was struck hard on the side of her body the moment she entered the Hall of the Gods. Caught by surprise, she fell to the ground clutching at her ribs. A second blow came a beat later as a bolt of lightning struck her, flipping her body face down and lancing her head, stealing her breath and causing her to bleed. She attempted to turtle against further assault, but none came. Instead the booming voice of her father shook the walls.

"Ignorant fool!" he thundered. "Did I not warn you this would happen?"

"Mighty Zeus, I do not understand the meaning of this attack!" she replied, hesitantly rising as the cuts on her head and side began closing. Though she would heal from any wound, it didn't mean she wouldn't feel the pain of them. She looked frantically about to see if there was anyone else in the room to help her. Not a soul.

Zeus shouted back, "You don't understand? You have neglected your duties and gone against our agreement. Did you think I wouldn't find out?"

Dike's mind raced as she tried to think of a way out of this situation. "For only a few human years have I not favored the linen. It is barely the length of a breath in the time of this world!"

"Do you find me so simple to accept excuses? You have not honored your role, you have neglected your charge and caused unnecessary suffering to humankind. You have allowed yourself to become weakened!" Zeus stomped over to her and roughly hauled her up from the floor by her hair. She barely resisted. "Give me the linen and show me what you have allowed to transpire."

Dike's heart sank as she handed him the soiled piece of cloth. It took Zeus mere seconds to view the scenes she herself had witnessed under the willow tree. Once done, he ripped the linen from his eyes and hurled it at her. A look of absolute fury on his countenance. "And look at what a mere fifteen years can wreak. You have allowed war and pestilence to run rampant with your foolishness."

"It is nothing that cannot be amended, Zeus!" she offered. "There is always war and pestilence among them."

"Amended? Did you not think Hades would come to me with his report? The river Styx is overflowing with human souls. Souls you were charged to protect!"

"It is the humans' weaknesses that have doomed them to these fates! They fall prey to evil faster than my fighters can maintain." Dike considered fighting back, but she would be no match against Zeus's force. She needed to keep him talking. "And there is nothing for me to do with the disease spreading like wildfire after a drought. What impact could I have had there?" Zeus's inner light glowed brighter with his anger and the walls of the hall danced with amber light.

"Ha! It is a weak being who blames others for their failings and neglect! You curse yourself as you cast them into despair. No, disease is not within your control to stop, but perhaps the human world would be better able to cope with it if it wasn't already so divided by war and civil unrest!" Zeus dragged Dike to the seeing window in the south-facing corner of the great hall. Sunlight filtered in so colors danced magically in the glass. "Look again into the void of evil you've allowed to fester!" The glass shifted and morphed in front of Dike, feet barely touching the ground as Zeus held her aloft. At once, the image showed hospitals filled to overflow, then angry people with guns marching up to a capitol building, and men and boys chained in a dilapidated building. Cities reduced to ash and rubble. Gunmen shooting children down in a school classroom. As more and more of these images – more extensive than those her linens had revealed to her – appeared and fled from the glass, Dike felt the full extent of her carelessness on display. The images tortured her, and she turned to look away.

"Do not dare avert your eyes!" thundered Zeus. "You have closed them to their perils long enough. You deserve to feel every single moment of anguish your neglect has created on the earth." Her head was in a vice and could not turn left or right, and he pushed her even closer to the glass. What seemed an eternity passed before Zeus stopped the stream of horror and let her drop to the ground in her misery. "What have you to say for yourself?"

"I did not know I had neglected so much." Dike sat pooled where he dropped her and placed her hands over her eyes to try to free them. A war was being waged in her spirit and mind. She was horrified at what she had just witnessed— all the suffering she could have helped them avoid, all the ways peace might have been brokered in place of war. She wanted to make it right, but a lingering sensation of selfish desire clung to her heart. What concession could she make that wouldn't have her lose Andrew, lose her fighters, but would be enough to make things right?

"That's not good enough, Dike!" Zeus roared back, striking her chest with his staff. Dike flew across the room, her flesh burning. "You didn't know because you were blinded by your selfish, infected heart. I warned you this would happen, did I not? Your folly was to disregard my cautions. Your ego led you to make irrational choices, and now look at the state of things!" Zeus stomped to his throne, and his staff pulsed with energy as if in response to his mood. "This ends now. Erase his memory and release the woman from your power, and every fighter you have abandoned in the last fifteen years will be given the same treatment. You have shown yourself as unworthy, not strong enough to wield such power. I blame myself for allowing it to begin in the first place. Your experiment is over."

"No!" Dike couldn't believe what she was hearing. He was going to ruin everything she'd built over the centuries because of fifteen short years of abandonment? This couldn't be happening. She had to make this right, make him see through his rage that there had to be another solution.

SUNDAY

Chapter 26: Victoria (me)

I screeched into my parents' driveway, nearly colliding with my mom's car. Philip's car wasn't there, and neither was my dad's. I flew out of the car and ran through the front door without even knocking.

"Mom? Are you here?" I shouted. My mother's startled form ran in from her sewing room.

"Victoria? What in Hades is going on?"

I moved toward her, looking around the rest of the house for my brother. "Are you okay? Philip isn't here, is he?"

My mother scowled. "Of course, I'm okay. I was actually getting through a very difficult stitching pattern when you barged in and I nearly ruined it." She crossed her arms over her chest. "What the devil has gotten into you?"

"Good, okay, good. I think we need to leave, get you somewhere safer. Grab your coat and your purse. Can you call Dad and tell him he shouldn't come home anytime soon?" A frantic energy consumed me, and I ran to move the curtains back over the windows. Visions of armed men in the black cars from the morning swam before my eyes. "Mom, you have to move, come on!" My mother was still staring at me wide-eyed with her arms crossed. She hadn't budged.

"I'm not going anywhere until you tell me what is going on. You barge in here shouting demands after attacking me so terribly last night at dinner. I don't know what's gotten into you, but I'm not really in the mood for more disrespect and shenanigans." Her nose rose another couple inches in the air as she stared me down. I had already forgotten all about my outburst at dinner the night before.

I moved closer, "Philip is involved with some really dangerous people. He was in trouble this morning, and I'm worried they will come here and could harm you and dad. Just please trust me and leave. Just until we can figure it all out?" I was pleading as I ran over and grabbed her coat from the hook. She took it from me forcefully and dropped it on the kitchen table, crossing her arms again.

"What on earth are you talking about? What dangerous people? Honestly, Victoria, you're being about as clear as a mud puddle!"

I took a deep breath. "I saw Philip this morning, Mom. At a drug deal…with lots of men with guns. Something happened, and they all started shooting at each other. I am pretty sure Philip and some of the men that arrived with him got out in their black car, but that doesn't mean the other guys couldn't have figured out where he lives or where his parents live."

My mom laughed loudly, "Philip—at a drug deal? That's the most ridiculous thing I've ever heard. Philip had a meeting this morning." Then her eyes narrowed. "Have *you* been doing drugs? I will not allow that behavior in my house."

This was not going well. "At a meeting? Mom, I'm telling you I saw him! Remember at dinner last night he said he was into something else? Something that would make him money and he didn't want to tell us about it? He's dealing drugs. He even talked about his drug dealing neighbor driving the Lexus, remember?"

My mother picked up her jacket from the table and walked it back to the coat rack. "Your brother would never be involved in something like that. How could you even suggest it? And where were you when you saw this apparent drug deal with men with guns?"

Rage engulfed me. "Why, because Philip's so perfect? He couldn't possibly do anything you would consider beneath him? He's the faultless child. I'm sure you wish he was your only child!" I regretted the petty remark the moment it left my mouth.

My mother put her hands on her hips. "So this is another attack on me, is it? Trying to make Philip look bad to me to make yourself look better? Really, Victoria, this is beneath you, this whole charade. And, frankly, I don't feel the need to subject myself to more baseless assaults from you. I think you should leave. When you're ready to apologize for how you've behaved, then we can have a civilized conversation about it." She turned to walk back to her sewing room.

I balled my fists at my side and mustered the calmest voice I could. "Mom, I'm sorry, that was uncalled for. I don't want to make this about me. I saw something scary just a couple hours ago. Something that involved Philip and people dying. I worried that some of those same people would try to find Philip here and put you and Dad in danger. If we could just leave for a little bit until we can talk to Philip about it, I would feel so much better. Can we do that, please?"

She turned back to me. "Victoria, I'm starting to think you might be delusional. Philip would not be involved with drugs. I would know—he would have told me."

Now I was seeing red. "That's right because there are no secrets between you. You tell Philip everything, you praise Philip for everything, you support Philip in everything…and I'm the stupid, lethargic, lazy, incompetent disappointment that you just had to tolerate in your house." There was no going back now. "I want to hear it from you. Did Dad lose your money? Cheat on you? Is that why you always treat him so miserably?"

She looked stricken. "Who told you this?"

"Philip, of course! Your confidante and best friend, who else? You couldn't tell me any of it yourself?"

Her face clouded with betrayal, "He should never have said anything. That was between your father and me, and I only told Philip because he was on a tear about us moving here. Yes, it's true that your father has lied and cheated and messed up our lives repeatedly. How does that make you feel, you who only ever had love for him? You who think the moon and stars revolve around your deadbeat father, while you hate me—me, who cooked and cleaned and made sure your homework was done and drove you to soccer practice and listened to every whine and complaint. You hated me and adored him. Never knowing what he'd done!"

"How could I know any of this since you didn't tell me!?" I returned. "You never treated me like you treat Philip. I was a constant disappointment to you while Philip shined on in his mediocrity. All I ever wanted was some kindness, some sign that you loved me at all. Instead, it was eye-rolling, criticizing, head-shaking, teasing…I can't remember you ever telling me I did *anything* right, or good enough. Yes, I adored Dad, because he adored me!"

"Of course, I pushed you. I had to! You were such a shy, fearful kid. I was terrified that if I didn't toughen you up, you'd end up getting bulldozed in this life. Your father coddled you, then went on to bankrupt us repeatedly and become someone I couldn't trust anymore. What good does it do you to have him as your example? Yes, he's kind, but that doesn't keep you housed, fed and clothed. You needed to learn responsibility, gumption, ambition!"

"The only one who bulldozed me was you. What's so bad about learning kindness and optimism and self-worth? Why did you have to be so relentless?"

"Because I didn't want you to turn out like me!" she shouted, panting.

"What are you talking about?" I asked her, confused. If she didn't want me to turn out like her, why did she insist on teaching me all her worst qualities?

My mother collapsed in a kitchen chair, her shoulders slumped, her head in her hands. I waited a long minute as she got her breathing under control. "It all got so out of hand." She cried. "The first time your father lost his job, and then gambled away our money, you were just a sweet little girl. But you were afraid of everything – the rain, a dog, bath time. I had the rug pulled out from under me and there was absolutely nothing I could do about it. I had no money or college education of my own. I went to live with your father right from my parents' house. I hadn't done anything in my life for myself, so I was trapped. Left picking up the pieces and staying in a marriage that felt like a lie, because I wasn't prepared to fend for myself. I knew nothing. I swore I was not going to let that happen to you. You would be able to fight for yourself even if it meant against me. But you didn't. You just kept turtling further into yourself the more I tried to force you out. I knew I was driving you to hate me. But I'd see you looking at your dad with such admiration and open love and realize he was duping you despite everything." She seemed so diminished sitting there, so small. "I was so worried. Worried you'd turn out like me, and worried you'd turn out like him."

I stood immobile. This was all so unfair. All I felt was anger. Anger at her for how she designed my life to fail. Anger at my dad for being the catalyst in the first place. Anger at myself for never looking deeply enough to see the truth. For being weak. For wanting more but never having the courage to try. Maybe being a fighter would be a better life for me, after all. What would it feel like to live life with conviction and confidence? At least I wouldn't feel non-stop self-doubt. My life would have direction and power and purpose.

Just then the front door burst open, and Philip came crashing through it! "Mom!" he yelled before landing on our depressed forms at the kitchen table. "What's going on in here?" he asked, looking between us.

Seeing Philip, I immediately remembered the morning danger and moved protectively in front of my mother's shrinking form. Philip looked at me confused and moved closer to us. "Has something happened?"

"Yes!" I retorted, "I know what you're doing – I *saw* you this morning at your 'meeting.'" I made air quotes. "How could you be so reckless? Endangering so many people?" I stepped toward him; he retreated.

"What do you know about it?" he asked, astonished. "It's not reckless, it's just giving kids some fun."

My mother gasped, "So it's true, what Victoria said? You're selling drugs?"

Philip frowned. "Drugs? What?"

"Don't try to deny it. I was there at the deal this morning! I saw the trucks, the guns, the armed men. How could you do it?" The urge to punish him grew, but I worried the scales would flash and I'd seriously hurt him. Or even kill him if what Andrew said today was true. I still didn't want that, did I?

He held his hands up defensively. "Vic, what the hell are you talking about? I wouldn't even know how to buy drugs. And guns?"

My mom stood up. "Then what was your meeting this morning? Victoria is convinced you're a drug dealer who got in a shoot-'em-up this morning and we're all in danger when the bad guys come looking for you."

Philip laughed at me. "Are you serious?" He looked himself over. "I mean, I know I look the part and all…" He gestured at his ill-fitting chino pants and wrinkled button-down. "But come on, Vic…drug dealer?" He walked over to the kitchen cabinet and pulled out the mug with his face emblazoned on it. I just stared at him, confused. Seeing him now reinforced that he *was* the one at the bottling plant this morning, even with the change of clothes. But he seemed so calm, so unbothered with me knowing. Was he just a really good actor?

My mom met him with the coffee carafe and filled his mug. "Then what was your meeting about this morning?"

Philip sighed, then straightened up, sweeping out his other arm. "Video games." He dropped his arm at my mom's confused stare. "I'm going to be a historian with this company making video games. Like, I'll help them keep the story, clothing, weapons, all of that, legit to the time period." Philip's smile looked forced. I stood there trying to make sense of his words.

My mother was the first to speak. "Like educational video games? For learning about history?"

Philip looked uneasy. "Not educational games, no. Though they'll get accurate historical background, clothing and weapons…like I mentioned. I'm going to be making three times what I make as a teacher." He looked at me for support, but I just stared at him, still unsure whether to believe what he was saying.

My mother looked ill. "But video games? Is there killing in these games? Or maybe they're the kind where you work together as a community to build houses and plant crops?" she asked hopefully.

Philip dropped the smile, sighed, and walked over to the kitchen table, sitting heavily and not looking at my mother. "It's a game where a knight had his whole family murdered by a demon, and he spends all of eternity hunting down said demon and anyone who gets in his way. Yes, it will be a killing game.

With historically accurate images, homes, even the mythological demons they believed in at the time. I'm not making the video game, they have programmers for that. I'm using my extensive historical knowledge to make sure the killing is as accurate as can possibly be."

My mother didn't respond. She just stood there with her mouth open as though Philip, her precious Philip, had been speaking a different language and her brain was piecing it together. I was just as confused. It had to have been Philip that I saw this morning.

"But video games rot kids' brains – you know how we feel about them. And the killing kind are the worst of all, a terrible scourge on our young people! You'll go from teaching young minds to corrupting them?"

Philip stood. "This is why I didn't want to tell you guys about it. I knew you'd overreact. I am tired of working so hard with nothing to show for it. This is a way for me to use what I know and actually have a little fun in the process, while being able to afford things like pants that fit." He gestured again to his outfit. "It's a way for me to get ahead and not resent my life!"

"What about your books? Will you keep writing?" my mother asked desperately.

Philip stomped over to the fridge to get the creamer. "My books. You know, I have spent countless hours, basically had no life, to get those books written. And what do I have to show for it? I don't know if I want to go through that again, to be honest. I'm just so angry about it all." He sat back down. "Look, I'm actually excited about this opportunity, okay? It would be great if you could be at least a little bit supportive."

My mother appeared hurt but didn't have time to respond before the front door opened again. My father stood on the threshold, one hand on the doorknob, frozen in place as he took us all in. "What the devil is going on in here?"

I looked at my dad in utter confusion. Black pants, black jacket, dirt on his face…same exact bulky frame as Philip. "Dad?"

My father came all the way in, throwing a quick peek behind him as he closed the door. Then, agitated, he moved into the room to throw a quick kiss on my mother's cheek. She turned away.

"Why don't you ask your son what he's leaving teaching for?" My mother folded her arms across her chest. Philip threw up his arms and my father raised his eyebrows.

I just stared at him. "Dad. It was you?"

He looked between our faces. "What was me?"

My mother made an exasperated noise to say "not this again" and flung her hand up in the air. "Victoria is convinced that everyone in this family is a drug dealer!"

My father paused just a moment to return my stare then gave a careful laugh. "What is this nonsense?" He mimicked Philip and grabbed a coffee mug from the cabinet, turning his back to me.

"Dad, I was there. This morning at the bottling plant. I saw the trucks, the men, the guns…I saw you. I thought it was Philip, but…now that I see you…"

My father stiffened ever so slightly before turning around. "Bottling plant? Victoria, what on earth are you talking about?"

My throat went dry. My father never called me Victoria. "How did this happen?" I responded. Then I remembered the bald man who was shot down running for his car. "People were killed, I saw it. Why did you let that happen? How?" I could barely breathe as my father turned to lock eyes with me. He stood there silently holding his coffee mug, his eyes begging me to stop talking. I could feel my own eyes beginning to sting with tears.

My mother moved between us and faced him, seeing for the first time his disheveled appearance, his black, dusty clothes. "Arthur, what is this nonsense? You can't tell me any of what she's saying is actually true. Arthur?" He looked down at her and shook his head. "What do you mean – use your words, you stupid man!" she shouted at him. My dad just shrank into himself, the coffee mug shook in his hand.

"I didn't mean for it to get this far," he choked out. "I just wanted you to finally have the life you deserved. The money you deserved. I…I wanted to try to make things right, so maybe you'd forgive me."

My mother looked at him in confusion. "You're telling me that what Victoria accused you of is true? Drugs? Guns? No. That's utter ridiculousness."

My father put his coffee mug down on the table and grabbed my mother's hands. "I didn't mean to, Marcia. I promise this wasn't the way I planned it to go. The business was barely staying afloat, and I panicked. I knew if it failed you'd leave me. When they came asking about renting my trucks, I figured I could do one job or maybe two and get back on my feet, and that would be that.”

“Arthur…the extra money? The gifts?” My mother whipped a hand up to her earring and inhaled sharply. “You’re telling me it’s from selling drugs?”

“I’m trying to tell you I didn’t mean for it to happen! I just did the one job and told them that was it – but they had all these pictures of me and the trucks…they said they’d turn me in if I didn’t continue working with them. Then they made me start supervising the deals. Corralling those fools they hired…it’s a whole operation, Marcia. Much bigger than me. Don’t you see? I had no choice!” He leaned down to be more at her eye level, imploring her to hear him. “What could I have done? They threatened you and the kids, they messed with my drivers. And then this morning…”

I was frozen. Everything was wrong. “I saw people getting shot this morning.” It came out as barely a whisper. “Dad, did you do that?”

My father gave me a tortured look. “I didn’t want to be there, Vic. I had no choice, don’t you see?”

My mother drew back from him, wide-eyed. “What are we talking about? What did you do?”

My father shook his head, and a slow moan escaped his lips. “I don’t know. I don’t know if I hurt any of them. I only fired one shot, in self-defense…it all happened so fast! I was pulled to the car and driven away—I didn’t see who was hurt.” He sank to his knees weeping, then raised his eyes to mine. “How could you have known about it? Why were you there?”

Before I could answer we were interrupted by a loud rapping at the front door followed by Teniese flying through it. "Vic!" she yelled as she entered. Seeing me, she ran over. "Are you okay? Still just you?" She picked up my hands, making sure they were empty of sharp objects.

Before my family could react to this stranger barging in, two more followed in her wake. The moment Andrew crossed the threshold, my father sprung to his feet and grabbed my mom and pulled her behind him. "No. Get the hell out of my house!" he bellowed. "I know who you are, Samurai!"

Andrew paused, startled. "You?" His eyes darted between my father and me. "This is *your* house?" He reached to his waistband for his gun, forgetting it was still in my car. Finding nothing, he grabbed Ana and tried to pull her back. "Ana, you need to get out of here now!"

Though Andrew hadn't found his gun where he expected it, it seemed my dad had, and now had it drawn and sighted on Andrew. "I said get out of my house, now! You three get out of here and go to the basement!" He gestured at me, Philip and my mom, who screamed in alarm then tried to grab at my dad's arm holding the gun.

"Arthur, what the hell do you think you're doing? Where did you get a gun?"

"Marcia, please, go to the damn basement!" He shoved her back toward Philip, who seemed completely frozen in fear. "This man is a murderer! He's been stalking us all, spying on us and killing people." He looked at Andrew, "That's right, I saw you. I put cameras on our trucks after what you did Monday. Everyone knows your face!"

Teniese ran over and grabbed Ana from behind Andrew. "Come on, we can't be in the middle of this!"

Andrew tried to grab her back, but Teniese threw a palm to his nose. "Back off! You want her killed?" Andrew had stumbled back slightly from the blow but was otherwise unfazed.

He took a half-second to look at the scene, then nodded at Ana. "Go with her to the basement."

They ran over to my mother. "You're coming, too." Teniese attempted to grab her arm, but my mom flung her off.

"The hell I am! I am not leaving this spot until someone tells me what the hell is happening here!"

My dad kept the gun pointed at Andrew but turned ever so slightly to look at my mom. "Please, Marcia, please just go!"

In that moment, Andrew saw his opening and ran in toward my father, startling him. A shot rang out from the gun. It should have sunk right into Andrew's stomach, but Andrew didn't even flinch. My mother screamed, and Teniese shoved Ana into the hallway, leaving my mother but grabbing Philip on her way. Andrew barreled into my father, knocking him into the kitchen table and sending the gun flying. They both landed on the floor, and Andrew straddled my dad.

"Stop!" I yelled and ran over to their struggling forms. I tore Andrew off my father and threw him across the room, then launched myself at the fallen gun. I got there first, but Andrew was already on me before I could even stand up straight. He tried to grab the gun from me, but I was still stronger and managed to flip him to the ground. I held the gun on him but the next moment, my dad flung himself between us and grabbed at Andrew.

"Stay away from my daughter!" He dragged Andrew up off the floor and threw a wild punch at his face, but Andrew's head moved out of the way just in time and in return he grabbed my dad and started kneeing him hard in the gut. I moved in and swept Andrew's legs out from under him. He fell back hard, and I straddled him above the chest, pinning his arms. He gnashed his teeth at my hands as I tried to claw the amulet from his neck. My father recovered enough to crawl over and try to take my place over Andrew, but he just got in my way enough for Andrew to have a chance to knee me in the back and launch me forward and off him.

"Run, Vic!" my dad cried hoarsely as I tumbled forward and he and Andrew fought for position on the ground. Andrew still knew how to use his body as a weapon, though, and my dad was no match for him even without Andrew's enhanced strength. And the amulet kept any blow from harming him in the least. This was getting ridiculous.

"Enough!" I yelled, grabbing the gun from the floor and yanking my father off Andrew, still on the ground. "Stay there! Christ!" I held out my hand in front of me. "This is getting us nowhere!"

My father's ragged breath came from behind me. "You don't know what he is, Vic. He'll kill us all if he can!"

We were a pitiful bunch. My body shook with adrenaline, but I was clear headed and not even a bit tired. Andrew was gasping for air but only from the effort of the fight – he didn't have a scratch on him. My father was in the worst shape – he stood hunched over, gasping for breath. I stood with my hands held between them, the gun pointed at Andrew, even though I knew it was useless while he wore the amulet.

"I know exactly what he is, Dad. And you can't hurt him, so it's not even worth trying. And you – " I looked at Andrew. "You know you can't keep fighting forever, even if you're not hurt, I'm stronger than you now and will outlast you and get the amulet back."

Andrew slowly stood, keeping the little distance between us, and pointed at my father. "He was never my target. Just another bit of scum in the pond that would lead me to the bigger fish. But he's one of them. He's embracing evil, can't you feel it?"

I was horrified to realize I *could* feel it, like an insect crawling up my arm. Small, but enough to demand your attention – not in a good way. In a way that makes you want to flick it away or crush it between your fingertips. I shook the idea from my mind. This was my father, not some demon. He looked pathetic to me, leaning there against the kitchen table, as though he'd aged ten years in the last ten minutes.

"He's not evil. He's my dad, and he just got caught up in something he didn't know how to get out of…right?" I looked at my father. Tears streamed down his face and a sob escaped him. "Dad?"

"I brought this on all of us," he cried.

A sound from the kitchen made us all jump. My mother whimpered and slid along the floor toward my dad. He fell over to her and wrapped her tightly in his arms.

"I'm so sorry, Marcia," he sobbed. "I'm so, so, sorry."
Andrew took a step forward, and my father started and quickly
stood back up. "Stay away from them! Vic, give me the gun
quick…and take Mom to the basement." He revived enough to
push toward me and grab the gun from my surprised hand, then
aimed it at Andrew. I snatched it back and held it away from
both of them.

"I'm not going anywhere, Dad! He isn't the Samurai or
whatever anymore…I am. Stop trying to get the gun, you can't
kill him anyway – he's still wearing the amulet."

"Amulet? That's right, the necklace! You were wearing
his necklace last night at dinner. Why did he give it to you?" He
looked at Andrew. "Try to get to me through her, you son of a
bitch?"

How could I possibly explain what we'd all been going
through this week? "It's complicated, Dad. Let's just say that
Andrew is someone who goes after bad guys, and the necklace
he has around his neck is magic. Whoever wears it can't be
hurt. His…his boss wants me to take over his job, wants me to
be a kind of vigilante against evil. I'm the one who looked for
Andrew…er, the Samurai…to find out what was going on with
me. I sought him out." I remembered our meeting. "He was the
one I stopped to help in the street during the storm Monday.
The one who I told you about."

My mother moved her head to look between us. "Did you
just say a vigilante against evil? I don't understand, Victoria."

Exasperated, I said, "Look, I know exactly how it sounds.
But it's what's happening. I've been changing since we met." I
gestured to Andrew. "And he's been tracking this gang that

Ana's brother was in, which led him to you, Dad, because he's trying to root out evil. Can we return to what the hell you were doing with guns at a drug deal?"

My father drew his eyebrows together. "I told you I didn't have a choice…and this man is the evil one. Do you know he killed six people just a few days ago? He is not your friend, Vic. He is a murderer!"

"I know!" I screamed in response. "And I'm going to be one, too If I can't figure out how to stop what's happening to me! I need *him* to help me figure it out. Frankly, I have no idea why I haven't tried to hurt you yet, or heard thunder or had a flash of scales in my mind that told me to harm you. I came here hoping to protect you from Philip because I misunderstood the warning I got last night at dinner. Andrew's boss was warning me about you, Dad. Not Philip. She said you were tipping the scales the wrong way. Yes – he is a murderer, but the people he murders are the worst of the worst of humankind. The ones who have succumbed to evil. Is that really you? Did you really let that happen? And for what – money?"

At that moment, Teniese peeked her head back in the room, "Has everyone calmed the hell down up here? Can we be civilized and figure this shit out?" she yelled.

"And who the hell are you?" my mother asked.

"Dad and Mom, this is my friend Teniese. She's been helping me, and has actually saved me a couple times. Things have been happening to me…I've…been out of control…"

Teniese inched out from around the corner. "Maybe I should hold the gun for now." She reached out her hand; it shook slightly. I didn't feel like relinquishing it and hesitated.

"Vic, just give it to me. There is no one present in this house who needs to be shot right now, you understand? And if you go to the dark side, I don't want you with a deadly weapon at your disposal." I kept my eye on Andrew as I reached to give her the gun.

"No! It's the only thing that will stop him!" My dad lunged for the gun, but Teniese got it first and ran backwards.

"Get back!" she shouted. "You really want someone to die here tonight? There's no guarantee it wouldn't be your wife or your daughter. I'm taking the icky, deadly weapon away from the kids, you understand. Now get back over there and figure this out!"

SUNDAY

Chapter 27: Dike

Dike couldn't believe the predicament she was in. As Zeus stared her down from his marble perch, she thought of all the fighters she'd counseled over the years, all the work she'd put into them. All the sacrifices they'd made in her name and in the name of justice. For the most part, it had all gone perfectly well. For millennia, she had had her own army working in the shadows to help the human race keep some semblance of balance between the evil always beckoning and the good that is their true nature. She was tasked with this duty, and it filled her with pride. And now it was unravelling at her feet. Zeus loomed, and she knew she needed to come up with a solution fast. Something that would make amends for what she'd done, but wouldn't put an end to everything she'd created. Everything they'd sacrificed. But what could she suggest that would satisfy him?

"Can you not sense what is happening to them right this very moment?" Zeus demanded. "Turn your attention to them now and see!"

The scene in the dining room would have been comical if Dike didn't know it was deadly and all her doing. Seeing Andrew with the amulet again enraged her – he didn't deserve it! With a flick of her wrist, she willed it off of him. Zeus struck her hard against the temple and she slid across the floor, stunned.

"Jealousy? Petty vindictiveness? It is you who escalated this situation, Dike. You are still so corrupted by your link to your fighters that you act against their best interests impulsively. You are not clear of mind. I will offer no further power for your army. The experiment is over."

"Wait, Zeus!" Dike cried. "It is only with Andrew that I fell. Only with him that my judgment was clouded." Dike got up to kneeling as the pounding in her head from the blow began to subside. Once the pain receded, a calm washed over her, and she looked around. While she had been prisoner to Zeus's tirade, the sky had darkened and storm clouds gathered all around the hall. Lightning streaked through them as wind whipped the trees around frantically. She had not seen him this upset in a very long time. In the distance, Dike could just make out the flowing branches of her willow tree. She was lighter now – the anger and bitterness she'd felt for the last several days was lifted. It was almost as though the narrow peephole of anguish she'd been looking through was cut open, and she realized there was a bigger world all around her that she'd been too distracted to see. "What did you do?" She stood and watched Zeus calmly and smugly sit back down.

Once seated, he settled his glowing eyes on Dike. "I have freed you. Disconnected you. Returned you to yourself. Now reflect on what you have done as a god, not as a human."

Dike felt stronger and clearer than she had in a long time. What a relief to be in control of her heart and mind again. She closed her eyes and exhaled as visions from the week flowed through her. What harm she had wrought on them all. Something else quietly lingered within her as well. "I still feel a trace of your power coursing through me."

Zeus stroked his beard. "I have severed your connection to them only momentarily. Long enough for you to return to your senses. Your fighters still maintain their changes. To remove your power would be to relegate all your fighters to the same fate as Andrew. You have already caused enough trouble. I have left you with enough power to retire them. Give them their new memories and the chance to live new lives."

Dike shifted her attention back to the house.

SUNDAY

Chapter 28: Victoria (me)

Teniese had the gun and moved to the far end of the kitchen; Ana and Philip lurked at the farthest end of the hall at the mouth of the basement, and I stood between my parents and Andrew. I was suddenly so very tired. My vision blurred, and I faltered on my feet. If only I could sleep right then and there.

My mother ran over to me. "Victoria, what's happening? Are you hurt?" I sank down to the ground.

"I just need to close my eyes, just for a second." Nothing else mattered in that moment. A tidal wave of fatigue crashed down over my head, soaking me through to my toes. I couldn't fight it anymore. I couldn't care about what was going on around me. If I just closed my eyes, everything would be okay. My head slumped down to the floor with the rest of me. I was aware that Teniese was speaking, but it didn't matter. Nothing mattered but sleep. I closed my eyes and let it take me.

SUNDAY

Chapter 29: Andrew

Teniese moved around Victoria, trying to rouse her. "What's happening to her?" She yelled at Andrew. "I can't wake her up! She's not supposed to sleep; the goddess told her that's when she changes for good. You have to help me wake her!" Teniese jostled Victoria to no avail. It was as though she'd gone into a coma.

Her dad ran over, too, and growled at him, "What did you do? Did you drug her?"

Andrew looked at the woman who lay before him. The woman who was taking everything from him. Fear gripped him. Instinctually, his hand flew up to the amulet, but it was no longer there. He clawed at his shirt, but the amulet was gone. Frantically, he slid to the ground where she lay and tried to move her collar, but her dad pushed him back hard. "What do you think you're doing?"

"The amulet, I don't have it anymore. Does she? Just look, please?" he implored.

Teniese moved one hand to her friend's neck and moved the shirt aside. The light caught the metal chain, and she pulled it forth. The amulet was back on Victoria's neck. She had taken it from him yet again. Andrew sank to his knees. Was that it then? Was he done being a fighter?

Victoria's brother and Ana inched in cautiously to see what was happening. The brother ran to Victoria's slumped form, while Ana went to Andrew's side.

"It's over," Andrew heaved. "She's going to be the fighter now. I won't be able to protect Julian, or you, or anyone anymore. I will be useless." Despair flooded him, and he couldn't look at her.

Ana grabbed his face with both hands and forced him to look her in the eyes. "You are not useless, you're free." Just then thunder rumbled overhead. "Oh no, not now!" Ana cried.

Andrew looked up just as Victoria shot up to sitting with a loud gasp.

SUNDAY

Chapter 30: Victoria (me)

I sat up abruptly. My father, mother, brother, and Teniese surrounded me. I felt so calm, so unconcerned.

"What are you all doing?" I asked. I had a vague memory of a fight. A fight with my father, with Andrew. My eyes canvassed the room and fell on his face. Instantly, the image of metal scales flooded my brain. Andrew was found guilty and justice needed to be served. I flew up to standing with the grace of a ballerina and casually pushed my family aside as I made my way over to him.

"Vic, are you okay?" Teniese tentatively asked. But I didn't even acknowledge her presence. I was focused on Andrew and the need for justice against all his evil coursed through my veins. A hand flew up to my neck, finding the amulet.

A slow smile formed on my lips. "You are no longer protected. Justice must be done." In a flash, I was on him. Ana fell back onto the kitchen table as I launched Andrew's form to the floor and started beating him. He held up his hands and tried to fend me off, but without the amulet, he had no chance. Power and virtue pulsed through me as I landed blow after blow to his head, arms, chest… I left Andrew's form writhing on the ground and moved over to Teniese, wrenching the gun from her hand as she squealed.

"Vic?" she squeaked. "Vic, are you still in there?"

"Of course I'm still in here. You all need to leave, there is nothing for you to do here." I held the gun and walked past their stunned faces, then grabbed Andrew roughly and easily by the neck and put the gun to his head.

"No!" yelled Ana. "Don't!" She tried to claw the gun from my hand, but I easily shoved her aside and aimed again.

"STOP!" a voice boomed in my head and in a flash of light, I was thrown off Andrew and to the opposite wall.

SUNDAY

Chapter 31: Dike

Not a moment after Dike had brought her attention back to the scene in the kitchen and relieved Andrew of the amulet, she was stunned to find the woman Victoria on the ground. The alterations were finally completed, Dike could tell. Victoria had transitioned. She was full. And immediately she had risen and began attacking Andrew. The girlfriend had tried to pull Victoria off him, but Victoria struck her aside so hard she fell into the other woman and they both fell to the ground. The scene was chaotic. Then Victoria had the gun to Andrew's head.

"STOP!" Dike yelled to her and flung her off Andrew's pitiful body.

Victoria just stood back up where she'd landed, unharmed. "What?"

"Stop now!" Dike commanded.

"I don't understand, why should I stop? The scales showed me. Evil has overtaken the good. Justice must be served."

Victoria didn't sound like herself. Her voice held little emotion, she was so sure in her purpose. Exactly what Dike wanted in her fighters. It was what made them so impactful. But now her energies were being brought down on Andrew, and Dike felt sick. He whimpered there on the oak wood floor, bloody and beaten. Dike had failed him in so many ways. She

274

had gotten too close, made him too dependent. Then when he betrayed her, she cast him aside like he was worthless just to make him suffer. And without the proper release of power and the changing of his memories, she had left Andrew prey to the very thing she trusted him with in the first place. The scales. Dike understood she needed to save him. Save them all.

Victoria waited patiently for instructions while Andrew rasped and bled, and her family and friends cowered around her. Dike felt Zeus's presence hovering above her, waiting. What could she do to make this right for them? She thought back to the day of the storm and Andrew's search to find a way to spare the girl's brother. She remembered then what Zeus had said all those many centuries ago. Free will. Humans and gods alike have it. All of them. The one universal. Andrew had sought it out. She had stupidly believed the scales would be enough to keep them chained to their duties, obediently ridding the world of evil. But Andrew had wanted more. He wanted his choice back. His free will.

Dike turned to Zeus with a new plan. "You were right. I had forgotten myself these last years. If you say I must relinquish my army, so be it. But let me allow them to choose for themselves how they wish to live out their lives. Give them the free will he sought. They will make it right through their own bidding. To simply remove all the fighters from humanity would be disastrous now. The world is too populous and they spread evil between them as the breeze touches leaves on a tree. You are right, Zeus, my judgment has been impaired and my duties neglected. This is the way to make it right. Allow them to feel their choices transparently again. Allow them to be in control."

"So you can fall back into the same predicament? You succumbed once, you will do it again." Zeus replied.

"No, I never again wish to experience life as a human does. But now that I have, I am better equipped to serve them. There is no need for you to once again be burdened with the daily judgments from which you have been free for centuries." This gave Zeus pause. Dike had guessed right that he'd forgotten how tedious their daily sharing of judgments had become before he agreed to give her the power to form her army of fighters. He couldn't deny the experiment had worked up until now. "What is needed is simple amending, not outright cessation. Andrew was the catalyst for my failure. We shared a connection that I see now was false and caused by my own weakness. But this can be changed. I can make certain that the fighters are always aware of their choice, even after they have agreed to join my army. They will always be able to change their minds and return to normal human life, perhaps even with a say in their alternate life stories."

Zeus thought for a minute, then dipped his chin in agreement. "From this moment forth, your fighters will neither be denied nor driven against their will in any capacity. Fix this now, and fix it for them all."

Dike turned back to the scene in the house.

"Dike?" Victoria said. "I know justice must be done – the scales have come to me. I understand what an honor this is now, and I am ashamed I resisted it all week. Let me rid the world of his evil." Victoria walked calmly back over to Andrew and held him captive beneath her. Only milliseconds had passed, and Dike was grateful she had paid attention before she was too late and Andrew's choice was taken from him beyond what she was powerful enough to undo.

"No. Allow him freedom to stand." Victoria, perplexed, hesitantly rose off him. Dike let her voice fill the kitchen so all could hear her. "I offer you choice. Andrew, I stripped you of your power and your duty and forced your memories and experiences upon this woman. This is not how it should be done. I have harmed you both and I wish to make it right." Victoria's father put his hands over his ears at the booming tenor of her voice. Her mother quaked. Teniese, Philip and Ana stared in fear and awe at Victoria and Andrew.

"In order to right this wrong, I give you both the choice. Free will is yours to command as it ever was, yet with its veil of fog lifted. Your lives are free to direct as you wish. Will you choose to be my fighters, both of you? Or will you choose to return to your human lives with no memory of this experience?"

SUNDAY

Chapter 32: Andrew

Andrew crawled away from Victoria and leaned on a chair to lift himself. He was miserable. Every physical part of him screamed with pain. Pain he'd been blissfully denied for as long as he could remember. It took up all the spaces in his mind so that even thoughts were laced with it. Why would anyone want to choose this? He looked at Victoria and knew what she must be feeling.

SUNDAY

Chapter 33: Victoria (me)

Victoria looked back. She wanted to finish what she'd started with Andrew. She knew in her veins he deserved to die. The scales had shown her, and exacting their justice was like drinking wine, intoxicating and freeing. She moved her gaze to her parents, crouched together on the floor, her brother clinging to the far wall in fear. How weak they looked. How much unnecessary suffering they had caused her in her life. Her father lifted his eyes to hers in that moment and she paused. All except for him. His face had always brought her peace. Brought her comfort. She trusted him fully. And look what had happened. Even he had not been strong enough to resist the scourge of evil on this earth. He surrendered for the weakest reason of all, money. She then took in Ana and Teniese. Ana, whose brother had caused the death and harm of so many, yet she still felt he deserved a chance at finding good again. Teniese, who did everything she could right in this world, but still suffered physical abuse at the hands of a man who wasn't strong enough to resist the evil inside him. It was everywhere, in all of them. What could be more virtuous than helping the gods fight this menace? What could be more right?

"I know what you're feeling," Andrew's voice came out haltingly. "It's so reassuring to have no doubts about your purpose, no question that you're living up to the highest potential. No pain or discomfort. No worrying conscience." One eye was bloodied and swollen shut, the other bored into Victoria. "I suffered so much pain when my father was killed that becoming a fighter was the sweetest relief. Like everything was right-side up again. And it was immediate. We humans are massive balls of suffering, and that was taken away the moment I said yes." Andrew's gaze shifted to Ana. "I never questioned any of it until I met you. My life was clear, I wanted for nothing." He shook his head. "The thing about being a fighter is that you trade that ease for not feeling much of anything else. All the emotions that make you human, the good and the bad, are muted, morphed into something different. Something less. But you don't care…don't even really notice. This week, I have felt it all. Every lightning strike of regret, shame, terror, fear. It's awful. It consumes you. Skews your thoughts so you don't know what's real anymore. I can't close my eyes without being bombarded with nightmares. But there is love, too. And choice. And when I saw you again today, Ana…just a little bit of hope. I have been remembering my mom. My dad. I hadn't thought of them in so many years." Ana moved over to his side, and she was crying. "I don't want to be a fighter anymore, but I don't want to forget you either."

Dike sighed in frustration. "You cannot have both. You have seen what torture your fully human mind wages on you with your memories. You will find no peace. No respite from the actions you wrought for justice. Your useless emotions will consume you and make you weak and vulnerable."

"I can help you through that if you stay with me," Ana entreated.

"You wish to help but do not understand how your selfish needs will torture him," Dike responded. "He will suffer and bring you into suffering with him."

SUNDAY

Chapter 34: Victoria (me)

I wanted to feel strong like this forever. To need nothing else. What life was I truly leaving behind? Nothing of consequence. Nothing of value. These last few days, I had worried needlessly about the changes taking over me. But they were wonderful! I am strong now. I helped people. I knew what was right and wasn't afraid to fight for it.

"Why would I want to live like I had been? This is so much better. Why would you choose to suffer again?" I pitied Andrew now. "You had strength and conviction and purpose. And you threw it away. This power. This confidence. I like myself far better like this than how I was before – weak, afraid, inconsequential."

Teniese moved towards me. "This isn't the only way, Vic." I raised one eyebrow. "Remember how you helped Jeannette? That was you, not this fighter."

I shook my head. "No, I was already changing. It was the amulet and Dike."

"You're wrong. You had it in you all along. I have always seen it – I wouldn't have wanted to be your friend otherwise. Wouldn't have wasted my time. Why do you think I kept pushing you? Do you really want to feel nothing anymore? Be less than human?"

"No! Not less…more. More than what I was."

"This is the wrong kind of more!" she shouted at me. "This is becoming a killing robot like you felt with the guard, like you felt at the hotel. This is eating stupid foods that you never liked, living a life alone without friendship, without family. How is that better? You won't laugh till you pee with a friend again. Won't go on a first date and fantasize about two kids and a picket fence and shit!"

"What about James? You found happiness with him and how did he repay you? By beating you. And you…" I looked at my parents. "Look what you've done to each other in the name of love. Of family. Look what Ana's brother did to his family. There is so much evil everywhere. I can change that. I can make the world a better place. I would never be able to do something so important if I remained the person I was before. Don't you see?"

"And you will have nothing for yourself. You will be an empty shell."

"I was already a shell," I retorted.

Teniese turned to Andrew. "Tell her! Tell her what you know, what you have done!"

Andrew shook his head. "It doesn't make any difference. I wanted it just as badly as she does. It's freedom from pain. We are doomed whichever way we choose."

Teniese roared back, "It's freedom from joy! Tell me how joyful you were as a fighter! Tell me what you gave up to feel that way! To feel nothing! But that still wasn't enough, was it? Because you are still mostly human. And love found you, and you chose that instead. Busted apart your whole, cushy badass existence just to feel that love again, didn't you? Because that's

what being alive, being a human, is about. You grow and you
learn and you shift and you try and you fail and you succeed
and you cry and you laugh and you dance and *choose*, dammit!
You choose who you are going to be! If you do this…become
this – " she gestured at me, "your life is no longer your own.
Someone else is in charge, and you lose everything that makes
being a human so wonderful. You will be no better than the
people you'll be bringing justice to. Please, Vic. You have to
listen."

SUNDAY

Chapter 35: Dike

Zeus emanated heat and power at Dike's back as she contemplated the scene unfolding before her. She knew his vision mirrored her own and could sense his anticipation. She had led these humans to this point and needed to prove she could make it right.

"Strip her of her power like you did the man. Only then will she truly understand the choice she is making," Zeus commanded.

"It will only confuse her further," Dike answered.

"You are the one who has been confused, Dike. You must return her to her natural state or her choice will not truly be her own. For is that not the arrangement we made all those years ago? Do as I say."

Dike took a deep breath and brought the power of the light down on the house.

SUNDAY

Chapter 36: Victoria (me)

A blinding light engulfed the room and everyone drew their hands up to their eyes to shield it away. I felt the flash pulse through me and doubled over.

"No!" I cried. The peace, the energy, the power from just a moment ago was gone. I brought my hands to my throat but they encountered nothing but skin. I frantically looked around as everyone slowly peeked out to see what had happened.

Then the voice of Dike returned: "A human must always make the choice to be a fighter. That is the way. I give you both the same option I gave Andrew on the day he accepted his role. If you decide to join my army of fighters, I will support you and guide you until the time you no longer wish it. You will want for nothing, and your life will be filled with the highest purpose. If you choose not to join me, I will burden you no further in this life. Victoria, you will return to your previous existence. Andrew, I will strip you of any knowledge of your time as a fighter or the silent shadow army of fighters that live among you, and you will return to a normal human life. What are your decisions?"

Andrew spoke first. "Dike, please," he begged her. "Why do I have to forget? If I don't remember Ana then none of this will have been worth it. You will be cursing me a second time!"

Dike answered, "You will find no peace with remembering. You underestimate the damage that will be rendered to you both. It is for your protection. Would you drag her down into your pain?"

Andrew's face contorted in anguish. "Every choice you give me has a cost."

"That is the nature of choice," Dike replied. "It can be both a gift and a curse. I should never have blinded you to it fully in the first place."

The room swam around me. Teniese was talking but it was hard to focus.

"Vic. Vic, can you hear me? You can decide to remember, too. Remember how it felt when you let yourself believe. Remember how it felt when you took control of your life and basically told Franklin to fuck off. You can have that without being her fighter. You can, I know it."

The confidence and virtuousness I had felt just a moment ago was stripped out of me like the bones of a fish. In its place, anger, confusion, fear, and doubt engulfed me again. It felt horrible.

"No," I sobbed and yelled to the sky. "Bring it back! I don't want to go back to feeling like this. It's torture!"

"Only right now!" Teniese grabbed my arms and made me look at her. "Only just at this moment. Do you really want to give up your family? Walk away from them forever?"

"What is she talking about, Victoria?" my mother asked with a quavering voice. "What does she mean, walk away from us forever?"

"There's no time to explain!" Teniese angrily replied.

"You're talking about my daughter leaving me – there bloody well better be time to explain!" my mother roared back. "Victoria, what is going on? Whatever this is, whatever choice you have to make, you can't leave us! Not like this!"

A crushing weight pushed down on my chest. "I don't want to feel this way anymore," I moaned. Having felt relief from all the negative emotions I fought on a daily basis was so absolutely freeing, that to have them back hurt twice as much as before.

Teniese shook her head. "No one gets promised a life without hurt. That's a part of life as much as love, as happiness. But the hurt serves a purpose. Gives you the opportunity to change, to get stronger, to love harder. You can't do that if you're an empty shell. You'll have power, yes. But nothing else. Remember, you're the one who stopped to help Andrew in the first place. You're the one who reminded me that I don't have to settle for someone who hurts me. You have it all in you, Vic. No fancy necklace required."

Could I just go back to being the same person I was before? The idea made me ill. But when I thought about the beating I gave the guard and Andrew just now, I felt even sicker. Being there for Teniese, standing up for myself against Franklin, against my mom. Jeannette's hug. Were moments like those enough to continue changing for the better? Were they enough to battle the negative emotions that had trapped me in a lifeless life before?

Dike interrupted my thoughts. "So be it. I leave it to you to remember or not, Andrew, but I have warned you both what remembering will do. It is time for you both to decide."

I closed my eyes. What did I want? What did I believe? I took a deep breath then made my choice.

Andrew took Ana's face in his hands. "I love you, Ana." Then he kissed her. "I'm sorry."

Once more, the lightning flashed.

ABOUT A MONTH LATER

Chapter 37: Victoria (me)

I walked through the door of the Blue Heron and scanned the tables. My eyes landed on Teniese in the far right corner, and she gave me a small wave. Her hair was cut close to her chin and angled forward, longer in the front than the back. "Wow – I love the new 'do!" I leaned in to give her a hug across the table.

"If I want to work my way up to creative director, I might as well start looking the part now." She laughed. Teniese was loving her new job, and I was happy for her. "You tell Ana?"

I nodded. "She isn't going to make it. They leave tomorrow, too, and she is going crazy with all that still needs to be done. I'm not surprised. I don't think she feels much like seeing us. Too painful."

When the light had subsided in my house all those weeks ago, Andrew was gone. Just vanished. Ana had lost her mind, yelling to Dike to bring him back. The goddess had simply replied that Andrew had made his choice, then she left us, too. We didn't know if he was a fighter again or just chose to forget, and I assumed we'd never find out. The only thing we did know for sure was he didn't choose to stay with Ana. I believed it was to save her. To save them both, really. Dike was right. Andrew was tortured by his past and would probably bring Ana down with him if he stayed. That didn't bring Ana much solace though. All she knew was Andrew had abandoned her.

"I was hoping she'd come say goodbye at least," I said, "but I decided not to push it. She and her mom visited Julian yesterday to say goodbye, and I think it messed her up quite a bit. After everything, she still feels like she's abandoning him, but what can she do? They need to make a fresh start."

The day after Andrew disappeared and I returned to my normal human status, Julian nearly overdosed from mixing his medication with other drugs and alcohol again. Ana and her mom were forced to bring him to the emergency room, where he was promptly arrested. This time, however, no Andrew came to his aid, and the police had found enough evidence in his apartment to lock him up. He was in jail awaiting trial and would most likely be there for years to come. Now that Ana and her mom didn't have to wonder where Julian was and knew they couldn't help him, they decided to move in with Ana's uncle and his family in Arizona. Ana and her mom both had jobs waiting for them there, and it was a way to try to move on with their lives. I had come to really like Ana and was heartbroken for her. Losing Andrew and her brother again in such a short time, she was really struggling. Hopefully, a change of city would help her start to heal.

"I'm feeling a little frazzled myself today," I continued.

"Did you visit your dad to say goodbye yet?" Teniese asked gently.

"Yes, the other night," I sighed. When the police found evidence in Julian's apartment, it only took them a few days to link him with the bodies found at the bottling plant. From there, it wasn't hard to figure out my father's trucking company was involved. My dad was arrested as well. Bail was set too high to bring him home, so he was also awaiting his trial at the jail. I hated seeing him there. He told us he would agree to testify against the bigger organization for a lesser sentence, though, so we hoped his time there would be short.

"Did your mom go with you?" Teniese asked.

"Not this time, no. I needed to see him on my own. He is still asking me to forgive him. I think I'm getting closer, but I'm not there yet." I was still trying to reconcile the different version of my dad with the one I believed as true only a month or so ago. Every time I thought back to a happy time with him, I had to look at it through a new lens. My therapist told me to take my time; rushing trauma healing doesn't release it, but rather buries it in our subconscious, just to come out some other way.

"I'm heading over to my aunt's for dinner tonight so we'll say our goodbyes then." Once my dad was arrested, my mom knew she needed to sell the house. She moved in with her sister while it was on the market because it hurt too much to sleep in her bed alone. "Did I tell you she is going to teach sewing? There's a class with the local park district she signed up to lead. She seems excited about the idea. I'm proud of her."

"Any buyers for their house yet?" Teniese asked.

I nodded. "A young family from Boston. The closing is right after Thanksgiving. Philip can help her finish packing what we haven't already cleared out. That reminds me. Guess who decided he's writing another book?" Philip quit his teaching job and had been working at the video game company for a week now. We talked on the phone pretty often these days, and he sounded happy.

"I thought he was done with writing," Teniese replied.

I smiled. "Suddenly he's inspired by ancient mythology and plans to write a fantasy novel about an army of fighters for justice on Earth. He figures no one will accuse him of stealing his ideas from Dike, so why not? He plans on calling you with a gazillion questions, by the way, so prepare yourself." Teniese laughed. She had been by my side nonstop since that night. I felt a lump in my throat thinking about what I was going to do without her. My eyes started to tear up.

"Hey, none of that or I'm going to lose it. We agreed, no tears today!" Teniese's eyes welled up too.

"I know, I know!" I wiped my eyes with a napkin. "I can't help it. It was a stupid agreement. Can't you come with me?"

"Ha! There is no room for me in your car! Besides, we both need to see what this next chapter will bring in our own ways." In the wake of everything that had happened to me, I spent a lot of time thinking about who I was and what I wanted. It wasn't easy, and therapy was a huge help. So much so that I finally decided I was going back to school to get my master's degree in counseling. Being there to help Teniese and Jeannette, and later Ana, through their problems had fulfilled me in a way I hadn't experienced before. If I could figure this stuff out, maybe I could learn how to help others get there too. I did a little research and there was a school in Pittsburgh that had a program I felt good about. I found a community college I could enroll in for January to knock out my prerequisites, and then I'd apply for the master's program the following fall. My car was already packed, and I was leaving first thing in the morning. Saying goodbye to Teniese was the hardest part about leaving yet.

"But I have a little surprise for you." She fiddled with her phone for a moment then slid it across the table for me to see. On the screen was a flight itinerary for mid-December.

"You're coming to visit!"

"Surprise! And then you'll be home for Christmas, so we'll see each other at least twice over the next couple months." She beamed. "I'm so proud of you, Vic. And I can't wait to see what's coming for you. For me, too!"

THE END
AND THE BEGINNING

Chapter 38: Victoria (me)

Pittsburgh was in the grips of a cold snap. The first couple weeks while I was setting up my new apartment and applying for jobs, it still felt like fall. Now a cold front had moved in and the first snow of the season was tumbling from the sky. I had just finished my first blissful day of work at a local independent bookstore and was slowly making my way back to my apartment, clenching the steering wheel hard and trusting my new tires wouldn't let me slip.

As I came to a stop light, a bright neon sign broke through the snow off to the right. It read "Martial Arts." My breath caught in my throat, and I immediately threw on my signal light and turned into the parking lot. Walking through the door, I felt an energy I hadn't in a long time. There was a class going on in the middle of the mats. Barefoot people with white pants and robe-like tops tied with belts rolled around together on the floor. It looked like they were trying to get dominant positions over each other. My pulse quickened and, suddenly, I knew I needed to be there with them. A woman at the front desk noticed me and walked over.

"Can I help you?" She smiled big.

"Hi, can you tell me what kind of martial arts you teach here?"

"Sure, this is a Jiu-jitsu class. It's a little bit like wrestling. We have classes in Jiu-jitsu, Judo, and kickboxing."

A pair of men was moving with intensity in the middle of the mats, and other students stood up and circled them to watch. We turned to watch, too, as the one man on the bottom did something quick with his leg and in a flash had gotten the other man in some kind of choke hold. Everyone cheered when the man in the choke hold tapped his hand against the other man's arm to signal defeat.

"That's the owner, there, if you'd like to ask him any questions about the studio. Hey, Andy, can you come here for a sec?" The man turned around and smiled at us. I froze. Andrew was casually walking my way.

"Andrew?" I gasped as he reached me.

"Andy, actually." He held out his hand and smiled at me. "I'm sorry, I didn't catch your name."

Though he moved differently, with an energetic happy step, and his face seemed lit up in a way I'd never seen before, there was no mistaking. Andrew stood before me. I paused a little too long while he held his hand out, and he threw a quick questioning glance to the woman who'd introduced us. I snapped to, and reached out to shake his hand, strong and solid. "Victoria. My name is Victoria."

"Well, welcome to Olympus Martial Arts Academy, Victoria." He grinned. "Pardon the dust, we only just opened two weeks ago. A lifelong dream of mine to own my own studio!" He swept his arms around as though he was giving the space a huge hug. "Have you trained in martial arts?" he asked.

I nodded, a giddiness creeping into my heart. "A little."

THE END

Author's note: Quote from Hesiod found at URL below.

www.theoi.com/Text/Hesiodworksdays.html